FOR BOOKS' SAKE
PRESENTS

[RE]SISTERS

STORIES OF REBEL GIRLS,
REVOLUTION,
EMPOWERMENT
AND ESCAPE

First published in 2016 by
Group Of
on behalf of
For Books' Sake www.forbookssake.net

A CIP catalogue record for this book is available from the British Library.
ISBN: 978-095666-517-1
Printed in EU by Pulsio SARL

CONTENTS

"THEY TRIED TO BURY US.
THEY DIDN'T KNOW WE WERE SEEDS."

MEXICAN PROVERB

INTRODUCTION

"A monster. You and your friends, all of you. Pretty monsters. It's a stage all girls go through. If you're lucky you get through it without doing any permanent damage to yourself or anyone else."

Kelly Link

"She is a loner, too bright for the slutty girls and too savage for the bright girls, haunting the edges and corners of the school like a sullen disillusioned ghost."

Eleanor Catton

No experience, no money. Ideas and ambition. That's the background of the For Books' Sake publishing imprint, and of For Books' Sake itself. Like all adolescences, there were growing pains, awkward phases and uncertainty. But there was something brilliant too. Despite our limited resources, we made something magical together. And slowly, slowly, without even realising it, we started to grow up.

Ever since we published our first short story collection in 2012, I was adamant that, one day, we'd do a YA anthology. It's been said that books can change the world. And when you're young, when your world is simultaneously too big and too small, confusing, frustrating, too much and not enough, books have a power, a magic all their own.

So we called for submissions, and they came in waves, from all over the world. The brief: stories had to feature teenage characters, and empower young women. The stories we were sent spanned every genre, style and subject. In the UK, we were smack bang in the middle of general election fever. People were hopeful, and afraid. In May, the Conservatives came to power, and with them countless plans and policies sure to cut deep. Women and young people would be among those hit the hardest. People raged. And wrote.

By the deadline, our inbox overflowed. It was the coldest summer we'd had in years. But the stories burnt and glittered; some giving warmth, comfort, a sense of security. Others searing enough to leave blisters, scorchmarks and scars.

We sifted through the submissions, and the world went on. Riot grrrl was two decades dead, but across the UK and beyond, teen girls were mobilising. Feminist collectives and campaigns multiplied, and everywhere there was evidence of girls' resilience and resistance. But even while girls were fighting back, the latest evidence showed that the world was still doing them damage.

Over 80% of girls feel adults don't understand the pressure they're under. Over 80% have experienced sexism in the last week alone. Anxiety about sexual harassment impacts three quarters of girls, influencing the clothes they wear and where they feel safe to go. Only half feel safe in their local area, a number that's falling further which each set of stats. Self-harm, mental illness and depression are among their top concerns. They feel pressure to look and act a certain way. Almost half have self-harmed after being bullied online.

(RE)Sisters contains works of fiction. But it also contains a lot of truth. The characters feel the same pressures and pains, fears and frustrations, and employ the same survival strategies as their real-life counterparts. Some of the situations depicted are extreme, but they are a reflection of girls' experiences, and to exclude them would be at best an omission at and at worst dangerous. No-one wins when we look at girls with rose-tinted glasses. (RE)Sisters explores girlhood in all its gore and glory.

"When you're young, you think everything you do is disposable," wrote Margaret Atwood in *The Blind Assassin*, "You move from now to now, to crumpling time up in your hands, tossing it away. You're your own speeding car. You think you can get rid of things, and people too—leave them behind. You don't yet know about the habit they have, of coming back."

In (RE)Sisters, some things come back; perfume that smells of mangoes and mint (*Upside Down*), an amnesiac's past (*Operation M*), and a runaway best friend (*Where You're Going...*). Some things are gone for good. For Della in *Kin Selection*, it's the habit of checking her shoes for scorpions in the mornings. In *Animal Heart*, it's the narrator's six sisters, now living in the woods, turned to stone. Sometimes, new things take their place. A girl with ultramarine eyeliner and a scandalous past (*Destiny*). A shot at education (*A Whole Plate of Biscuits*). In *Vientiane*, it's an unlikely friendship with a mysterious stranger who knows a secret trick, and in *Disharmony*, it's a baby, Mila, and 'the light from the window roars a fire in her eyes.'

Like today's teenage girls, the stories in (RE)Sisters have the power to shock, seduce and manipulate. They're sometimes subtle, sometimes crude, and almost always subversive. From a spelling bee that stings like a wasp and an abandoned bathtub seen only in passing, to an indefinite hospital quarantine and schemes for survival on a council estate, the girls in these stories feel everything fiercely; isolation, alienation, love and loss. Euphoria and defiance.

RE(Sisters) aims to champion writing by women while paying tribute to girls; their strengths, their stories, their potential and power. It's a testament, a prayer, a snapshot and a celebration. But most of all, consider it an invitation. To find your sisters, and resist.

Jane Bradley
Editor

KIN SELECTION

ELIANA RAMAGE

Bones, Stars, Dinosaurs, Weather, Rocks for Jocks. Those were my choices.

At least I'd thought they were. It was a week before the start of sophomore year before I even glanced at the course listings for my science requirement, and by then all the easy classes were full. I quickly requested permission to take a senior-level Bio course in Animal Behaviour, not because I was qualified but because I'd always wanted a dog. Jess and Hailey would be in Introduction to the Universe together—"Stars"—probably passing notes during the lectures and helping each other study in their pyjamas. Sandra would bear with her Chem classes, in the name of being a doctor back home.

Back home. To go back home was to go back better, smarter, braver. That's what all of us wanted, officially. We said it again and again. "I just gotta get out of here," we'd say. "There's so much needs doing back home."

The Native American Programme had a special guest flown in the night before the first day of class. An elder, so far always an elder, except the time they brought in the couple who'd taught themselves their Native language, and except the time they had a business school alum talk about his plans for an all-Indian investment company. This one was from Oklahoma. He had long, black-streaked grey hair tied back in a worn-out elastic. You could tell because it slid down a little when he bent over to burn the sage and sweetgrass. He used a beaded cigarette lighter.

We sat in a circle around him, our backs to the dining room windows. With the lights on and the sun off, standing outside the Native American House could be clear as watching a silent film. I cupped my hands and waved the air over the burning braid of sweetgrass, pulling it towards my chest. I brushed my palms across my face. Felt the oil forever on my skin. I was breathing in and breathing out and thinking shit, we'll look crazy to any passers-by.

The elder, Mr. Stillwater I think his name was, talked for a long while about how college isn't just an opportunity for us but an opportunity for our nations. That whatever we do, we do carrying the hopes and dreams of all the people who love us, and the ancestors who were killed trying to protect the people, and the land and the… I'd heard this all before. Said it, too.

That night, Mr. Stillwater had us go around in a circle and say how we were going to use our college degrees to strengthen our nations. The room was thick with the smell of singed sage and the fluorescent lights beat white-green shadows on our skin. Sitting up straight, I gripped the bottom of my chair, let go and gripped again. Watched my knuckles turn white, red, white while Sandra talked about how IHS was a joke and what the folks back on her rez really needed was a qualified doctor from the community. What they needed was her, she meant, but she didn't say that. Jess wanted to start a literacy program for Alaska Native youth, and she thought the next step might be to take some psych classes and get better prepared to deal with all the suicides up there. Hailey took a long time to make her point—something about a theatre troupe that would promote positive representations of the sovereign Indigenous female body—and then it was my turn and they said, "Della?" I nodded, put on a coughing fit, and excused myself. Safely in the bathroom, I locked the door behind me. The mirror was fogged-up from a recent shower, and I couldn't see myself in it. I sat down and stared at the laminated periodic table someone had taped to the door.

It was unclear exactly how I planned on changing the world. It was unclear whether I even knew where "back home" was. My most interesting days were behind me, and I wasn't sure I had what it took to accomplish anything on my own. I'd scrambled my way to good grades in high school, some of them more deserved than others. When I was down on myself, which was often, I'd stare at the frayed college acceptance letter I kept in my sock drawer and I'd wonder if that, too—my so-far greatest achievement—had something to do with my fame. They say that fancy New England schools like ours kept files on every student, and that they held onto them until we died. This was in case we were to become remarkable alumni, at which point they'd want to claim their part in that. I imagined my file to be remarkable already, though not for anything I'd earned.

I was born to Albert Begay, and some white woman who didn't stake a claim to me even when shit hit the fan. Albert's Navajo and he hates it when I say I'm half-Navajo, but I figure he was lucky I started to claim that half at all—it's that half of my DNA that set me up for trouble from the start.

When Albert's fling put me up for adoption, Albert signed away his parental rights. Of course this was until he and Grandma found out my new parents were a white couple from Chicago, at which point he called in the Indian Child Welfare Act. He won his case, got me back, lost Mom and Dad's appeal, lost me. Front page news. Drama, drama, drama. Remarkable.

All in all, I was given away by my biological parents, taken from my adoptive parents at age two, raised on the Navajo Reservation until age five, and then returned to Chicago just in time to start kindergarten not quite sure who my parents were.

Depending on whom you ask, I was either the brave little Navajo girl stolen from the homelands, or the sweet baby returned home safe to the only people who had laid a claim on her from birth.

I learned a lot of this on late-night Google searches, my left hand steady on the computer plug and ready to yank if Mom and Dad should wake up and come downstairs. It was on those nights that I learned what the world had wanted me to know; everyone splashing their opinions across the net so they could sit there until the girl in question learned to read and sneak and wonder.

Before that, though, I had known enough. I knew that Grandma liked the right side of the bed, and with the left pressed against the wall with the window I could listen to far-away coyotes in the safety of my head on her chest. I knew the sting of shampoo in my eyes, Mom dipping a plastic cup in the bathwater and pouring it over my head as I howled and thrashed. Albert—Daddy, back then—shooting a rattlesnake again and again, blasting holes in the living room floor while Grandma and I screamed for him to stop. Christmas pageants in Chicago, and piano recitals in Chicago, and first communion in Chicago and before I knew it there was no world but Chicago. I stopped checking my shoes for scorpions in the morning. I stopped leaving a space in my bed for Grandma.

I didn't flush, not wanting to ruin the mood they'd all nestled into with the prayers and dreams and smudging. Not wanting them to remember I was there. I held the bathroom doorknob all the way to the left, clicking it slowly, softly back into place. Pressing my bare toes to the carpeted staircase, inching away from the warmth downstairs, I could hear them laughing. And then in bed, the room so cold and quiet I lay down with the blankets pulled over my face and my hands firm against my chest, it was like I could hear them, huddled in close, breathing, not saying anything at all.

Sandra walked me to my first class. She must have known I didn't know where the science campus was, must have known too that it wasn't anything to be ashamed of in my still-undecided major status, but she didn't mention that. Instead she talked about labs and nerds and grading on a curve, all the things I'd have to know about taking science beyond high school.

"Show me all your essays before you turn them in," she said. "There's a totally different format for scientific papers, so everything you think you know is wrong."

She left me standing in front of room 405. The tables were long shiny black ones, that connected all the way down the row. I'd come early, and still most of the seats were taken. The front row was crowded with extra chairs people had pushed in, eager to get close to the action. I hadn't seen anything like it before, and I'd been in all three courses famed for being easy or—God help us—fun.

I took an empty seat between two girls in daring clothes—a backless lumberjack shirt, a puffy sweater that was oddly sexy. Until the professor walked in, these girls would hunch in close and talk to each other across my face. Later I'd learn they lived in an off-campus bio-major house specialising in weird experiments and weekly science show-and-tell. Later I'd learn that they were hopelessly nerdy and yet exceptionally cool—a nice kind of cool. A kind that would let almost anyone from anywhere in, if you would just meet them halfway. I wouldn't.

Professor Andrews was her name, but everyone called her Lucy. I thought that was a bad idea on her part, seeing how young she looked already. I spent the first few minutes of class calculating how quickly a person could get out of grad school and secure a teaching position, then moved on to other concerns. Professor Andrews was black, and I was distracted. Being technically brown myself, I still felt a strange need to get used to her being who she was. Had I ever had a teacher like that before? What did I mean by "like that" anyway?

Professor Andrews mostly told stories about animals. She used the stories as a jumping-off point for terms I couldn't place: Dollo's law, warning colouration, the Bruce effect. I knew I was missing a lot of the stuff that mattered, a lot of the stuff that heads were nodding to all around me. But the stories shook me awake. Some of what I was learning about everyday animal life was dark and upsetting. A lot of it was funny. I felt myself relaxing into science every time I laughed, easing into it even if I really only understood things on the surface. Professor Andrews talked about a study on tadpoles. Related tadpoles in one pond, unrelated tadpoles in the other. The finding? Related tadpoles didn't mate as much. Why not?

"Incest," I said.

The professor looked at me, long but not unkind. "Yes. But in the bio department, we like to call that inbreeding."

I felt people laughing at me just then—people who weren't. The shame was in my head, but that's the only place it has to be to make its mark. To bang just one more nail in the fence I carried with me. Three years later, on the night before graduation, I'd run into a few of these students and they'd teach me to lick salt off my wrist before throwing back my neck to a shot of tequila. We would laugh and laugh together, I'd be cracking them up, I'd be on fire, and they'd say they had always wanted to get to know me better—that they had tried. That it was a shame, how alone I'd made myself.

A female cuckoo bird will lay her own eggs in the nest of a bird from another species, so that some other mother will have to care for her young. Long after the female cuckoo is gone, the cuckoo hatchlings drop the mother bird's own eggs out of the nest. As the only survivors, the cuckoo hatchlings are the sole focus of the surrogate's parental energy.

My own adoption was desperately wanted, wanted with medical bills and paperwork and lawyers and an almost violent longing when I was taken away. And if my biological mother did just drop me off and move on, if she did think I wasn't worth any great investment in parental energy, does it matter? With all the many pulls on my heart, I tell myself it doesn't. With all the many pulls on my heart, I tell myself it can't.

We were supposed to find our own groups for lab, and I was genuinely surprised when no one came and swooped up my silent, no-fun, no-bio-major self. Everyone was grouped off together, had been since they arrived on campus with all their goals in order. They lived with each other, ate with each other, sometimes even dated each other. They volunteered as lab assistants and counted out live crickets for feedings, and if there were money and research in it then they seemed to be happy enough doing this type of thing as long as they lived. Most of the class was just coming back from an off-campus programme logging fire ants in Namibia, and they had whole troves of stories about ant attacks. Ant attacks on the feet, ant attacks on the hands, literal ants in their pants. I just wanted a damn group.

It was the night before we were due to start our research projects, and Professor Andrews announced in class that day that all but one person had a lab group and we needed "to take care of that." Unbelievable. She didn't actually say my name, but she might as well have. There was pity in that room.

When the college bells tolled, I tore out of class and went straight to the Native American House. I liked that I could find almost all of us, almost all the time, right there. I liked that I could just walk down the hall banging on doors one-two-three and soon enough we'd be spread out on the thin-carpeted floor eating an entire package of double-stuff Oreos.

Jess said, "Remind me what this is about?"

I stopped myself. I'd been talking about animals again, talking about how female zebra finches will lay big, nutrient-rich eggs when their mates are really unattractive. About how they mate for life, and the female has no incentive to save her resources for someone better down the line. "That gives the offspring a better chance at life," I'd said, to which Jess had said, "Remind me what this is about?"

Sandra laughed. "Cut the animal crap, Della. You need a lab group; no one cares about compensatory investment."

"So you were listening," I said.

Sandra read out a list of names.

"Jake Mallory. Good guy. Andy Jaraz. Hilarious, but you'd be three-wheeling his girlfriend. Celia Green, Abel Willhelm, Sarah Jones. Take any one of those kids and you'll be fine. I know them from bio pre-reqs."

Jess asked what I'd been thinking. "How's Della supposed to just take them?"

Sandra groaned. "Seriously?" She rolled over, pulled out her phone, and sent a text.

"No," I said. "You did not just helicopter-parent me."

Her phone buzzed. She checked it without looking up at me. "It's Jake," she said. "He'll let you in his group tomorrow."

Once a year, grey whales migrate from the coastal waters of Mexico to their Arctic feeding grounds. The mothers cannot head north until their calves are strong enough. The older whales and male whales leave and the mothers stay behind for weeks, nursing their calves until it's time to make the journey together.

Sometimes, this is when the orcas come in. Sometimes, this is when a pack of orcas will coordinate an attack, each taking part in an hours-long battle to separate the calf from its mother. Sometimes the mother fights and swings her tail and beats away the danger. Sometimes the calf is separated from its mother, and killed, and left behind as the mother swims on alone.

I'd known about this for a while, but it was the footage they made us watch in grad school that would come to haunt me. It's online now, and I watch it when I'm being unkind to myself. Sometimes I think, what would it be like to be loved like that? To be protected? And sometimes I think, it would be a mangled rattlesnake on the living room floor and locks on every door and voices lowered when you walk in a room. It would be what it is now, which is a love built more on fear than comfort.

I came into the lab with my eyes to the floor, like I didn't deserve to be there. I looked anywhere but their faces: the bags of fish in a row for another group's experiment, the dry mud in the grooves of Jake's sandals, the smooth rocks lining our lizard terrariums.

There were microscopes and Bunsen burners, scales and chunky protective goggles. There was a showerhead for when you get chemicals on your body, two fountains for when you get chemicals in your eyes. Everywhere warnings, everywhere signs.

I found my group leaning across a couple of lab tables, and to his credit Jake didn't make a big deal of me joining. He did quick introductions and started right in, like I was supposed to be there.

"Here's just an idea," he said, "and y'all can tell me if you think it's worth pursuing." He looked at us one by one, Celia-Abel-me, and I liked how I felt heard, even without saying a thing.

"I was thinking we could design an experiment around lizard mating," he said. "Since you know how violent that can sometimes get"—I didn't know that, and it turned out not to be true—"I thought we could manipulate the situation to look at some of its causes."

"Hunger," said Celia. "If we don't introduce the female until the male is experiencing hunger, that might heighten its sense of danger. You know, put him in survival mode." Also not true. Not that I knew it then. If I'd known our findings would be so far off I would have agonised over these plans, but as it turns out science is all about being wrong.

"Competition," said Abel. "We could ask Lucy for a few more males, and we'll see how they react to being in a tank with two or three competing males."

They looked at me. "I like the hunger idea," I said, though I didn't. It would be up to us to starve the thing. But I also knew it would be up to us to put a few males together in a small tank, and I didn't want to see any blood first-hand. In the end we went with the competition plan, because getting the lizard seriously emaciated would take time that we didn't have—Abel had looked up our project due date in the syllabus.

By seven o'clock we had a pretty rigorous schedule planned out. I'd known to expect multiple trials, but there's multiple trials and then there's science teacher butt-kissing. I didn't complain though, just tried to be invisibly helpful wherever I could. I looked for physical tasks I could take over, so I wouldn't have to talk as much. But they talked to me anyway. People always did.

Celia said, "It's a nice surprise, you being here."

I nodded, looked down the lab sheet at our numbers.

Abel said, "My cousin had a bad adoption once. It all worked out, though. Not in the history books, I mean." He laughed softly, then gave a little cough.

This was exactly why I didn't like new people. I didn't look a thing like that little girl in the faded newspapers, but our school was small enough for people to get excited when they heard my name. Campus celebs included the boy who was once a yellow Power Ranger, the girl who briefly dated Josh Groban at summer camp, and me.

"I'm glad to hear it," I said.

Jake said, "You guys signed out the lizard yet? I heard there were three other groups studying Carolina anoles, and I want a good one."

We selected our male—browner than the lime-green I had for whatever reason expected, firm where Albert's lizard-shaped fish bait had been fantastically gooey. I'd wanted to name it, but Celia said no. "Things happen in labs," she said. "This isn't a pet."

The four of us got quiet after that, their almost-camaraderie towards me caught on a line. Jake cleared his throat. "Wanna get a bite to eat?" he asked.

Abel and Celia said yes, but I pretended to have a big test to study for in Spanish. Before their goodbyes—bigger and friendlier than a less chilly team might have warranted—Abel reminded us to meet early the next morning to run trials.

The female poison dart frog lays eggs on the rainforest floor. The male fertilises them, then stands guard until they hatch. Tiny tadpoles wiggle up onto the mother's back, and she starts a days-long journey up into 100-foot trees. She carries them slowly up to a safe haven, to pools of rainwater collected in thick, green leaves.

As a child I demanded I be carried. The Navajo Nation social worker and then the Chicago child psychologist said that it was a perfectly normal reaction to early childhood trauma, that it would fade with the baby talk and the whining and the hiding my face in my fathers' pant legs. Whatever the cause, there are times when I miss it. Seeing clear above the low-to-the-ground world I'd known, being free to sit tight on a bench through steadily climbing waves of court decisions and microphones in the face. I could sit there in pinching, patent leather shoes, I could look straight ahead, and when it was over someone would pick me up and carry me away. Mom or Dad or Albert, someone would just lean in close with open-wide arms and take me.

College was hard—gone were the easy As of my public high school, gone was the constant praise of teachers familiar with my case, willing to overlook a few late papers in the face of all I'd suffered. In elementary school, I'd been put on a float in the Chicago Christmas parade. There were songs written about me in the Navajo Nation, and a bestselling tell-all book by Mom and Dad's lawyer. Away from those stories, away from what I had and hadn't been allowed to know about myself, I had trouble knowing exactly what I was here for. My greatest achievement had been almost overturning the Indian Child Welfare Act, and I hadn't intended that. Now I was off on my own, and people expected me to do something meaningful with my life.

High school had been about staying in good graces. Being a good and easy child, being worth the loans Mom and Dad and Albert paid back each month for their five-year stretch of legal fees. College seemed to be about more than that, though. About myself and what I cared about, which I wasn't sure of. I did notice, though, that I had fun in Professor Andrews' class. I did notice that I stayed up even later than the usual late studying for her midterm, partly the usual panic and partly because I was enjoying myself. London cab drivers had enlarged hippocampi, just like animals that have to cache foods over a large area. Peacock evolution was driven by sexual selection. And flatworms could change sex, and there was something called the sexy sons hypothesis, and inbreeding was avoided pretty much across the board.

I fell asleep in Hailey's bed with my textbook over my face, every so often Jess saying across the room, "Go to bed, go to bed. It's just a core course req, go to bed." Hailey saying, "What's wrong with this kid; her own bed's like ten feet away."

I failed that test. Completely tanked. I didn't tell Albert—we weren't close enough to do bad news with each other. Mom said it must have been a mistake, and Dad decided I wasn't focused. What he really talked about was my bad-influence friends in the Indian house, and how we drink and go out when we should be studying. But what I played in my head was, "Do you know how much we're paying for that school? Do you know how deep you got us in with the lawyers?"

As for Professor Andrews, she summoned me to office hours. She said, "Your mid-term."

I said, "Yes."

She said, "Was there a death in the family?"

Parental investment is not equal across the board. Human males invest years of energy into the extended childhood of feeding, protection, and education we have come to ask of them. Human females, too, though it's considerably less heroic.

And then there's the minimum. The minimum investment required of a human male is the fertilisation of an egg. Without medical support, the minimum investment required of a human female is about 37 weeks' development in utero.

Years down the line I'd know all about foetuses, and one of my own would develop in utero. What struck me most was how much that time counted. I knew enough about foetal development and the risks of miscarriage in the first trimester to call it "the foetus," something that drove my husband up the wall. What struck me, though, was how the minimum investment wasn't minimal at all. How, when no one was around, I called it baby and sweetheart and love, and love, and love. I spent two thousand hours lying in bed with my arms wrapped around myself, wrapped around her, and I knew that the woman who gave me away had felt this once. Somewhere in Arizona, sometime in two thousand hours already thirty years gone, I had been loved.

The lizards didn't like to mate with our faces pressed up against the glass. We set up Abel's laptop in front of the terrarium. We sat under the table and huddled around Celia's screen. We Skyped the computer above our heads and watched the male lizard flare up and approach the female. I squinted at its toes, its back, its tail, the way its feet raced forward and then froze, raced forward and then froze. I couldn't look away.

After the deed was done, we began again. I'd come to love that. I loved how everything we thought we knew had to be tested into oblivion. I liked how we never tested the same lizard twice in one day. It was worth the cost of the extra lizards because exhaustion would skew the results. Also, I knew what it was to be tired.

I scribbled down the data from our fifth trial of the day and jumped up. I wanted to set up the next trial, something Celia and Abel and Jake were always rushing to do themselves.

All three heads shot up at me from under the table. "We can take care of that," said Jake. "It's a bitch trying to get a hold of those guys."

"No thanks," I said. I already had a corner of the mesh terrarium top open. I was already inching my hand down the glass walls, hovering above the male. It froze. Waited. Ran.

My arm swung to the side, sweeping across the length of the terrarium in a race against the short, blurred legs of the lizard. It was almost at the top of the tank, almost at the open corner roof that rested on my arm. I slapped forward, catching its tail in my hand.

"Got it," I said. But Celia and Jake and Abel didn't respond. They were reaching out their hands and throwing themselves on the floor, cupping their hands and cursing when they missed. There was the lizard, speeding across the floor until Celia caught it and held it against her chest. I was still holding the tail.

Abel walked back over to me. "That happens," he said. "It's why we try to never touch a reptile on the tail. Unless it's, like, all tail. I mean, like a snake."

He didn't say, "That's why we don't want you to have anything to do with our research," which was a nice thing to not hear even if I thought that might be what he meant.

"So they just drop off?" I asked. "Anyone tries to pin them in place, they can lose the tail and run?"

"Pretty much," he said. "But it's never something we want to let happen. Growing back a new tail takes a shit-ton of metabolic energy, and life in the lab is stressful enough. Plus it won't grow back as bone. Just cartilage."

I looked at the lizard, released into its own tank. Alive, but still. Hidden under some leaves in the corner. We did five more trials with different lizards that afternoon, and every few minutes I'd stand up and look across the room at what I'd done. It hadn't moved. After our work was done for the day, Celia invited us to dinner. I told her I had to study.

It was only a little bit because I felt stupid around them. I really did have to study. Not just study, but study with the professor. After that failed midterm, Professor Andrews had sat me down and read me the riot act. There would be no writing off of her class, not even if it was the last science I'd ever choose to study. She had never let a non-major take her course before. "It would be a shame," she said, "if you were to make me regret my change of heart."

That's what she'd said. I wondered if it was because she and I were the only minorities in the classroom, and if she felt that women-of-colour kinship I hadn't known back in Chicago. And then I wondered if it was worse than that. What if she felt bad for me? What if she was just one more fan, another 1990s tabloid-reader come to offer special attention?

Professor Andrews said I had to turn in a first draft of every lab report and short essay, giving Josh-the-teacher's-assistant enough time to make comments and give me another shot before the deadline. I had to record her lectures on my phone and listen to them "at the gym." Of course I'd never had the discipline to step foot in a gym, so I started bringing headphones and listening to her descriptions of sideways flanking and mate choice during group beading sessions at the house. I still sat on the floor with the other girls, but I was somewhere else. They were probably talking about boys or class or the state of things back home, but I wouldn't know with all the biology pulsing through my ears. Ring species. Food caching. Concealed ovulation.

Once a week, Professor Andrews made me come to office hours. I had to give her a ten-minute summary of what she'd taught us. At first, I made the same mistake I'd made on my midterm. I stayed on the surface, murky and full of human bias. "When a male lion joins a pride," I said. "First thing it does is kill off all the defenseless cubs. And when a baboon—"

She stopped me, setting her hand down firmly on the desk. Her nails were short, neat, and manicured with see-through nail polish. She wore her hair in hundreds of thin braids, and if that weren't enough she had them swept out of the way and pinned tight to the back of her head. Everything about her was clear, sensible. "Hold up," she said. "Why are you telling me this? What's the point of the lion story?"

I glanced at the bookshelf behind her. Ten shelves of science journals. Each one probably had at least ten scientific papers, which meant I might be sitting in front of thousands of studies on thousands of animals. For just a second, I forgot what a hard time I'd been having with the studies we had to summarise for class. I wanted to take over her office and read them all.

Actually, no. I wanted to have someone tell me their stories.

"The lion…" I started. Stopped. Started again. "Well, we were talking about kin selection today, which is all about helping your shared genetic material survive and get passed on. This new lion, the head of the pride, he has nothing in common genetically with the random cubs around."

"Take it further," she said. "What does that mean?"

"Survival is difficult, and the burden of defending the pride and feeding it is going to fall on him. The lion doesn't want to spend his energy fighting for genes that these cubs got from random lions."

Professor Andrews leaned back in her chair.

"He'll also probably have his own offspring soon enough." I was careful not to say "children." I knew better than that.

I said, "Once he starts mating with the lionesses, he'll produce his own cubs, and he can invest parental energy into feeding and protecting cubs that will pass on his genes."

"And there you go," she said. "I know you could probably recite back to me every story of the semester. And that's good—most people don't realise how important a sense of story is in a scientist. But you need to focus on analysis now. When you're reviewing your notes, try to clarify what lies behind the story. I want you to start asking yourself why things are the way they are."

Kin selection.

Kin selection means doing what it takes for your shared genetic material to survive and be passed on. According to kin selection, tadpoles are more likely to eat each other when they're third or fourth cousins than when they're first cousins or siblings. According to kin selection, there's a reason stepdads are on average more abusive than real dads. According to kin selection, Albert has a deep biological need to take care of me and see me be safe in this world. And yet nothing feels safe like my face buried in Dad's thick-sweatered shoulder, and I don't have a theory for that.

It was the last Sunday night before reading period, and the Native American Programme brought in another guest. He was a Navajo poet—a young, attractive one from the looks of the event poster taped to the house refrigerator.

"Oh look. I'll bet he and Della get on well enough," said Hailey, three-time Miss Cherokee and all-the-time ass when it came to getting all the good ones. I ignored her.

Jess was still looking at the flyer. I looked with her. Straight nose, broad shoulders, clear skin with neutral undertones. Before I'd gotten so caught up in bio, we'd filled out a quiz together in Cosmo. The upshot: people with neutral undertones will look good in literally anything.

"Looks good," Jess said. "I say you come down here a little early and get him talking about the stuff you have in common."

"What stuff we have in common?" I said.

"You know," said Hailey. "Traditional food, major families, dirty, dirty tribal politics."

We laughed, though mine came out more like a sigh. These were my closest friends in the world, and they didn't always get it. Maybe this poet and I had some shared genetic traits. We were both short and tan and potentially lactose-intolerant. Maybe we had evolved to tolerate desert heat better than your average New Englander, though I was pretty sure evolution didn't work that fast. Maybe we even had some way-back family connection, and kin selection would force him to save me from an oncoming train.

Kin selection be damned. When it came down to it, I didn't have any of the stuff that makes a Navajo kid. I was pretty waspy, for a somewhat-Indian. I'd been raised on Mother Goose and embroidered sweater sets from The Children's Place. Hot Poet and I may have both been born on the Navajo Nation, but I'd always be a long ways away.

That night, I waited to come downstairs until I was sure the dining room was full. The poet read some of his work. I had always had a tendency to zone out when it came to poetry, and that's what I did, but his time my thoughts were anchored by the pair of hands I was staring at. They gripped the open book of poetry so hard the veins stood out, and as I looked at them I thought about risky things I'd never do, like what if I were to come onto this man ten years my senior, and what if he were to figure out who I was, and what would "coming onto him" even look like. He shut the book; I snapped out of it.

The poet answered questions, talked about his inspiration and process, talked about the rough time he'd had growing up, and how much his grandmother had meant to him when he was abandoned and she raised him up herself in the desert. Honestly, it was a bit much. At least I thought it was. The visitation agreement had only given me about five hours to spend in Arizona each summer, so if I thought this poet's grandma sounded too stereotypically hardy and Indian-stoic then that could just mean I didn't know enough Navajo grandmas. When would I know enough about us to be mixed up in it like the other girls, to curse the tribal councils and spit sharp-edged jokes about Indian Country's most downtrodden?

We went around in a circle towards the end and talked about what we wanted in our lives. It amazed me that every speaker was so desperate to know what us kids had in mind for ourselves, but here I was being asked to answer. I stayed, but lied. I said something about getting involved in social work. Back home, of course. There are a lot of families having a hard time back home.

Sandra followed me up to my room afterwards. She slammed the door behind her. "You're full of shit," she said. "Over my dead body will you major in Psych."

"You know," I said. "I grew up around a bunch of social workers. A lot of them were Navajo Nation employees. Who knows where I might be today if it weren't for—"

"You'd be here, Della. Now go be a scientist."

I stared her down. Sandra was tall and thin, but muscular in a way that was so grown-up, so strong, she looked like she was better equipped to face the world than any of the rest of us girls. Like she could just push her way through anything, like she was doing with me now.

"I don't want to be a scientist," I said.

"You want to be a scientist," she said. "A behavioural ecologist. All you do is talk about studies you've read. Then you talk about the same ones over again to the same people. Jess says you have thirty issues of Animal Behaviour checked out from the library and hidden under your bed."

I told Sandra I wasn't any good at science. "No one is good at science," she said. "It's just the scientists who stick with it. The highest average in Chem IV right now is a C. Fuckin' Divyanka."

I told Sandra I needed to do something for my tribe. I said, "The last thing the Navajo Nation needs is a sub-par behavioural ecologist."

Sandra sat down on my bed and fell back. I lay down next to her. There were glow-in-the-dark stars on the ceiling, a gift from Albert when I was five. Dad had helped me tack them on when they arrived—a rare acknowledgement of the person who'd mailed them to me. I used to look up at them in the first few months after Mom and Dad won custody. I used to pretend they were the same stars I used to look up at with Albert and Grandma, back before I learned we all get the same stars everywhere. Dad had helped me take them down and pack them up the year before. When he drove me to college, he stood on the bed and got a crick in his neck trying to stick them to the dorm ceiling.

"I've got a friend back home," said Sandra. "A really good woman. She said to me once—I was probably talking out my ass about something—she said I had to stop thinking of our tribe as its history. She said that we've always been changing, what with migration and horse trading and whatever, and that's part of our story. What's happening right now—reservation life and urban Indians and whatever— that's all a part of our story."

Downstairs we could hear the drum circle start up. The boys liked to practice on Sunday nights and the beat never failed to thud through the entirety of the house. Out of the basement, through the kitchen, up the stairs. On the other side of the wall, Hailey was playing this awful Somali-British punk album on her laptop. Downstairs, the boys reached back their heads and sang, "...You're myyyyy heya, heya, NDN gi-irl heya heya heya..."

I said, "A Navajo behavioural ecologist. You think that's crucial to the story."

She nodded, yanking the pillow under our heads as she did. "You're crucial to the story, Dell."

We looked at each other. Sandra was holding her lips tight at the corners, like she knew how lame she was being as the words came out of her mouth and she was too late to stop them. We burst out laughing.

"Oh, Sandra," I said, "I am unworthy of your sweet, sweet Indian wisdom!" We were on our sides now, hearing our voices over Jess's playlist and then laughing harder at that.

"Sit at my feet, young Runs-from-Passion, and I shall share the ways of cheesy motivational speakers across Turtle Island," Sandra said.

We laughed until Hailey turned off the music and banged on the wall. "DINNER?" she called. I stood up and stretched. I said, "SURE."

Sandra followed me to the door, stepping back into her shoes as she walked. "I did have a point, you know."

"Oh?"

"Just do what you want, Dell."

A week later, I went to Professor Andrews' office to pick up the take-home final. She gave me her cell number and told me to call if I had questions. She said she'd keep her phone with her for the next thirteen hours while I worked through the test.

I got a B- on the exam, a C+ for the semester. I went out dancing with the girls on the night the grades came in. We were all one step closer to something, whether or not we knew what it was. For that night, anyway, we stood close together in a circle and danced through the throbbing in our calves and the underfoot sticking-unsticking of years of spilled beer on the frat basement floor. We all went home together that night. We went to bed sometime around four, wrapped up in sleeping bags because our upstairs rooms were too far apart.

At nine, I shot awake. I showered and jumped into sweatpants and flip-flops, nearly tripping on Hailey's outstretched arm on my way out the door. I ran to the Biological Sciences building, where Professor Andrews gave me a talking-to about the challenges that lay ahead. Then she signed my major card.

I walked back to the dorm, my feet itching in the dew-soaked grass and the morning air blowing straight to my skin through my loose-knit sweater. Before letting myself back in, before the other girls had woken, I stood outside to call my parents.

UPSIDE DOWN

ALAINA SYMANOVICH

The kiss burst like a camera flash, so startling and fast that Kate only knew it by the whisper of blindness, the disorientation it left behind. She thanked the dark hallway for obscuring her face as Ari pulled away and helped her stand; she didn't need a mirror to tell her what she looked like. She wore the sepia softness of someone in love—eyes so fuzzy, mouth so slack, it exposed her feelings about her photographer better than any picture could.

Kate realised why the moment unfolded: unlike other first kisses, unlike opening doors and shimmering horizons, Ari's kiss meant The End. It meant neither girl had anything to lose; it meant they would never see one another again. And like a photograph, Kate would keep it tacked to her heart long after Ari moved away in the morning, long after time and sun bleached it white.

Because for one flashbulb instant, the world had stood right-side up. Kate had been crying into the blackness, careful not to let her tears mar Ari's leather jacket, when Ari approached. Kate wore Ari's clothes, and Ari's perfume, and heartache. *You'll break me when you leave,* she wanted to say, *without even trying.*

She didn't say that.

She said: "I can't be this person," gesturing to the leather encasing her arms, the layered polos and suede pants she wore. "I'm not you."

Ari's face always changed in dim light: it was one of Kate's favorite things about her. In the after-midnight hours, when the girls lowered their voices because it felt right and shared beers just because, Ari didn't look like the jaded girl everyone thought she was. She became the confidante who held Kate's hand when she was drunk, the one who knew how her mother's weekly phone calls drove her to tears, who understood why she worried her nose was too pointy, her arms too flabby.

Ari leaned close and traced two warm thumbs over Kate's cheekbones, erasing her tears. "You," she whispered, "can be anything."

As Kate shook her head, she marveled at the feeling of Ari's hands cupping her jaw, at the two of them moving in tandem.

"So you can sit here and cry all over my clothes," Ari said, her mouth flirting with a smile, "or you can come finish your drink and have a good time with your friends."

Then Ari kissed her. She kissed her and pulled her to her feet and they rejoined the party, and all Kate could think was that her tears were lingering on Ari's hands, the way Ari's kiss was ghosting her lips.

*

Springtime again: pollen allergies and perspiring underarms. The apathy that overtakes college campuses as May nears. This year Kate will join the seniors' exodus, a thought that inflames her with enough passion to kiss Devon back like she means it. If she's learned one thing over the past year, it's that girls pine to be swept. Swept off their feet, or into the gutter like bowling pins—doesn't make much difference.

Kate pulls her mouth off Devon's for a moment, nodding toward the cinderblock wall where several couples grind in pairs. "Up against the wall," she shouts over the music.

Hesitation dims Devon's eyes. "It's kind of public," she says, glancing around the crammed basement. The band clots in one corner, surrounding by gyrating bodies. The only hands empty of beer bottles are those, like Kate's and Devon's, laced around a partner.

"Come on," Kate lowers her voice and her lips, pressing her mouth against Devon's neck so she feels the words resound through her body. "I like it rough."

Devon bites her lip and surveys the room a final time, as if double-checking for acquaintances, before she grabs Kate by the shoulders and steers her to the cinderblock. Kate feels the usual bloom of hands on her hips, the trailing and squeezing over her waist, ribs, chest, and—inevitably—hair. Devon's hands linger over the back of her neck, the slope where downy hair fades into skin. The long-haired girls always ravish the nakedness there, try to drown their fingers in the buzz cut, cup its warmth in their palms. They used to do the same to Ari; Kate remembers her razor tone when she complained, *they're obsessed with short hair because they're scared of it—scared of how much they want it.*

Kate lets Devon continue to paw her hair, lick her neck. *They only like you as much as they like themselves*, Ari had said, her voice pinched. *And they're obsessed with themselves.*

"You're amazing," Devon gasps between kisses, pressing her pelvis forward. Kate grunts, noncommittal. Reminds herself to mimic Devon's excitement.

She closes her eyes and smirks as the bass explodes to their right. She imagines Devon stumbling back to her dorm later, collapsing on mussed sheets, grinning about the night. She won't turn Kate's words around in her mind, won't examine them side-to-side and upside-down as she should. Won't realise that, under the right conditions, "I like it rough" and "I don't give a fuck" sound one and the same.

*

Ari led them through the same playlist every party, and since she'd finalised her plans to move West after graduation, *California Girls* gained a permanent spot in the rotation. Drink in hand, legs spilled over arm of the pleather couch, she would lead long-winded discussions on everything from solipsism to genital piercings—until "her song" pumped through the speakers. "*Dance*," she coaxed Kate as the bubblegum beat swelled. "It's my last night."

Kate pursed her lips, but allowed Ari to pull her upright. She remembered Ari talking about moving West since they first met, months ago. Like most things in Ari's life, Kate never doubted that the plan would yield to her desire. Even without a trust fund and a kindly uncle in San Francisco, Ari would have gotten herself to California. Ari always got where she wanted to go.

"Remember how much you used to hate dancing?" Ari laughed as she shimmied her shoulders and reached for Kate's hand.

"I didn't hate it," Kate argued, trying to mimic Ari's fluidity, the sinuous snaking of her hips. "I just sucked at it."

Ari laced her fingers through Kate's, drawing her in and spinning her as the last verse faded out. "You still suck," she said with a broad grin, leaving their hands loosely intertwined as she led Kate back to the couch. Their friends continued dancing, to one of the few electronica tracks Ari would tolerate at her parties.

"Clearly you don't remember the fall," Kate said, surreptitiously peeling the label off her bottle and sliding it into her jeans pocket. She tried to save as many mementos of these nights as possible, touchstones to keep her moored after everything changed. She kept a box in her bedroom where she stored fossils of Ari: handwritten notes, water-bottle caps, movie ticket stubs. Tangibles she could keep with her.

"So maybe you were even more awkward—*maybe*," Ari conceded. "But you still don't have any confidence."

Kate's smiled faded. She kneaded her hands. "You know why."

"I do," Ari nodded, giving Kate's shoulder a quick squeeze as a silence lapsed between them.

"But," she said, "sometimes you just need to say 'fuck it all' and let yourself go, you know? Like, in all the time I've known you, you've never just thrown your shirt off and stopped giving a shit and had fun. *Never*. And, hanging out with me,

I didn't think that was possible. But you managed."

Kate blinked. "I've had more fun with you than I've had in my life."

Ari clunked her bottle on the windowsill behind the couch, reaching for Kate's hand with surprising strength. Kate felt the flex of tendons in Ari's wrist, the clamp of insistent fingers; she grabbed her the way she'd grab their friend John, the one whose body moved like flames across the dance floor. She grabbed her like they had something to accomplish.

"Then show me," she said, leveling her gaze at Kate. "John," she shouted over her shoulder, "give us something we can dance to."

There was something unnervingly vulnerable about dancing, Kate thought. People pretended to like it, pretended to feel beautiful as they shook and swayed, but she always felt spotlighted by the beat. Even in the darkest rooms, her every movement felt magnified. She wondered if she was on beat, if her arms looked stupid, if her stomach rippled in paunches when she twisted. But she danced anyway, if only to watch Ari. Ari emanated an ultraviolet confidence, so luminescent Kate thought she'd get burnt by her skin. Ari's body could become a colour, a wave, could force itself into your cells if you let it.

Kate let her hips grind against Ari's, finding the rhythm there and clutching it tight. Ari's hands scaled her arms, so Kate mirrored the motion; Ari danced low, so Kate followed. It was like that "How to Be a Good Kisser" article she'd read on WikiHow: the first rule was to observe. People showed affection the way they wanted to receive it. It made Kate glad that she'd spent so many months waiting on the sidelines.

She watched Ari rise out of a low move, wiggle her hips, and strip off her shirt in one flourished move. Ari joked that most of the students on campus had seen her in her underwear, and Kate didn't doubt it. If she looked like Ari— honeyed Greek complexion, sleek stomach, muscled limbs—she'd probably take her clothes off, too. She had none of those features, but Ari's blazing eyes were enough to make her forget it.

"Fuck it," she announced, and the scene went dark for a moment as she pulled her sweater over her head.

Ari gave a whoop of approval, then pulled her closer, pressing their stomachs together. "Oh, my God," she said into Kate's ear. "You've got a *body*."

Kate rolled her eyes, trying to focus on the ceiling and not the unfamiliar draft on her abdomen. She felt the bravado of the moment fading fast.

"Well, don't stare," she crossed her arms over her stomach. Ari waved them off. "John," she called. "Holy shit. John, check out Kate."

John's eyes widened as he took in Kate's rose-colored bra, her pale torso. "Damn."

Kate swiveled her eyes back to the ceiling. "How come the room doesn't freeze when you take your shirt off?" she asked Ari.

"Because I don't go around in old-man sweaters and sweatpants," Ari said, looking Kate up and down again. "I'm one of the hottest people I know, so I own it. Why don't you?"

Kate shrugged, still avoiding Ari's eyes. They both knew why.

"Come on," Ari said, linking their hands again. They ran into the bedroom, Kate stumbling to keep up. A mess of unsealed boxes peppered the floor, Ari's life compartmentalised and ready for transport. Kate looked away, out the window, then realised with a pang that she could only see outside because the makeshift curtain—a Seattle Seahawks blanket tacked to the wall—was gone. Except for the crooked line of holes freckling the wall, Ari might never have lived there at all.

"Here," Ari said, still rifling through a box. She threw a jacket and several shirts at Kate, who recognized the brands as ones she couldn't afford even on clearance. "And this." Ari lobbed a pair of suede pants at her.

Kate held up the shirts. "Which one—?"

Ari took the clothes back. "Sit," she gestured to the bed, "and take off your pants." Kate raised her eyebrows, but did as commanded. The shock of her floral underpants on Ari's sheets made her blush. She slid on the pants and stood up quickly, wondering if Ari was watching her, if she would remember the image of Kate stripped to her underwear.

"You need layers," Ari said, handing her a t-shirt. She shook her head when Kate yanked it on, taking it upon herself to rearrange the neckline and shoulders. "There," she said, smoothing the fabric around Kate's hips. They repeated the process with a polo and a vest, until Ari's hands had tucked and tugged the fabric on every inch of Kate's body. When Ari handed her the finishing touch, the leather jacket, Kate felt a flush of something like drunkenness.

Ari steered her in front of the full-length mirror. "Look at you," she said, smacking her butt. "You're hot."

"What did you do to me?" Kate heard the awe in her voice and wondered whom she was really questioning. As Ari graced her with a spritz of perfume, something clean-smelling, mangoes and mint and herbs, Kate thought they looked like doubles in the mirror: two short-haired girls, candy-coated in layers and buzzed with alcohol. The moment struck Kate as vaguely tragic, like the crumbling last minutes of a dream when you feel yourself dissolving back into reality.

She studied their reflections as Ari hovered her lips behind at the nape of her neck, whispering so Kate shivered at every word. "Seriously," Ari smirked at the mirror, meeting the reflection of Kate's wide eyes, "*I'd* fuck you."

And then she was gone, flitting out of the room and snapping off the light switch and yelling for everyone to dance.

*

Kate dodges Devon's kiss, ducking out of her embrace even though she moans and tries to wrangle her back inside. Her back itches from pressing up against the cold cinderblock, from Devon's hands raking the skin under her shirt, greedy as someone who has never run her hands over a girl before. And maybe she hasn't, Kate considers with disdain. Inexperienced girls annoyed her more than the experimenters; they latched on fastest, believed the first girl to grind against them was The One.

"I need to find my friends," Kate lies, pretending to scan the room. Her roommates left around two o'clock, one for a frat party, the other for phone sex with her long-distance boyfriend. Kate starts to walk away, leaving Devon blinking and swiping her hair out of her face.

The crowd almost muffles the girl's voice. "Meet you upstairs—?"

Kate waves a hand over her shoulder, a gesture Devon could read as dismissive or assenting. *Let her decide*, Kate thinks, weaving through the groups of dancers. Another band has taken over, an electronica one that Ari would hate. At that thought, Kate raises her wrist to her nose and inhales the scent there. Even after the hours of dancing, after being mauled by Devon and several girls before, the trace of mango and mint lingers. Ari probably thought she lost the perfume in the move, probably replaced it without a thought. She'd never know that Kate still kept that bottle, used dry, in her fossil box along with the bottle caps and gum wrappers. She'd never know that Kate still wore the scent like holy water.

*

Ari pried the cap off Kate's first beer, sliding it to her across the kitchen table. John joined them, already on his second glass of wine, and nodded for the girls to sit.

"Cheers," he said, "to our last night." He wasn't leaving for his Ph.D. program until August, but everyone knew the group wouldn't be the same once Ari moved. She tethered them, pouring enough drinks to make Kate relax, taking John's drink away when he started threatening to drive drunk or curse out the neighbors. They both needed her; they both feared her absence.

"Cheers," they repeated, clinking their drinks. A few friends would join them later, but until then the room was quiet.

"Truth-speak," Ari announced, folding her legs underneath her. "What's one thing I don't know about you guys?"

John swirled his wine in its fingerprinted glass. "I thought the point of hanging out with lesbians was avoiding these heart-to-hearts."

Ari rolled her eyes. "I'll go, then," she sat up straighter. "Did I ever tell you about the only time I got grounded? I was really young, playing with my sister— she must've been three, maybe four. We were on the swing set. And I went to give her an underdog, but I pushed her so hard that her entire swing flipped upside down. And she just hung there, yelling for me to help her."

John shook his head, laughing. "Jerk."

Ari smiled. "Aren't I? So there I am, laughing my head off, and my mom looks out the window. And let me tell you, I've never seen her angrier."

John and Kate laughed as Ari impersonated her mother running out of the house, screaming and calling Ari by her full name as her little sister swung, pendulum-style and upside-down, tentacles of her hair trailing in the dirt. Kate wondered how long the sister dangled like that, feet overhead and heart in her throat. She wondered if she'd seen the betrayal coming, or if it shocked her as much as the swing's overturning: the sudden inversion of space, the vertigo of seeing the world wrong. She wondered who helped the girl down, in the end. Kate gulped her beer, letting the carbonation sear away her conviction that it hadn't been Ari.

"Kate," Ari snapped her fingers in front of Kate's face. "Your turn."

"Oh," Kate wrapped her fingers around the bottle, absorbing its chill. "I don't know. I guess, the only time I was grounded? I was six or seven, and it was when McDonald's was still giving away Hot Wheels cars in Happy Meals."

Kate smiled as she remembered the plastic scent of chicken nuggets, the french-fry salt pearled on her fingertips. She remembered listening to U2 with her dad as they waited in line at the drive-thru; her mom never condoned any trip to a fast-food restaurant. She probably stayed at home, eating her low-carb dinner in tiny forkfuls in front of her soaps. She would frown at Kate when she saw the Happy Meal container in the trash, stare pointedly at her daughter's waistline and suggest she go for a bike ride, or a walk.

"Well, I was playing with those Hot Wheels in the living room, and I left one laying out." Kate bit her lip, looking guiltily at her beer—guilty because of the smile quivering at the wings of her mouth. "And my mom fell."

Ari burst out laughing, lifting her hand for a high-five. Kate met it, bashful.

"You don't understand," she argued, trying to protest but breaking into giggles. "She's got osteoporosis and shit—she could've been really hurt." They ignored her; John snorted into his wineglass, clutching his side as laughter wracked his body.

Ari waved Kate's words away like a bad smell, setting her drink down and pressing her palms on the tabletop. "Kate. Listen to me. Maybe if your mom wasn't a fucking cunt who told you that you needed a nose job when you were eleven, I'd have some sympathy. Okay?" Ari raised her eyebrows, daring Kate to tell her otherwise.

"Frankly, I wish she'd broken a leg," John said, raising his glass again.

"I'll cheers to that," Ari said, nodding for Kate to join. As Kate took another drink, letting the alcohol flood the grottoes of her mouth, wash her tongue, she could finally name the feeling in her stomach, the freefalling sensation that coloured moments like these: she felt lucky.

Lucky, and out of control.

*

Kate bums a Marlboro off a sophomore on the patio, savouring its smoke in her lungs. It makes her feel sterile, torched clean on the inside. She knows it's not supposed to work that way. She knows she probably sees everything all wrong.

Devon doesn't find her until the cigarette burns low enough to warm the space between her fingers. She doesn't look up when she hears Devon's voice— just watches the orange eye, smouldering and ready to close.

Devon hoists herself onto the patio's railing, swinging her legs back and forth from her seat on the warped wood. She says something about the night—a thank-you, maybe—and it takes Kate a few moments to realise she wants to exchange phone numbers.

"I'm moving away in a few weeks," she says, flicking her cigarette over the railing. She'd been saying it all year—*South, I'm moving South*—and she revels in its now-definite truthfulness. She has a job arranged, a life awaiting her in Louisiana, and she will go alone.

"That's cool," Devon nods, as if Kate said something inconsequential. "But we've got a little time…"

Kate frowns at the darkness, feeling like she could cry, or scream. She laughs instead, a rough, dry laugh that sounds like her mother's.

"We don't have time," she says, staring at the spot on the ground where her cigarette died. "So let it go."

The best part of the long, black walk home isn't the silence, or the nudging breeze on her neck, but the thrill of leaving Devon dumbstruck on the porch. Kate imagines her waiting there long after the party winds down, silent, feet dangling in empty space. Devon will never hear from her again, will never feel Kate's hands on her waist or smell the trace of mangoes and mint on Kate's wrists. And that, Kate thinks, is the way it ought to be.

THE ORIGINAL

KATIE M. FLYNN

Condensation has formed on the plastic sheeting. On the other side, Mom sleeps in her chair. I can hear her snoring over the whirr of the machines, pumping and measuring. I text Lara even though I know she's in class. She gets back to me immediately, just a single question mark, as if to say, what? I send back two question marks because what does she mean, what? I could be dying here.

Luckily, Lara gets back to me during free period. "You're all right, aren't you?"

"I'm not dying."

"That's not funny."

"I don't want to talk about that."

"Well, I only have a few minutes. What do you want to talk about?"

"Everything."

After she's told me about the horrid trig quiz she bombed, the awful rhinoplasty June got, and the totally killer party she's going to this weekend, she says she has to go.

"Well, call me after."

"Fine," she sighs, and then she's gone.

But not before I've heard it in her voice, how tired she is of me, stuck in my bubble, showing no symptoms of the sickness I pass to others like breath mints, just a slip of the palm, a cool lick of my breath.

It's not my fault.

"What'd you say?" Mom stirs in her seat, sits up. "I'm sorry, sweetie. I must have dozed off." She touches her hair, adjusts the zipper on her swishy lavender jogging suit.

I search my name on my phone. The first hit that comes up is an exposé about asymptomatic carriers of infectious diseases. "And what happens to these so-called super-spreaders," the blonde newscaster with enhanced everything smile-speaks into the screen.

I sign off. "Mom!" I holler. "I want—" The sentence floats there unfinished in the plastic-encased air.

What do you want, sweetie?" She sits forward, ready to reach into her very insides to give it to me.

I huff, roll onto my side, reach out and touch the plastic.

"Now, Ginger, you know you're not supposed to do that."

I lean further off my bed, stretching, shaking the plastic, making waves.

"You could get out of bed. You have ten whole square feet in there. We could exercise. I'm feeling pretty stiff myself." She stands and stretches, smiles at me as if to say, what fun!

"This is a form of protest." I bat the sheeting with my hand.

Mom stands over me now, her nose breathing white clouds onto the plastic. "You know what they'll do. Do you want to sleep, is that it?" I shake the sheeting some more and the nurse comes, working her magic at the machines until I am a tranquil turnip, a cold collard green. I go places in that syrupy sleep. Before I'm gone, Mom reaches in with the plastic arm, pawing at me. I let her hold my hand because even this, her plastic grasp, is better than nothing at all. I squeeze her hand and disappear.

*

This time it's my fifteenth birthday. I'm sulking, hiding the sunny dress Mom bought me under Dad's old plaid Pendleton. I won't eat the cake. It's not vegan and I specifically requested a vegan cake.

"The first one I made was vegan. You saw how it turned out." Mom is pleading, kids crowding around us, annoyed because they want their processed sugar fix. But she won't let them have it until I take a bite. She holds out a fork, and I snatch it, stuffing a too-big bite into my mouth.

"There," I say, spitting cake, "feed the savages." They eat. I listen to their gnawing jaws. We all dance.

But what matters comes later. The kiss I steal from June in the garage as we search for more plastic cutlery. Amid the stacks of cleaning supplies, crates of canned soup and bottled spring water that Mom keeps in case the world crumbles, I take June's hand. Her fingers flicker back, her mouth locking onto mine in the darkness.

Later she'll claim that I came onto her and she laughed me off, but it doesn't matter then, in the dark.

I'm on an island, slathered in SPF, sleeping off a hangover on the beach. I partied big-time the night before, at a disco that erupted right out of the sand. Mom tells Carson it's food poisoning so he won't be mad. I watch them make out in the surf, pretending I'm asleep. June won't text me back. She posts a not-so-blind item about a totally psycho stalker on all her feeds, and I sign off, shoving my phone deep into the sand.

Carson and Mom are married that night. We're all barefoot and burned, decorated with local flowers that have a too-sweet smell. I snap pics for my followers. Mom cries. Carson tries. He can't eke out any real tears, but I have to give him points for effort. I hate him in that moment, the linen shirt he wears open, his smooth hairless chest, the board shorts hanging so low I can see his pelvic bone, the little leaping dolphin tattooed on his left hip. It's not until later, too late really, that I learn to love him.

After, we sit near the hotel pool. They serve an unrecognisable sweetmeat. We all dance.

Three days pass before the first outbreak. The newscaster looks constipated as he tallies the dead, twelve cases on the island where we stayed. Seven hours later there are outbreaks in four cities, but they don't make the connection for another five hours. By then it's loose.

I return to Pathways with a tropical all-natural tan and a new last name—Lane. It sounds fancy—Ginger Lane—and I repeat it over and over under my breath, trying to calm my stuttering heart as I climb the steps.

I see the wealthy Nevelle twins at the entrance, stop to flirt with the cute one. His brother, used to being the alternate, holds the door open for me, and just for fun, I touch his hand, squeeze it really, hoping to stir something up—though I don't know what. In Earth Sciences, I dissect a worm with three girls at my lab table. We take turns, passing the scalpel between us. I pretend to be grossed out like the others, but I love pinning back the worm's skin, poking at its reproductive organs and plucking out its five hearts as the girls squeal.

I spot June in the lunch line. She ignores me, slouching her way to a back table crowded with girls who whisper and giggle and gawk. Lara is out that week with bronchitis, so I eat alone, plugged into music of the angry variety, killing the sound of them all.

I see my favorite teacher on the stairs. Sister Grace congratulates me on my mother's nuptials, bending bony arms around me.

Meanwhile, Carson starts coughing at work. He manages the product line Close-u at Mor Pharmaceuticals. He likes to talk about how his product helps people overcome grief with few known side effects, including but not limited to nosebleeds and fits of rage. I know because Mom took it after Dad died.

When Carson succumbs, Mom's therapist calls in an emergency prescription for Close-u, but Mom refuses to take it. She tells me, "I want to feel it this time," and I can't begin to understand.

The next day there's an outbreak at Pathways. The Nevelle twins catch it—even their brawny bodyguards can't protect them from this. The three girls from Earth Sciences and Sister Grace—she's the first to succumb. They say her old age sped up the process, but I think it was the close physical contact. There are others too, some I've never met, a social network of lost souls.

But I don't know this as I'm role-playing with Sumi, a foreign exchange student from Japan, for Conflict Management week. She is the religious hostile; I am the undeserving target of her aggression. They call me to the nurse's station, and Sumi looks so relieved to break role. Later, she'll realise she was role-playing with a super-spreader and blast about it on her feeds in broken English, earning hundreds of new followers.

A woman from the CDC is waiting for me at the nurse's station. She gives me a blood test, her trained face barely registering the results on her handheld device. She asks me to accompany her to the hospital.

"Oh my god. Am I dying?" And she dares to assure me that it's only a precaution.

I get into her car, feeling lucky to miss class, like I'm getting away with something. I don't know it now, but this is my last moment of freedom. At least I enjoy it, windows down, a cool dry breeze gliding over my skin.

Then, I'm in my garden. I always go here in my sleep-state. From the lush beds of clover erupt long curved zucchini, wide webbed fans of kale and red-veined chard. Tomatoes droop over the lips of their pots, some as big as baseballs, others the size of a baby's fingertip. Pea shoots crawl up wooden posts, the trunks of the fruit tree, a splice of apricot and plum that's never grown right. Its leaves are holed and edged in brown, curling inward like arthritic claws. Once, I took a trio of leaves to the nursery. The owner, a woman with nice silver hair swept up in a banana clip, said it was a fungus and gave me a spray. I applied it faithfully, dutifully following the directions until the bottle was empty. Still, the tree never flourished, never fruited. Mom said we should cut it down, plant something new, maybe avocado, but I begged for more time.

The splice tree shakes in the breeze, an old abandoned web in its nearly bare branches, dirty with insect bodies and debris carried to it from lord knows where. There's the start of something in a cluster of leaves—maybe it's a fruit—but I don't inspect it too closely, afraid to be wrong.

*

When I return to the world of the living, Mom is waiting on the other side of the plastic, knitting a scarf. She looks up, sees me staring, smiles.

"Want to play cards?" Before I can answer, she digs the deck out of her big bag of distractions.

She plays the cards for both of us, showing me my hand, turning her head in this exaggerated way to prove she's not cheating. She waits patiently for me to tell her what to take, what to discard.

"This is stupid." I search my name again on my phone. The first hit comes up:

Typhoid Mary 2.0! "Who's that? She sounds god-awful."

"Ancient history." Mom waves her hand in front of her face as if she's smelled something unsavoury.

I stream two minutes on Typhoid Mary, get the idea. I look up at Mom through the plastic. "They kept her in isolation for three decades before she died. And not of typhoid. She never caught it, and she never understood why she was being held. Can you imagine?"

"Good lord, would you put that thing away? Nothing but junk on there."

"Everything is on here."

"Oh, honey."

"What?"

"Want me to read to you?"

"No." I slam my fists down into the bed, something bings, my heart rate quickens—I can hear its heightened pace on the machine. I could unhook myself, pull the tube loose, refuse nourishment. But I know what will happen. Two of the nurses will suit up, struggle me down, stick me with a needle. And, anyway, the tube is what connects me to the magic. "Calm down." Mom starts to put her hand into the plastic arm, but I tell her no. She steps back, looking injured.

"Why aren't you in here?"

She shakes her head, bites her lip. "I don't know. They," she points at the door, at the doctors beyond it, "don't know, either."

"They'll keep me here until I die. Then they'll cut me open and study my insides." I wonder what will happen to the rest of me, my skin, my hair, all the trimmings. Will they stuff me like a taxidermied animal, keep me for an exhibit?

"No. They'll keep you here until they have a vaccine."

I stare at the wall behind Mom, shimmering in the plastic, turning like the skin of an opal in the sun. I'm tired, so I reach out, give it a shake. Mom eyes me from her chair. She knows what I'm doing. After a while, the nurse comes in, performs her magic, and I'm gone.

*

This time I don't go anywhere. I wake after what feels like a long stretch of black. My head hurts. Mom is there, curled up in her chair, still in her swishy lavender jogging suit. She smiles, says hello stranger. I know she smells like hair spray. I wish I could touch her hands, feel the cool papery skin along her wrists.

"What did they give me?"

Mom shrugs. "They're tired of your shenanigans."

"Well, it was no fun at all." The blackness. It felt like death, what I imagined death to be anyway, stretching, never giving. I couldn't fight my way back.

"I think that was the point." Mom takes out a magazine that she's bought at the gift shop. Today it's *Nature*. She shows me the cover: the barn owl. Ghost face, dark stone eyes staring. I nod, and she reads.

But I don't listen. Instead, I look up soul on my phone. The hits that come up go on forever. I don't know where to start, so I choose at random.

According to St. Augustine, the soul is "a special substance, endowed with reason, adapted to rule the body."

In Jazz slang, soul is "an instinctive quality felt by black persons as an attribute."

To Buddhists the words "I" or "me" do not refer to any fixed thing, but an ever-changing entity.

The Greek word for soul is derived from a verb, meaning "to cool, to blow."

I look up at Mom, still reading her magazine. "I miss wind chimes."

"Yeah, well. I miss your father."

"Not okay." He died when I was seven of a brain aneurysm. And now, every year, I have to get my head scanned to make sure I don't have one too.

"What? I thought we were truth-telling."

"Why not Carson?"

"Don't get me wrong. I miss him too. But your father, he was the original."

I close my eyes, try to go to the garden on my own. I can't see it as well without the magic, but I can control what happens. This time I bring him with me. He's wearing an old t-shirt from his college days, pulled so thin over his hunched back that his earth-brown skin shows through. He tugs the splice tree out of its plastic pot, the black cone of soil crumbling as he places it in the hole we've dug. It's still new, its branches green-tipped, its leaves waxy and smooth.

Together, we bury the tree's roots with more soil, packing it down. I try to remember the feeling on my fingers, cool and moist, the smell of dank earth, but it's so hard without the nurse's help. He takes off his baseball cap, wipes his forehead with the sleeve of his t-shirt, the sun gleaming off the bald spot at the crown of his head. I want to remember more, to hear him speak, but his voice—it's gone now. I can't find it anywhere. I huff. Shake. The plastic crinkles.

"Stop that," Mom says, "You'll unplug something."

"I'm just so—"

"Mad?" she cuts in. I shake my head. "Furious? Enflamed?" I laugh. I can't help it. She does too, relief relaxing her shoulders. "Someday we'll look back on this and cry."

"I doubt it," I say, "I doubt we'll ever look back on this." And then she is crying, head in hands, as if thinking about it made it so. "Those are tears of happiness, right?" She shakes her head. "Joy? Ecstasy?" But she just goes on crying and shaking her head. "Mom, it's alright," I insist, "I'm alright." Sobbing, she's sobbing now, as if to say it is so not alright.

I sit up, swing my legs off the bed. They are numb and tingly from not being used, the floor cold on my bare feet. The IV tube they stuck me with when I stopped eating is coiled around my ankle. I kick free.

"Come on, Mom. Get up."

"What are you doing?" she asks through sobs.

I lean down, touch my toes, my spine crackling back to life. I come up light-headed, little electric snowflakes clouding my vision. "I'm exercising." Mom dabs at her eyes with a tissue, daintily blows her nose. I see now how fragile she is, how she needs me.

After she's led me through a session of low-impact calisthenics, I flop back onto my bed, exhausted from the effort, the tube running down my leg like a tail.

"Should I continue?" Mom holds up her copy of *Nature*. I nod. She goes back to reading aloud, her voice floating away on the whirr of the machines, pumping and measuring. I pick up my phone and search for my name.

A WHOLE PLATE OF BISCUITS

ANGELA KANTER

If Hornett doesn't know by now that there is no point picking Jem to answer a question, it's not my fault. Everybody knows Jem puts up his hand only because he likes the sound of his own voice and he never has a clue what the answer is. It isn't up to me to put old Hornett right.

So why am I bursting to stick up my hand too—or even worse, to shout out the answer?

I'll tell you why. Because I am tired of sitting at the back of this classroom and knowing the answers and being treated like I don't exist.

"So, Jem, what is Shakespeare trying to show us about Othello in this scene?"

"If I could make a comparison, sir, with the political situation in…"

"No, Jem, you could not. Now answer my question," says Hornett. He ignores my hand, wavering from the effort of holding it up for so long. "Or maybe Hugh would like to give us his opinion."

Hugh tries to hide behind the enormous zit on his nose. Jem waffles a bit more.

I stretch my hand higher and struggle not to make infantile sound effects.

"Anyone like to help?" Hornett's gaze sweeps the boys, not taking in Heather, Grace and me at all.

"Very well, I—"

"Shakespeare's showing how Othello really is noble, because he stops a fight instead of joining in!" I shout. Then I clap my hand over my mouth. I can't believe what I've done. Hornett looks at me like I've just vommed all over the classroom floor and to be honest, I feel like I have. In the boys' section, someone snorts.

The only good thing is, Hornett can't tell me off without admitting I'm in the room. If he wants to pretend he can't hear my voice, he'll have to let me off. I'm shaking, but I try to give him a steady stare.

Hornett draws breath.

But then, the classroom door opens and a girl steps in. She comes through the boys' door, into their section and nobody's looking at me any more.

The girl's thin, but tall. Her uniform loosely skims her body, so she looks like a doll in a paper bag. Her curly hair's the absolute minimum length a girl is allowed in this school—she can barely strain it into bunches. I catch her eye, trying to communicate that she should go out again quickly and in through the girls' door if she wants to survive. I want to go into the boys' section, put my arm around her and lead her to safety.

The boys snigger. Hornett signals to the girl to go out and come in again the other way. She looks like she's about to sit down next to a boy. But then she steps out of the room—and in a minute she's sitting next to me.

"Now, these are the key points," says Hornett, picking up the orange marker and writing on the board, as if nothing had happened. But he is getting his revenge. He knows I can't read the board, especially not when he uses orange. Not that I could copy down the points anyway, because the pencil I scavenged is all used up.

Jem sucks his pen, Hugh doodles. I could smash through the barrier now, reach for Jem's mouth and twist out the pen, still glistening with his spittle.

The new girl smiles, then takes a pen and a scrap of paper from her pocket. Where did she get those? Tidily and small, she writes: "Matty" and pushes the pen at me. I write "Isha". Matty nods.

*

"I want to show you something ," Matty says, as soon as school is over. "Can you come back to mine?"

I don't know anything about this girl. But I say yes, without even thinking.

We wait ages for the bus. The first two are packed and there are no seats in the women's section, so the driver won't let us on. While we wait, I show Matty how short-sighted I am, pointing out posters and shop signs I can't read. I exaggerate my hopeless vision, to make her laugh.

We get on the third bus, but when we push past the dividing curtain, there's only one space, so we squash up together, in the hot seat over the wheel.

Matty lives in a thin, terraced house. The step is grimy, the hall is peppery with dust and the carpet lies dark and flat.

Matty jerks her head towards a door.

"Mum's in the kitchen—I'll introduce you after. Come on up." She pulls me up the narrow stairs.

Matty's room has postcards stuck all over the walls, around the sink, all over the desk and the cupboard. I don't think a single one of them is straight. I sit on the bed and Matty starts tearing off her clothes—I stare around at the wonky postcards, the window, anything but Matty until she says: "Ready" and I look up. Matty in boy's clothes—jeans, a plain black t-shirt, hair sprung loose from its bunches.

"What are you doing?" I ask.

"You'll see. Lie back on the bed. In a minute, you're gonna be so happy, I promise you."

Matty goes to a drawer and I hear her remove something, which she puts by the bed.

Then she washes her hands.

"No—don't sit up."

Her mother is downstairs. I think about screaming, but if Matty is a maniac, her mother is probably in on it. Why did I come home with a stranger?

Matty's on the bed, straddling me. I'm shaking.

"Look up and relax," Matty says and softly she holds open one of my eyes and puts into it something like a raindrop. I blink. She does the other eye. Then I look up again, and:

"I can see! But that's because you're so close. No—I can see far away, too. I can see the postcards on your other wall! That one's an angel fish! That's Shakespeare... What have you done?"

"Contact lenses."

"But they're for boys..."

"You can get them if you know the right people," says Matty. "I can get you lenses—nobody will know, as long as you pretend you can't see the board. I'm wearing lenses now. Look."

She puts her face close for a moment, then pulls me up from the bed.

"Come and meet my mum!"

The kitchen's a mess. Stacks of newspapers on the floor, books on the table. A woman in a dusty green jumper is sitting at the table, reading. She looks up—she is wearing glasses.

"Hi, I'm Frances," she says. "Here—biscuits." She reaches under a pile of papers and pulls out a tin. But I don't want biscuits.

"Go on, then—" Frances has noticed. She gestures towards the books.

Suppose you were born in a world without biscuits. And then, one day, someone offered you a plate with all these chocolate digestives and shortbread and jammy rings and chocolate marshmallow teacakes...

Matty is making the tea. She turns.

"Isha, is it true what they said in the cloakroom—you spoke in class today, just before I came in?"

"Yes, it's true," I say, touching the cover of a book.

"Oh, Isha!" says Frances. She gets up slowly—looks like it hurts—but she moves around the kitchen, collecting books, muttering about her choices, then

35

she presents them all to me. She sits down again, hunching over the mug Matty brings her.

"My mum had a bad time with the police," says Matty.

"I wouldn't take these books home, Isha," says Frances. "It wouldn't be safe. But come here any time and read them."

I try to thank Frances but my throat is full of dust.

"I teach girls, Isha," Frances says. "Really teach them, I mean. I help them to get into university. It's okay, you know—I mean, there's no law against it, because they reckon no girl could ever get the grades. But if you wanted, I could teach you."

I couldn't tell my mum and dad.

"Will it cost much?"

Frances shakes her head. "The struggle will cost us plenty, Isha. But not money."

She is mad. Do I really want to keep coming here?

Matty is watching me. Now that I have contact lenses, I can see my reflection in her eyes.

*

This isn't going to work. I come to Frances' every day after school. I factorise equations and interpret demographic transition models and analyse sonnets and feel a constant screaming inside my skull from trying to understand them. Matty factorises and interprets and analyses while drawing complicated doodles in the dust on the table.

We've both applied to uni now, but what if only Matty gets the grades? As Frances patiently explains ionic bonding to me for the fifth time, I catch Matty looking bored.

I throw my pen on the floor and storm out.

Next day after school, Heather comes up to me in the cloakroom.

"Grace and me are going to buy dresses for the end-of-term dance," she tells me. "D'you want to come?"

"I can't—I have to…"

"Go home with your girlfriend. Yeah—we know," smirks Grace.

Heather makes a face and Grace makes a gesture to match. They turn away and start to talk loudly about what their favourite film stars wore to the Oscars.

"Wait!" I run after Heather and Grace. I allow them to whisk me to a boutique. I'm free. My most difficult questions are: sequins or lace, pink or red?

I pull on a sparkly dress and step into high heels, then pose in front of the mirror. I am all girl, and I dance to the changing room music.

"You going to the dance with Sam?" Heather asks Grace, as she squeezes into a silver top and cranes round to see the label. "Oh, I love this—but look at the price!"

"Sure am. He's going to do law at uni—gonna get a really good job. I'll be able to buy all the outfits I want when we get married! I'll be able to buy this entire shop!"

I flip. "And what are you going to do, Grace? You going to do law too?"

"Yeah, right. Law! You'll be telling me to try on trousers next."

I take a deep breath, to stop myself shouting. But that's a mistake. I inhale the sweaty scent of the dressing room, then pull the suffocating dress over my head. Something rips and Heather laughs—"you'll have to buy it now!" But I throw it on the floor.

I shove the curtains aside and run. I make it to Matty's, my face slick with sweat and tears, I lean on the bell till she opens the door and I fall into her arms.

She closes the door behind me, hauls me in and up the dusty staircase; we're on her bed in seconds and she's straddling me again and this time my eyes are closed but the rest of me is all open.

*

Matty and I open our letters together and scream. We're going to uni.

Matty leaps around. "Let's go and shove these down Hornett's throat."

We can't wait for the bus; we half-walk, half-run to school. It's still really early, but there are loads of people in the driveway, swapping results. We crash into the crowd and sing out our grades. Jem actually makes the thumbs-up sign.

"What d'you get, James?" I can smile at him now.

"Three Ds," he smirks. "It's cool. Hornett'll talk to the uni. They'll take me."

Hornett's car sweeps through the school gates. Matty and I leap out, banging on the window, yelling and waving our results letters.

Hornett has to stop. He has to at least swerve.

He drives straight at us, I dive sideways, pushing Matty ahead of me. Metal hits my shin and I slam into the tarmac.

I can't move; keep my eyes shut. I hear a car door slam.

Ten seconds.

Twenty.

Thirty.

Then I open my eyes and I'm looking straight at Hornett, smelling his huffy breath, seeing his taut face perfectly.

He turns away, but it's too late. I've already heard him say my name.

DISHARMONY

TANVI BERWAH

It's my fault, of course, but I'm grateful I don't have to carry the burden for too long now. For fifteen years, I've lived in darkness. Watching the perfect, glassy blue of the sky from the small window at the back of the room. I'm so glad the government perfected the cure for the skin's darkness, and that once I take it, I'll be able to go out too. My skin's so dark, sometimes it burns red under the yellow sunlight. To be clear—I'm not breaking any laws, my courtyard is roofless and sometimes mother allows me to spend time there. She's kind, kinder than I am, and more righteous, more perfect. Her procedure was flawless, she has brilliant pale skin, with a tinge of dusty yellow around her collar. When she steps out of the bath, her hair's straightness births envy so deep in me, I'm afraid of myself. If the government heard my thoughts, I'd be put down.

But I can't help it. My mother can almost pass for being born with beautiful skin.

Me? I'm exactly what society is afraid of. A dark-skinned spectacle. A reminder of the ugly days that plagued our society for so long. I can't wait. I can't wait to have the procedure done and become fair. Fair like all those people who strut down the streets, fair like my mother, fair like my older sister who's now married.

Married.

She became so pretty someone wanted to marry her.

Marriage is the kind of luxury beauty affords you.

In our part of the town, marriage is the grandest luxury you could hope for in life. When Dina was married, the whole neighbourhood congratulated my family. But not without murmuring about me.

"Don't worry," a neighbour said. "If you and Dina are anything to go by, her procedure should be fine too."

"Yes, but," my mother wiped her brows. "She's so much darker. The lighter, the better, you know?"

"You're such a good mother," the woman assured her, patting her hand gently. My mother nodded, her glazed eyes passed over the house. She couldn't spot me in the darkness. I'm glad she couldn't. I didn't want to embarrass my beautiful mother.

*

There are some people, in this time and age, who fight against the procedure. Sometimes, you can hear army trucks with brittle tires rolling down the street. In the night, their hammering on the road sends waves of anxiety so deep I'm worried they're here for me. Someone told them I'm so dark that even the procedure won't do me any good.

But then, thankfully, there's a scream. It's almost always female. You hear the screams, the nails on the wooden doors, the thud of the butt of a gun, the thump, the silence. The truck loads. The truck vanishes.

It's disgusting, people defying what's good for them. I can't wait to get this colour off of me. I want my mother to look at me like she looks at Dina. And I want Dina to be my sister again. As children, we played together in the darkness. She braided my hair; she told me—secretly—that she loved the fierce brown colour of my eyes. But after the procedure, when her eyes became the colour of the sky, she averted them. She couldn't look at me the first time she returned home from the lab. That night, she'd slipped me a pamphlet with more information about what the procedure is like. You can get this pamphlet at the school. But schools are only for the treated or naturally lighter-skinned. There are no weird experiments, sending a dark kid to an all-white school. The nerve of people, back in those days. What were they hoping to accomplish?

My jaw tightens. No, that is not how we behave. I coax myself back to proper order. The pamphlet listed details of how the brown and black skinned were out in the society, tarnishing the beauty of Mother Nature. It included short stories about how the faithless tried to access public space, leading to brave state forces curbing them, leading to mass hysteria, leading to trouble and more trouble. Damage to public property. Protests. Riots. Civil wars.

These are terrible words.

If one simple procedure can take away all the pain of the world and fill it with beauty, why shouldn't it?

*

My father is a doctor. It's the only thing that allows us to own a house with an open courtyard, and the slight leeway of letting me see the sun. It's also inconvenient because, though I hide myself well with scarves, chances are someone will glimpse me. It's mortifying. Forget the name-calling—I'd much prefer that—it's the adults' faces paling with sheer horror at laying eyes on an untreated child that gets me really bad.

Especially since last month, when an underground racket that had destroyed over a thousand strips of the special anaesthetic and syringes from the procedure lab was exposed. You'd probably think it's a bad thing, rounding up people and hanging them until death—it's been thirty years since death penalties were outlawed. But what else would it be revived for, if not for people bent on destroying the harmony of society? What was the alternative? Just go back to being a segregated society? Fighting for our lives? Separate townships? Working below someone else, being paid less than half of the lowest salary a fair-skinned gets? Being spit at or being dragged from beds in the middle of the night? Getting up in the morning and ignoring the streaks of dark humans' blood on the street. Kids playing on blood-laced streets, immune to the harsh reality. Just letting it be, just letting it be. Barbed wires and curly hair, heavy guns and brown skin. All stuck inside and away. Away from a fair-skinned, blue-eyed world. And if you step out, stay away. Don't drink the same water, don't eat the same food, don't travel in the same bus, don't go to the same school, don't talk back to a police officer, don't get a fair-skinned's blood transplant, don't touch his Religious Book. Especially that. God hasn't made all humans equal.

I mean, we're still separate, of course. But that's only until the procedure. Then, it's freedom.

Freedom so beautiful.

Freedom through blue eyes.

*

My father comes home late. My mother's still up. I watch the midnight sky and listen to them both.

"They're ready to do her procedure early."

My flesh rises. My heart beats like it hasn't, ever. Not in fifteen years.

"Oh, good," my mother sighs. "Oh, good. I'm so tired of working alone. If she can go outside, I'll get much more help in the house. Dina's due next month. Perhaps she can babysit."

Dina's going to have a baby?

A knife twists in my heart.

But why does this bother me? I wouldn't want my niece to be seen with a dark-skinned babysitter. The child must be lighter. Dina's husband was a natural light-skinned. I wouldn't want to ruin her life.

"Of course," my father says. "But it'll still take two months. Two months is fine, right?"

"Better than another three years."

I wipe my tears, tasting the salt in my mouth, and quietly send thanks to God. I've never been happier.

*

Seven days after Dina's due date, something is very wrong. The doors are shut. My mother's trembling voice demands I shut the window too. I sit quietly in the dark, running my hand over the familiar plastered wall. The damp mustiness of the corner is growing stronger and stronger as the daylight outside dims.

A chair scratches against the floor. The main door opens and shuts. What's going on? Did my dad get laid off? Will we have to vacate the house? I can live with that. This house is a luxury anyway. I wish this could've happened after my procedure, though. It's easier to calm the nerves when your doctor father is around. I won't admit it, but I am nervous about the procedure. The side effects include dementia, fatally low blood pressure, grotesque failure that ruins the structure of your bones, handicaps, haemorrhage, coma. And of course, death. But death isn't mentioned as a side effect. Death is just the next best alternative to the procedure. A small price for harmony and peace in society.

The knob rattles. I straighten. The door opens. Someone steps in. The door closes. Treated people have a curious, pleasant smell. A child cries.

"The bed's still our old one?" Dina asks.

My voice is stuck. I scramble and stand, gathering the folds of my muddy skirt. If I'd known my beautiful sister was coming to visit—coming to visit this room—I'd have cleaned up.

"Yes. Yes, it's the old one."

I see her silhouette in the faint fluorescent ray issuing from a crack in the door. She gently lowers her child on the bed and sits beside it.

"Is it a boy or a girl?"

"A girl. Would you like to hold her?"

That's when I know something is very, very wrong. A treated woman's child cannot be tainted by the touch of an untreated.

*

The baby's skin is black. She's me, just more blue than red. Every morning, she wakes me up with her incessant crying. She's hysterical when she cries. My mother takes care of her, Dina has gone back to her house. "So generous," my mother whispers as she changes the baby's diapers. Or feeds her through tiny tubes. Or washes her tiny feet. "Never thought he'd take her back."

It's a big deal. Dina's husband forgiving an unfaithful wife. Dina hasn't been unfaithful. She said it over and over again through clenched teeth, refusing to look at the baby. "I don't know where she gets it. Probably your side of the family." She turned an accusatory eye toward our mother. Three weeks after, her husband had sent word. "Come if you want. Leave it." Dina was gone by afternoon, leaving the child in the dark room with me. My procedure has been delayed, owing to the drop in my father's reputation, so I have nothing to do but take care of the baby.

As much as I want to hate the child—for what's a dark child unwanted by its parents—I can't help but notice her little smile. She has a full lower lip, giving her a spectacular smile. Even without a set of teeth. Children are weird. She has large, brown eyes. She's not allowed out. But even the slight light from the window roars a fire in her eyes. Most nights, she grips my fingers with her tiny ones and dribbles all over my hand. I pushed her away the first few nights, but soon grew accustomed to her baby noises. She has a peculiar smell, something very natural, that I don't think I've ever experienced before. But I wouldn't know much about children. As an untreated, I haven't seen many babies.

It's a month and a half after the baby came, and it's raining. It hasn't rained in six months in this part of the settlement. Water is directed toward the main town for most of the prescribed rain days, anyway. But even by that standard, we got less rain. I sit at the edge of my bed, watching the water dripping off the window sills. The baby is awake, but quiet. This is her first rain. I wonder what she thinks.

"It's raining," I say, gently nudging her. She looks me in the eye, then gurgles with laughter.

She's so beautiful.

*

She's so beautiful.

For a week after, I roll the words around my head. It's the same, day in and out, as the date of my procedure gets obscured by the shame my family lives with now. But I have the baby. The baby, who I think is beautiful. At first I panic. What's happening to me? Is it our family? First Dina. Now me. How can I think an untreated baby is beautiful? I hear a tired cycle groaning outside, its rusty gears protesting. And I zap out of my daydream. The baby is pulling at my hand. I lift her, coo at her, brush her already-curling hair back. Her hair's like a crown. It's funny. There's no questioning it. Dina's baby is lovely.

What happens when she gets the treatment?

It startles me.

To imagine the baby not looking like this. Why on earth would anyone want to change what this baby looks like? And who, in their right mind, would think she was ugly?

It's a blur. Words and orders and announcements and more orders. All saying the same thing. The same thing. Be beautiful. The cure treats anything ugly.

Become the best. Take charge of who you are inside. Pale is pretty.

My heart stops.

I want to scream.

Flames are burning inside me. Every little touch from the baby—she's getting hungrier—sends pulses through my blood. I won't let anyone destroy her.

"Mila." I name her in my hoarse voice. "My lovely Mila." I squeeze her against me. She cries. I let her go, she's still crying. I don't know what I'm more afraid of, my painfully angry heart throbbing in my mouth, or her and her loud cries, her sheer defiance of how an untreated baby is supposed to be.

"We've got to go, okay? Then you can cry as much as you want, laugh as much as you want, and see the skies as much as you want." She sneezes, then coughs, her tiny nose wrinkles, her little balled fists wave in the air. I pat her clumsily, then lay her down. Immediately, she grabs at the damp, soft corner of the sheet. My hands tremble as I withdraw. In the darkness, I can't see them shake as I quietly gather the things that we'll need.

*

Blood rushes in my ears as I land softly on the mud outside. Mila, strapped to my chest, sleeps through. The night sky is a deep, inky black, like the colour of the font on official circulars. I have an hour and a half before the patrol returns. Fear blazes in my eyes as I slip outside the gate, colours blending together, the smallest of noises sending waves of terror through me. This is the farthest I've ever been from my confinement. I place a hand over Mila's head and pull her closer, thank the stars I don't look like my mother or Dina. Gravel cooperating and staying muted, soon we're hurrying past the last of the lower town's houses. On, on, on. I urge my feet to walk, stamping down the pain shooting up my legs. How do people walk so much?

The rolling tanks are emerging into town again, in the distance they groan over the gravel. A cool breeze blows, carrying the scent of oil and gas. The houses on either side have given way to tall, wild grass and an occasional dry tree. Up front, there's nothing but the empty road. No place to hide. Several miles lay between the edges of the lower town and the city's fence. If I make it over the fence, Mila and I have a chance. A chance to live, to breathe, to see—as we are. And none of it matters if we're caught. My heart races at the thought. What if we get caught? What would happen? The procedure would be last of my worries.

I duck toward the grass, off the vision line of anyone hunting us. Mila jerks awake and sneezes.

"Shush," I whisper, patting down her soft hair. "We'll be out of here soon." But she doesn't listen. She's wailing, slowly at first, then at a speed to rival my quick strides. Tears sting at the back of my eyes. Damn it, Mila, stay quiet! I wrap my arms around her, muffling her voice, and break into a run. Sweat drips into my eyes, blurring my sight and making me stumble. Pain lashes in my limbs but I push past it, past Mila's hungry yelling. The sky lightens, too early for dawn. Lightens a little too much. As if they're increasing the radiance of every fluorescence slowly, slowly. And it lights up suddenly, a stark white washing away the colour of darkness. I halt, staring at the sky, its unfamiliarity leeching life out of me.

Once, on one of the good days, my mother had told me the story of a man who was sent to earth to preach goodwill and peace. Some people back in the days before the cure said he was brown-skinned, and I'd laughed. A brown-skinned messiah? That makes no sense. In what world could that be? But brown-skinned or not, the man was hammered onto a cross and he died, before being resurrected. I don't think I've heard of that kind of brutality even from those performing the cure. Then again, I've never experienced the treatment. Perhaps that's what they were doing. Making him whiter. Where was he in the in-between? Heaven. What's heaven? A beautiful place above the clouds, washed with a brilliant white light, with no problems in your heart, and a peace that you couldn't know anywhere else.

I clutch at Mila, I clamp my eyes shut. Maybe we reached heaven.

UNDER THE HOLE

IONNA MAVROU

It was that time of year again when there were more red days than green, and when my mom would not let me go out at all. I would beg, cry and plead, or even try to reason with her but it would always end the same way. "Red means stay inside, Nadia," she would say, and that'd be all she wrote. Every question always answered with another question: "What does the Sign say?" sometimes followed by the command: "Turn the TV on and look."

I hate the Sign. The Sign ruins everything. Last week Joseph, who had never talked to me before, did. On our lunch break, he said, "Hey, a bunch of us are gonna hang out at the video arcade later," but then the Sign was all red so she wouldn't let me go. I tried to tell her that red actually means 'stay in the shade,' and that the arcade is indoors but she started talking about my skin burning in five minutes and how I'm fair and photosensitive (these are the words she learned from Doctor Ozono who every other Thursday informs us on the State of our Hole whether we want to hear it or not—I vote for not), and how it's not worth taking a chance for some silly date with a silly boy at some silly arcade, and that, if he really likes me, he'll ask me out again soon, which of course won't matter unless the Sign by some miracle points to green or yellow.

On red days the sky is the color of eggshells and every single smooth surface reflects light; a harsh, cruel, blinding light, and if you look at the sun directly you could go blind.

At least, that's what Ellie told me. I've never ever been allowed to go out during a red day. I swear if there was an emergency on a red day and we absolutely had to leave the house, my mom would dig a tunnel with her ladle sooner than let me walk out into the sunlight.

From morning to night, every year for as long as I can remember, the Sign rules our lives. And it's not just on TV either. It's on the street, outside the school, in the centre of town, up on the hill, dozens of sign-clones everywhere, directing our lives like the traffic. *Stop. Go. Wear a hat. Put on sunscreen. Look like a dork.*

I don't mind the sunscreen, but nobody else comes to school in a hat big enough to house a circus. A couple of kids have baseball caps, and Ellie's been wearing this ancient fedora she got from her dad, but I'm the only one who has to watch for narrow turns or kids bumping into me in the halls. In case you're wondering, not wearing the hat is not an option. Because for a while the great-dictator-also-known-as-Mom was all ready to make me home-schooled until Nana put her foot down, and Nana is not here to intervene anymore.

Nana told my mom: "This is crazy, you either pack your things and go, away from this place, or you learn to live in it and you let her live in it too."

She died two months after that, from the disease, halfway around the world alone. She spent her last days sipping martinis sitting out by her hotel's pool, they told us, and all I could think of was the sun reflecting off the blue water and my grandmother's glass sparkling like the very best day in the world.

*

Another week went by, and Joseph wouldn't even look at me at school anymore. He probably thought I didn't care about him, and I couldn't tell him she was the reason, that she wouldn't let me go. No one else in the school had this problem, no one else in the entire town. I'm fifteen and she treats me like a ten-year-old. And it seems to be getting worse. Like on Sunday, two days after the whole arcade fiasco, I begged her to let me go out with Ellie.

"Please, mama. It's only three blocks down, four at the most."

And she totally lost it. She started shouting about how she can't afford taxis, and how my grandmother squandered my inheritance on martinis and plane tickets and expensive hotel rooms, after my dad left us very little to begin with when he took off.

"At least they had the guts to go somewhere," I shouted back at her as I ran to my room.

And it's true. I don't know why we stay in this place, this experiment we call a town. Ellie said we should make a pact and just go. Right after graduation, pack our bags the night before and take off to anywhere, just as long as anywhere is far away.

She said, it's a big world and we'd be stupid to stay here. This place is cursed, broken, over. It's so over, Ellie said, this place, and all of the people here are in denial. We all should have left years ago, all of us, the whole town, just taken everything that wasn't nailed down and moved the hell out.

She recited this speech often, and I couldn't help but think of big cranes lifting up some of the houses while others were being pulled away by cars. Trains pulling the mall and the aquarium, with all the townspeople following partnered up in twos, holding hands on one side and on the other holding up their parasols, waiting for that special moment when the leader would give the signal and we'd all throw the parasols up. And then the wind would blow them away, or maybe they would all float up in the sky like balloons or like the graduation caps we saw in ceremonies on television on the days the Sign said we couldn't go out.

But no such luck. Instead I was left counting the time for when spring would finally be over, when December became January and I wouldn't be the only person in the world who didn't get to go out.

*

A month after Nana died, after we got that Miami phone call in the middle of the night, I found her letter in the mailbox.

"I miss you both so much," she had written on the back of a postcard with a cheesy picture of a couple walking on a beach with palm trees. "Remember when we used to go to the beach? You would love it here. I wish you were here. Nadia, I'm sending you a seashell necklace to wear to your next school party."

Later, I found out it was postmarked the day after her death. A cleaning lady had found it in her hotel room and mailed it. I imagined her just falling asleep with her martini glass beside her, content that she'd had a good day, because I didn't want to think about everything in her body shutting down, breaking, none of the pieces that were her working anymore. I wanted to think she was happy. And I wondered where that seashell necklace was.

*

In the beginning there was just me and Mom. I suppose Dad was there too, I mean, I've seen pictures, but I don't remember him being there at all. I didn't even really know much about him, until I met Nana when I was about five.

"This is your home too, now," she'd said, then proceeded to show me everything: my father's room and things, her clothes and the collected memorabilia of her already long life. Nothing was off limits, and for a while, before I started school, Mom would let me spend my mornings there, and Nana would let me do anything, look at everything, turn her whole house inside out for one of my games, she didn't care. She'd do her chores, go visit neighbours, cook, work in the garden and let me roam around in my own little worlds.

Sometimes, after lunch, she'd show me old pictures of the family. Ancient pictures from the times before cars, before the internet, before the hole even, if you can imagine such a time. Everyone would be all dressed up in those pictures, smiling, even the little kids.

"See, this is your dad," Nana would say. If Mom was there, sometimes she would look at her instead of me, to see her reaction.

Which was always the same; face hardening for a moment, inevitably turning into: "Come on, Nadia, grab your stuff. We'll be late."

She was almost pretty then, Nana, old but okay looking. She was the light to my mom's eternal black cloud, the whimsy to her seriousness, and always in my corner no matter what. She'd even convinced Mom to let me go to the beach one time, like a normal person, in the summer. But all that, as they say, is now history.

*

It was weird that it worked out that way, but Nana's sixth-month death anniversary fell on the night of the Multicultural Fiesta, the one town event my mom always insisted we go to. I always suspected that even in the smallest, dullest, most over places in the world occasionally something happens worth writing about.

Obviously you'd have to start with the Tale of the Fifteen Tacos. For a relatively slim girl, my friend Ellie could put away an impressive amount of food. For Ellie, eating was a passion, a hobby, a finely tuned and disgusting skill that you wouldn't notice if you just spent recess with her, but you'd definitely know about if you ran into her in the ice-cream shop or the taqueria. Sadly Joseph (remember Joseph? The guy I used to have a crush on?) was lactose intolerant, and preferred burgers and fries to tacos. So when he overheard Ellie order seven tacos on the night of the fiesta, he made fun of her.

"Look at fatty here," he told his friends. "Hey fatty, you're going to eat seven tacos? Aren't you afraid of getting fat?"

"I could eat double that if I wanted," Ellie said. And when Joseph and his flunkies laughed, she added: "I bet you I could eat fifteen tacos, right here, right now."

The laughing stopped and Joseph got serious. "If you do, I'll give you all the money I have." He took out a bunch of crumpled notes from his pocket and put them down on the counter. "My whole allowance," he said.

"And if she loses?" one of the guys asked.

"If she loses, she and her freak friend will have to be my slaves for the rest of the month."

(What I ever saw in this guy is beyond me. Was I crazy, on medication, temporarily body-switched with someone really dumb?)

"You're on," said Ellie, more fierce than ever, ordering the eight extra tacos and going to work on the first of the seven that had already started coming.

I forgot to tell you that one week before the fiesta, before Nana's sixth-month death anniversary, my father had suddenly showed up. He had come to see about the house, my mom said, to see if there was anything worth selling, probably; but part of me hoped there was more to it than that.

I had waited for the day of his return so long that I'd imagined it happening a dozen different ways, all dramatic and exciting and life-altering. Like, he'd show up a rich man and invite me and Mom to go live with him someplace far away. Or, if me and Mom had recently fought, he'd just whisk me away and leave her behind. Or my very favorite: He'd come back crying and begging for our forgiveness, and we'd wait a little and make him sweat before we all made up, and hung that big 'happy ending' sign outside our door and faded into a fuzzy peach-coloured sunset.

In reality, when it happened, it was all different and boring and more disappointing than watching one of Nana's telenovelas. His appearance, for one. When he left, when I was five, he looked like Che Guevara, rugged and handsome. Now he looked like someone's lawyer. He was like some guy I used to know, like Emanuel, the grocer who used to give me orange-flavoured chocolate when I was little but then moved to Caracas with his family.

And on the night of the fiesta, sometime between Ellie's thirteenth and fifteenth taco, my so-called father decided to have it out with my mom, in front of everyone.

"It was because you were so controlling," he shouted at her. "That's why I left. Because I couldn't stand you telling me what to do all the time. And I was lucky that I got out. I mean, look at her." He pointed at me. "Look at what you did to her, turned her into some kind of freak."

And right there, in front of everyone I knew, was when I found out that even though he was partly right, my father was also a jerk. And that, with Nana gone, except for Ellie, I really had no one else. I started to run, Ellie chasing after me, fifteenth taco in hand, Joseph chasing after her, shouting: "If you don't finish eating them at the stand, you lose, you fat freak!"—followed by a gasp from some nearby townspeople that I guessed was about Ellie giving Joseph the finger as she ran behind me. And then suddenly, there it was, a safe place for hiding: Raul's hot-air balloon—Raul who had rewarded himself for finishing med school with a half-completed trip around the world, to fulfill his childhood dream of living like a Jules Verne character. His balloon, empty, unguarded, just sitting there: a perfect hiding place for me and an even greater prop for Ellie's next crazy scheme.

"We should just take it," she said, finishing her taco despite being out of breath from all the running. "We should just go. I know how. I've seen it on a show."

It was obviously a stupid and dangerous idea, and we both knew it, but somehow just saying it out loud made doing it unavoidable. So I just sat back and watched Ellie take all the necessary steps: light the fire, discard the weights, say some parting words, and before anyone could stop us we were hovering above the town.

The sky was all rain and lightning. Everyone crowded under the gyro and Greek coffee tent, oblivious to anything but the sudden rainstorm. I couldn't see where my mom was, but I didn't care anymore.

"Adios, suckers," said Ellie, and smiled at me. And I said it too, to all of them that far down, "Adios, suckers." Goodbye, stupid pathetic little town.

*

They say that change happens slowly, without you noticing, like the UV radiation slowly eating away at your skin without the weather even feeling hot. They say it happens under clouds, comes from the stratosphere through the hole that's not really a hole, but a thinning in the ozone layer the size of North America above our town when it's spring here in the bottom of the world. They say wind happens when energy from the sun acts on the earth's atmosphere, or something like that. I never paid that much attention in science class.

I looked at the sky as we drifted, trying to imagine it, El Agujero, the big stupid hole that ruined lives—*our lives*—one part ultraviolet, all parts evil, destroying tiny little organisms in the ocean, and on land dreams, and families.

Below, I pictured the mayor at the entrance of City Hall, handing out sunglasses to schoolchildren and their families, same as every other Sunday. Probably saying, "Remember, wear them every day," knowing that they most likely would not, touching his neck where the skin cancer used to be before his operation. Getting the kids to wear sunglasses was like convincing them we're all made of starch, and that the rain would melt and carry us out to sea. Like when mothers tell their children to eat fruit because it has vitamins, but you can't see vitamins and you can't see UV radiation, not until it's too late anyway. Sometimes you can't wait for graduation to see how things will turn out.

After that, we drifted south. And then there was no more town.

*

On the way back from Argentina, I tried not to think about how close to death we had come, or how I would spend every day for the rest of high school locked up.

I could tell you about the balloon swooping down over the water, suddenly plunging with me screaming and Ellie saying something in gibberish followed by a moan about too many tacos, and how the balloon amplified the sounds of the rain and our singing all the way to that moment of sudden fall, but there are some things I'd like to hold on to for when Mom bans me from watching television, which you know she's bound to, no doubt.

Our rescue you probably heard about, anyways, or saw on the news, or will when the Chilean and Argentinean Coast Guards figure out who got there and fished us out first. I did wonder whether the kids at school would mock or hero-worship us, but in that moment it was all trivial and incidental somehow.

As Ellie snored the rest of the bus ride home, I lay back and watched the world go by outside my window, big, shiny, new; and I dreamed of the day that I would live in it again, bravely, and not under the hole anymore.

A GRAND ADVENTURE

VALERIE HUNTER

"Well, look what the cat dragged in," Ma Evans said, looking Garnet tip to toe. Garnet watched her eyes linger on the empty sleeve, but Ma's expression didn't change any. "Come on in. I've got supper on the stove, I reckon it'll stretch to another mouth."

"Thank you," Garnet said, pulling the words from somewhere far back in her throat. "I appreciate it."

Ma Evans gave a little nod, acknowledging Garnet's appreciation was necessary, that she might be getting a free meal but she shouldn't expect one. That was Ma's way. She wasn't actually anyone's mother, not that Garnet was aware of, nor was she particularly maternal, but this was home, more or less.

Inside, the kitchen seemed smaller and the children particularly young, even though Garnet knew a few of them were only three or four years younger than herself. Seven kids total, including four little 'uns in various stages of squirminess. Some faces were familiar, but most weren't. Children came and went at Ma Evans' place, and Garnet couldn't keep track of all the names and faces from over the years. But she and Jules had been constants. Ma Evans used to say that neither of them were ever going to be wanted anywhere else because Garnet was too ugly and Jules too simple, but Garnet had never wanted to go anywhere else, secure in the knowledge that she would stay, and that she had Jules.

"Where's Jules?" Garnet asked, trying to keep her voice normal even though she didn't know what normal was anymore.

Ma Evans ladled out the stew. "She joined up a couple months after you left, once she turned sixteen."

Garnet sat down and ate because that was easier than thinking about how wrong it was. Ten months, and her old life had all but disappeared from her head, but Jules had remained. She hadn't come home to Ma Evans; she had come home to Jules. So how could Jules be gone?

She got through the meal, somehow. Ma Evans invited her to stay the night, and Garnet went up to the loft she'd once shared with Jules and looked at herself in the mirror, trying to remind herself who she was now. It had only been ten months, but the time stretched like pulled taffy, with none of the candy's sweetness.

Her hair nearly reached her shoulders. No longer army-short, but always flopping in her face. Soon it would be long enough to tie back, but she wasn't sure if she could manage that one-handed. Nor did she particularly want to cut it and look like a soldier again.

She pushed back her hair from her face. The scar ran the length of her left cheek into her neck, jagged and purpley red. The rest of her face should have been the same, but wasn't. Her eyes looked like they were still seeing the past year, all of it, all the time. Like she was some kind of ghost. No wonder none of the little 'uns would look her in the face at supper.

Ten months ago, she'd had two arms and two long braids. Ten months ago, Jules had said the war was none of their concern, that men in the Territories weren't required to fight, and women weren't drafted anywhere. Why volunteer? Jules hadn't gone on about it—she never did—but she'd wanted Garnet to stay.

But Garnet had been swept in by the eloquence of the recruitment officer. She couldn't even remember his name anymore, but she could remember his fanciness, that smart looking uniform with the shiny buttons. It made her burn with shame now to think how she'd fallen for those buttons and his words, his lies about how she'd help win the war.

Jules had seen through him then. If Jules was going to change her mind, couldn't she have done it sooner? Couldn't they have gone together?

It was stupid, but all Garnet could think about now was that maybe the war wouldn't have been so bad if Jules had been with her. Maybe she would have stayed whole and safe, if only Jules had been there.

*

Garnet arranged with Ma Evans to stay on and work for her keep, in addition to giving her the piddling money she'd earned from the army. There weren't any other girls older than five in the house now, and Ma said she could use the extra pair of hands. After she said that, the phrase hung in the air, mocking, but neither of them acknowledged it.

Garnet could still pump water, but she was slower hauling it, one bucket at a time. She could still rassle the little 'uns into their clothes, though she was rougher about it, using her knees and hips to do for an extra hand. She was clumsy and slow in the kitchen, but she got done what she had to.

All the time, though, Garnet was aware that Ma Evans could manage without her. At any moment Ma Evans could deem her unnecessary, and then where would she be? She tried not to think about it, but it crept in anyway. She didn't belong here. Ten months had changed everything.

One afternoon when the little 'uns were napping, Garnet went outside with nothing to do. The inactivity didn't sit right—in the army, even when you weren't doing anything the feeling that something might happen at any moment lurked behind you, adding a sense of urgency that life at Ma Evans' lacked. She tipped her face to the sun, and tried to remember how to relax. Eyes closed, she pretended she was younger, with two arms and Jules by her side and—

"Garnet?"

She opened her eyes and jerked her head around, hardly able to process what she was seeing before a pair of arms engulfed her, spinning her around in an enthusiastic hug. "I didn't know you were back!"

"Caro?" Garnet asked dazedly, taking in the dark curly hair tangling its way out of an aviator's cap as Caro let her go. Caro had been one of Ma Evans' kids, eight or so years older than Garnet. She'd left years ago, but came back to visit occasionally, particularly since she became an aeronaut with her own steam balloon.

"Aren't you a sight!" Caro said, her tone some odd cross of sad and joyous. At least she was looking Garnet in the eyes and not staring at her empty sleeve.

"Where's Apollo?" Garnet asked. She always found it amusing that Caro had named her balloon.

"Stashed him at the livery stable."

"Are you staying long?"

"Few days, maybe. I'm waiting for a shipment I'm supposed to take south. Say this for the war, it keeps me busy. Keeps the money coming in, too."

Well, at least someone benefited. "You coming in?"

Caro shook her head, sending her hair into further disarray. "Just thought I'd mosey by, see if anyone I knew was around." She grinned. "Didn't figure it'd be you. Been back long?"

"Two weeks."

"Ma don't mind you staying on?"

"Guess not. I help out," she added quickly, even though she knew she didn't have to justify herself to Caro.

"Course you do. You always were a worker. You want to walk to town with me? Go for a fly?"

"Yes," she said, with more enthusiasm than she'd felt in a long time. "You going in to say hello to Ma first?"

Caro looked away for the first time. "Nah. Ma and me, we had a falling out last time I was around."

Garnet bit back a why? Caro hadn't asked about her arm, after all. She briefly considered letting Ma Evans know where she'd be, but Ma wasn't expecting her in any time soon. Besides, she was a grown girl now; she didn't have to account for her every action.

So she walked into town with Caro, listening to her chatter on about the courier service she worked for, unaffiliated with either government and therefore able to profit from both. Garnet got the idea that some if not all of the transporting they did wasn't above board, but Caro made it sound exciting rather than dangerous, and Garnet didn't ask questions.

Caro had spent part of a summer bunking at Ma Evans' a few years back, after she'd gotten the balloon, and she'd taught Garnet the basics of flying during that time. Now, as she climbed into the balloon basket and Caro took them up, Garnet remembered how much she loved it, how there was nothing better than that little whooshy drop in the pit of her stomach as they ascended, nothing better than looking straight ahead and only seeing sky.

Caro had once told her that you had to take things one moment at a time when you were flying. Garnet wished she could live her whole life like that, in a balloon.

"Do you think…" Garnet kept her eyes focused on the horizon, where anything seemed possible. "I mean, is there any way I might be able to get a job as an aeronaut?"

In the hesitation before Caro spoke, Garnet steeled herself for the disappointment she knew must be coming.

"Can't fly without both arms." Caro sounded apologetic. "It's in the blasted manual I had to study to get my license. Makes sense, I suppose. You need two hands to do the trickier parts."

Garnet knew that. She shouldn't have asked. She shouldn't keep asking, but her mouth opened anyway. "What if I had a mechanical arm?"

Caro turned to look at her, eyebrows raised. "You getting a mechanical arm?"

"Army promised me one, once the war ends and they have the supplies again." Assuming the army held true to its promise. Assuming the war ever ended. She shouldn't hold her breath over either.

"Maybe. I dunno. I could ask, if you want."

Garnet wasn't sure what she wanted. What she should allow herself to want.

"I'll ask," Caro said firmly, as though Garnet had replied. "And if you get your license, you could come work with the service I'm at. Graham has extra balloons; he's always looking for pilots. Be no time before you could save up for a balloon of your own."

Garnet shook her head, more for herself than for Caro, who had already turned back to the sky. It was too much to hope for, but the seed had been planted, and it was hard to uproot.

"You planning on staying with Ma Evans till the end of the war?"

"Nowhere else to go," Garnet said.

Caro glanced over at her again. "There's something I should tell you."

Garnet could already tell it was something awful, something she didn't want to know. She wished she was on the ground again, with earth under her feet. "What?"

"I only found this out afterwards. After you and Jules left. I…"

"*What?*" Garnet demanded.

"That recruitment officer didn't come on his own. Ma Evans invited him. If you hadn't agreed on your own, she would have signed you over to him. That's what happened with Jules. Ma claimed to be her legal guardian, and the officer was just fine with it. Ma was boasting how she got twenty-five dollars apiece for you, and that's when I lost my temper with her."

Garnet held onto the rim of the balloon basket, staring at her hand. It looked small. She *felt* small, like a gust of wind might tumble her out and into the sky. Ma Evans had done this to her. Ma Evans had done this to Jules.

"I won't ask you if you're alright 'cause I know you're not," Caro said. "You're welcome to go back to Holtby with me when I go. I don't know what kind of work you could find…"

Likely no one in Holtby wanted a one-armed slip of a girl any more than anyone here did, but she nodded anyway, nodded over and over as though this might rid her of the knowledge of what Ma Evans had done. But when the balloon landed, Garnet went back to Ma Evans' place, arriving in time for supper. She put on her soldier's face, a mask she'd developed over the past ten months. In the army she'd used it to mask her fears, but now she used it to hide her anger, to hide that anything was wrong at all. The secret was to try not to even think, to keep your head as empty as your face. Garnet could never completely succeed in that, but she did her best.

Maybe her mask had cracked in the weeks since she left the army, or maybe Ma Evans was just good at noticing such things, but either way Ma grabbed her by the arm once the dishes were done, her long fingers digging into the flesh of Garnet's elbow. "You've been talking to Caro."

Garnet didn't say anything as she mentally tried to adjust her mask.

"You think I don't know when that balloon's in town? You think I don't know when you're upset?"

Part of her wanted to ask what gave her away so she could change it in the future, but anger kept her lips clamped shut.

"You just remember that you're the one who said yes to that recruitment officer. You could've refused him."

The truth of that coiled around her, tight enough to strangle. She fought it off. "And if I had? You would've just sold me to him anyway. Like you sold Jules."

Ma Evans neither confirmed nor denied this, just looked Garnet hard in the eyes. "But I didn't have to, did I? You agreed. You signed your name. And now you're in a twist because it wasn't what you expected, so you're laying the blame on me as though that'll change something. It won't. The past's over and done.

You need to learn that, girly."

Garnet knew that, she did. There was no undoing the last ten months, no undoing her arm, no undoing her signature on the recruitment officer's crisp paper. And yet if the past was done, why did she still have nightmares? Why could she still feel the ghost of her arm? Why did she see Jules' face every time she closed her eyes?

Ma Evans continued to look at her. "And if you can't learn that, maybe you ought to just fly off with Caro."

She didn't respond, just went to bed and lay there, waiting. She didn't want to close her eyes, to risk falling asleep, but she thought of Jules anyway, how when they were little 'uns, tagging along after whoever was older and would let them, they let themselves be tied up or stowed away or buried under hay or leaves and waited patiently for their saviours because that was how games went. But when they got a little older, they played their own games. They called them Grand Adventures—Garnet couldn't remember how this particular phrase came about, but she loved it—and together they vanquished the world, fighting imaginary foes and always coming out victorious. It didn't matter that Garnet was puny and funny looking, that Jules couldn't do sums and never said much. Together, they could do anything.

After everyone was long asleep, Garnet got up and shoved her things into her sack, then crept into the kitchen. Ma Evans was guarded with her money, but Garnet hadn't lived here for sixteen years without learning most of her tricks. Sure enough, there was still a stash hidden in the false bottom of the flour barrel, nearly a hundred dollars. Garnet pocketed her army pay, then the twenty-five dollars she'd been worth, and then, after a moment's hesitation, twenty-five more.

The walk into town was dark but not scary. The dark didn't scare Garnet, not anymore. She found the balloon basket in the shadows of the livery stable and curled up inside, telling herself she was safe over and over until she fell asleep.

She awoke to Caro shaking her shoulder. "You been here all night?"

"Near about."

"I'm still waiting on my cargo. Breakfast?"

Garnet followed Caro toward the only restaurant in town. Her stomach felt tight with something, though she didn't think it was hunger. The extra twenty-five dollars smouldered in her pocket.

"Can we go find Jules?" she blurted out.

Caro stopped walking. "And do what? Steal her away from the army?"

People deserted all the time. Most of them got found and dragged back. First time you went it was just a whipping. Second time you got executed. With a balloon for a getaway, a second time probably wouldn't be necessary.

"We can't steal her away from the army," Caro insisted, like she could read Garnet's mind.

Garnet had run once. Almost everyone did, eventually. Most all of them were caught. The whippings were public and vicious, but quick. They wore their scars like badges of honour after.

She hadn't had any plans when she'd run. She'd just snapped one night and gone because she couldn't stay any longer. Been caught within an hour and found she could stay after all. That hour was a blur. She hadn't felt free. Hadn't felt scared. Hadn't felt much of anything.

Caro didn't understand what it was like. Garnet wasn't sure if she could ever explain, the fear and the doubt and how the longer you stayed the more it felt like you were meant to. How the days started to run together until you lost everything except the marching and the mud, the shooting and the blood. And there was no one to rescue you, no matter how hard you prayed. "I just need to see her," she said, because that was easier. "To see if she's all right."

Caro frowned. "Well, maybe. But it'll have to wait a day or two, after the cargo run. Do you even know—"

"Caroline Motts?"

They both turned. The constable approached, his long stride gobbling up the distance between them.

"Yes?" Caro said, like she was stopped by constables before breakfast all the time.

"You waiting for a shipment from Loms?"

This time Caro didn't answer, but the silence didn't stop the constable from taking her by the arm. "Come with me."

Garnet took a step forward to do something, anything, but Caro shook her head as though to say *stay out of this* while asking the constable, "What have I done? Am I under arrest?"

"Until you tell me about that shipment you are. Let's go."

Caro shot Garnet one last look as the constable dragged her away, not quite panicked but approaching desperation. "Apollo," she mouthed.

Garnet nodded and slipped back to the livery stable. She half expected to find the balloon already seized, but it sat there the same as before, just an inconspicuous basket with the envelope folded inside. No telling when someone might come for it, though.

Caro was clearly trusting her to take care of the balloon. Probably she hadn't meant for Garnet to fly it, but what else was she supposed to do? Barricade herself here and fight off one-handed anyone who came for it? Drag it away piece by piece?

Flying would be easiest.

She tried to ignore the watery feeling in her stomach as she set about checking the fuel and attaching the balloon envelope. Her one-handed knots were good enough for boot laces, but there was a big difference between a loose bootlace and an envelope detaching mid-flight. She used her teeth as an extra hand, the thin rope rough and nasty in her mouth but the knots taut and sealed with saliva. She checked and double-checked, repeating everything in her head that Caro had taught her years ago.

Back then Caro had called her a promising pilot. No reason why she couldn't still be. No reason at all.

Once the balloon was inflated, she triple-checked the instruments and then reeled in the tethers. The take-off was a bit wobbly, but not terrible. She could do this. She was doing this.

It wasn't until she had leveled off at nine hundred feet that she realised she didn't have a destination in mind.

She kept going because she had a full fuel tank and no desire to be anywhere close to Ma Evans' place. She kept going because she owed it to Caro to keep the balloon safe. She kept going toward Hopestown, where the Territorial War Office was located.

Landing the balloon gave her several bruises, and it took a passerby to help her tether it. He gave her a look, but thankfully didn't question her right to be flying a balloon. She changed into her uniform and went to the war office like she belonged, asking for the regiment of one Julianna Robbins, and then asking where that regiment might currently be located.

The second flight took longer, though not nearly as long as it seemed it should have. The war was a world away from the Territories, they said, but she traveled the distance in a few hours. When the army camp came into view, Garnet couldn't help but stare at how insignificant it looked from above, how small and surmountable.

She landed well away, a little more smoothly this time, and deflated the envelope rather than tethering. The balloon had to remain as hidden as possible.

Entering the camp made her skin feel crawly. She knew no one was going to mistake her for an active soldier, not with her sleeve rolled and pinned, but being here made her feel like one, as though the uniform and the atmosphere held all the fear and confusion and monotony of those ten months.

Whatever else it did, the uniform helped her button things away. Put it on, and she was some other Garnet, not herself at all. So she walked into the camp with her head held high and her legs strong beneath her, and asked for Jules's company in a voice that didn't falter.

Once she knew where it was located, she tried to make herself invisible and hid behind the latrine. Jules would need it eventually.

It was a long, pungent wait, but at long last she saw her. Jules looked funny with short hair, funny and beautiful, and Garnet wished she could just drink the moment in for a moment, but instead she hissed Jules's name.

"Garnet?" Jules's voice held a wonder to it, and she looked so confused that Garnet wanted to laugh. Jules put her hand on Garnet's arm as though to ascertain her realness.

"It's me," Garnet said.

Jules nodded, squeezing her arm. "What're you doing here?"

"Fetching you."

Jules looked at her, her gaze going to the pinned-up sleeve and staying there. "Fetching me where?" she asked finally.

"Away from here. I've got Caro's balloon."

"Caro's with you?"

"No. She got taken in by the constable. Probably not for long, you know Caro. But I can get us away."

Jules was quiet again. Then, "I'm not supposed to leave."

Garnet's anger bubbled, and she struggled to tamp it down. After all, it wasn't Jules she was angry with. "Says who? Do you want to be here? Did you agree to this?"

Jules shook her head.

"Well, then. It was Ma Evans's agreement with the officer, not yours, and I don't see her here. Let her fight if she's a mind to!" The anger went from a trickle to a gush in an instant, bleeding out hot and red.

Jules tightened her grip on Garnet's arm. "I stay, I can make us some money. Get us a real home when the war's over. Lieutenant says it won't last more'n another six months."

Garnet shook her head, wisps of short hair brushing her cheeks and reminding her who she was now. "You stay, you'll end up dead or broken or hopeless. The war might end in six months, but six years is just as likely, and either way you'll be in it in the meantime. We need a home now. They're giving away land out west. I've got a little money, enough for us to get set up farming, and I bet Caro'd agree to fly us out."

In truth she wasn't sure if any part of that plan was sound, but all of it seemed better than Jules going back to fight and herself going… she didn't have a plan for just herself. She couldn't exactly work a homestead on her own. Or maybe she could, but she didn't want to. It wouldn't be home without Jules.

The fact that Jules herself seemed to have the same dream made her warm inside, though she ignored that for now. She needed Jules to agree first, needed them both to be well away before she could bask in that.

Jules just stood there. Not saying yes, not saying no. Garnet outlined her plan in whispers. It wasn't difficult at all; Jules just had to slip away to the balloon in the dark of night, and they would fly away together.

"You're sure?" Jules said finally.

She'd flown with Caro at night a couple of times. Granted she hadn't done the actual piloting, but Caro had shown her how to navigate in the dark. She was pretty sure she could do it. No, she could definitely do it. She nodded hard at Jules.

"All right, then." Jules gave her the quickest of smiles and turned to go, and it was then that Garnet noticed the threadbareness of her shirt. Noticed the hole, and through it, a scar.

This would be Jules' second attempt.

Hardly anyone tried deserting a second time. In Garnet's ten months in the army, three had tried it. Two had been caught, their rotting bodies displayed to the camp. As if they weren't used to dead bodies.

Hardly anyone tried, but Garnet reckoned they all thought about it. She had, anyhow. Imagined it over and over again, all of the scenarios. Most of them ended in death, but maybe it would've been worth it, that hour or so of freedom. Maybe this time she would have appreciated it.

But she had never gotten to find out. Never been brave enough to try. How could she expect Jules to risk it when she hadn't herself?

"You don't have to come," Garnet said to Jules' retreating back.

Jules turned and looked at her, in the eyes this time. Garnet hadn't realised how much she'd missed those eyes until now, the depth of them. Jules might not say much, but those eyes were always speaking. "I'll come."

And Garnet didn't try to change her mind.

*

That night, Garnet waited so long on the outskirts of the camp that it started to feel like some other night, like she was the one escaping. In the darkness, she was a soldier again, finally ready to run for the second time.

When Jules finally arrived beside her, face looming pale in the dark, they didn't speak; it wouldn't be wise and anyhow, words weren't necessary. Garnet latched onto Jules' hand and pulled her in the direction of the balloon. They were just two shadows, nothing more. They would get into the balloon and disappear into the night and everything would be all right.

Then Jules stumbled.

It wasn't a full fall, more of a lurch, but a tiny, surprised sound crossed Jules's lips and magnified itself through the quiet dark. In that long instant, Garnet was struck by the irony that Jules, always so quiet, was going to get herself killed for being too loud.

"Halt!" a voice yelled, but it was far behind them and Garnet didn't listen, just grabbed Jules by the arm and ran, dragging her, stumbling. Quiet didn't matter now. There were more yells, and then the crack of a bullet, and they just kept running.

Garnet sensed the balloon more than saw it, throwing herself into the basket as Jules flopped in behind her. Another shot, closer, and Jules said something but Garnet couldn't make it out. Her ears buzzed, or Jules voice did, maybe both. She pulled up the tethers wishing she had six extra arms; nothing was fast enough, a nightmare of fumbles and slow. They ascended, but slowly; she could see the silhouette of the soldier beneath them, gun raised, and she pulled on the acel lever as hard as she could and screamed, as though her voice could stop the bullets.

The balloon lurched and dipped, a wounded animal. Hand still on the lever, Garnet twisted to look at the fuel tank, hissing steam from the tubing, so much steam. Caro had never told her what to do if Apollo was wounded.

What had she done? Why had she ever thought she could do this?

Jules' hand gripped her shoulder, the shoulder that had no arm, and her voice was close to Garnet's ear. "What do we do?"

Jules' voice was loud but surprisingly calm, like she expected— no, like she knew—Garnet would have an answer. Garnet's own panic crested, and she clung to Jules' voice as she looked for something to staunch the steam with. She wrestled herself out of her shirt and gave it to Jules. "Wrap this around the hose. Try to stop the leak. Don't burn yourself."

Jules did as she was told. Garnet kept her hand on the acel lever, holding it steady with every ounce of the strength Jules' voice had given her, standing on tiptoe and snapping with her mouth until she caught the valve line in her teeth. Then she held that steady, too, clenching down on it fiercely until the balloon calmed its death throes.

She spat out the valve line, jaw aching, and turned to look at Jules, who held the shirt bandage firmly over the fuel line. The glowing dials on the dash said they'd already lost a lot of fuel, but they weren't on empty, and that was something.

Jules's voice came through the darkness again. "You ever run?"

It took Garnet a moment to realise what she meant. "Yes. Didn't last an hour. How long were you gone?"

"A day."

Impressive. Garnet tightened her grip on the lever and tried to imagine it. Did the numb feeling wear off after a few hours? Had Jules been able to appreciate her freedom? Had that made it worse when she'd finally been caught? She wasn't sure she should ask.

"I maybe could've gotten clear away," Jules went on, "but I didn't know where I was supposed to go. All I could remember were those games we used to play. I just wanted to go on a Grand Adventure."

Garnet hadn't really had a destination in mind, either. But after, when she'd dreamed of that second attempt, of all the possible outcomes, the few that hadn't ended in her death had all ended the same.

"When I pictured running a second time, it wasn't to a destination," she said. "It was to you. But I was never brave enough to try."

There was a pause, then Jules said, "You're trying now."

Garnet opened her mouth to protest, then shut it. Maybe this was her second attempt after all, maybe she should just enjoy her freedom, the way she'd always sworn she would if she tried again. Maybe she should just take one moment at a time.

*

When the sun was just beginning to poke above the horizon and the fuel gauge had nearly hit empty, Garnet touched the balloon down behind the livery stable. She felt done in, like she would never be able to fill herself with enough food, enough sleep. But there was something else, too, something warm and promising jangling through her sleep-starved mind. A mission accomplished, a rescue made, a game won.

"Well, look what the cat dragged in," Caro said. It was one of Ma Evans' expressions, but Caro managed to infuse it with a tenderness Ma never had. "Looks like you took Apollo on quite a trip."

Caro's eyes flickered over the shirt tied around the fuel tube, but her gaze lingered on Garnet and Jules, not her beloved balloon.

"Everything worked out with the constable?" Garnet asked.

"Not entirely. Shipment got confiscated. Graham's about as furious as you can get with a person through telegraph. I'm figuring on laying low for awhile."

"Could you maybe lie low while flying us out west?" Garnet asked.

"As soon as I change that fuel pipe, I think I could be persuaded to transport a couple of fugitives. What's out west?"

Garnet looked at Jules, reached for her hand, held it tight. "A Grand Adventure."

VIENTIANE

ELIZABETH BYRNE

Red dust scuffs up from the road as I stop and turn round in a circle, trying to see where I missed the turnoff. Yesterday I found the café by accident in the dark, but I know the turn came before the paving stopped. I take a step backwards onto the jagged end of the path. The rest is just missing, as if it's been bitten off. A lot of this city is like that—buildings of crumbling pink stone and peeling white plaster, or grand fronts of carved marble with missing pillars and corners, and taped up glass in the windows. They're not spooky, just fading and tired in the hot sun. But there are bright flowers in every garden, and trees in every courtyard that give patches of shade from the heat. The air is warm and sweet.

I see a mansion with a dusty French flag over the doorway; it might be the Embassy. I push my sweaty hair out of my eyes, and risk a peek in my guidebook. Sorcha told me that if they see you looking in a guidebook they know you're lost and they'll mug you—or worse. Darina started giggling then, like she always did at anything even vaguely hinting at s-e-x. Sorcha had ignored her, and looked me up and down, from my round face to my fat body. In her sweet voice she said, "I guess in your case it would probably just be mugging. But be careful, Lou-Lou, you know what you're like!"

I know she's looking out for me really. Forever besties, since I can remember. Since kindergarten, all through school, and—if we get the right exam results—we'll be university in September together too. Sometimes I think she'll be beside me my whole life.

The building is definitely the French Embassy, so if I go back about a hundred yards I'll be at the corner of Khon Viang. Turn left, through Talat Sao market, left, and I'll be at the café again... and maybe the old woman will be there. If she'll talk to me, maybe I'll be able to find out how the trick works. I put the book away carefully in my bag and start back down the road.

We came here to Laos to escape from Vietnam. We hated it there, and felt like it hated us too. Sorcha's brother had said it was like the most epic place he had ever been. Maybe it was different for guys. I know I've never heard of a place where gangs of girls stand around on every street corner, watching and leering and shouting at any guy who walks past. But everywhere we went in Vietnam, that's what guys did to us.

It was like walking past snarling dogs. Guys our age and older, big groups of them, looking and shouting and laughing, calling dirty comments to each other in Vietnamese, and gesturing with their hands. Then, worst of all, following us and calling out after us in English.

"Lady, lady, hey! You come with us? You have a boyfriend? You want a boyfriend? You want beer? Hey! Lady!"

We always just sped up, folding our arms and staring at the ground, focusing on the slap, slap of our sandals, waiting for them to get bored. But every time my hands were in fists, my shoulders went up and my face turned deep dark red. In my throat was lava, all the things I wanted to turn round and roar at them like a dragon breathing fire, see a bit of fear on their faces. But I'd swallow and keep the flame coiled up inside me, walk on, and say nothing.

Even Sorcha hated it. She started wearing her blonde hair pulled back, and a lot less make-up, and kept her giant D&G sunglasses on all the time when we were out. Little things, but I could see they were tiny cracks in her bulletproof cool. One night we got back to the hostel and she curled up on her bed, facing the wall.

"Sorcha, are you okay? Do you... do you think they know it's actually scary and awful? Like, they just have *permission* or something..."

Sorcha turned around to stare at me. Her expression was blank and cold.

"I don't know what you're talking about, Louise. I'm just sick of this place. We should totally have gone straight to Thailand. This whole stupid country is a dump."

She put her earphones on, turned her music up really loud, and rolled back over to face the wall. I watched her for a few minutes, trying to understand why talking about it had somehow been the worst thing I could have done. Then I went down to reception to get us out of there.

We got a cheap flight to Vientiane, planning to catch a boat up the Mekong River to Thailand. Sorcha wanted to get to Phuket, where the trip would finally deliver perfect beaches and full moon parties. She would find the right clubs and bars; she always made friends with cool people really quickly.

"So how long do we have to stick this dump, Lou?"

"The next boat's Wednesday. But there's stuff to do here, the guidebook says..."

"You and your guidebook. You've got to stop being such a massive nerd."

Sorcha stretched out by the hostel pool, flexing her slim arms over her head. Darina lay out beside her, and looked up at me.

"Don't you feel like sitting down, Lou?"

The loungers were flimsy wicker. Darina was laughing. I flushed, walked over to a lounger and very carefully sat, trying to pretend I didn't notice as it creaked loudly under my weight. At least it didn't collapse. Sorcha yawned.

"There has to be something fun. Show me that stupid book, Lou."

I reluctantly handed it over. Sorcha was a page-bender and a spine-cracker.

"Dull... stupid... no... fucking dull..."

She carved up the whole city in seconds. She stopped, and looked up at me with interest. Like a spider is interested in a fly.

"What's this? 'Plain of Jars'? Why's it all marked up and highlighted...?"

I felt caught, but I tried to explain.

"See, it's these fields covered in huge stone jars carved right out of ground, and nobody really knows what for. There were people buried in the jars a thousand years ago and nearly all of them were the exact same age as us when they died! The fields were bombed and bombed by America, more bombs than anywhere else in the whole world. Most of the ground is still ticking under the earth, ready for a footstep. People are killed sometimes. But the jars are still there. And America didn't win..."

I trailed off at the look of utter incomprehension and scorn on her face. I mumbled,

"It doesn't matter... probably stupid."

Sorcha stared at me for a few moments, perhaps waiting to see if I might struggle a bit more. I stayed quiet. Abruptly she lost interest, turned to Darina and threw her the book.

"You pick somewhere, D".

Darina chose the Buddha Park.

The tuk-tuk driver took us through the centre of the city, weaving in and out of the traffic, and drove around a giant archway in the middle of a crossroads. He seemed inordinately proud of it, pointing and smiling back at us.

"Triomphe! Vous voyez? Triomphe Lao! Triomphe de Lao-lum!"

"What the actual fuck is he going on about?" said Darina.

"I think it's meant to look like the one in Paris?" I said.

It was concrete, not carved stone, like a child's sandcastle copy of the real thing.

"That's totally retarded. I've been to Paris like four times. It so doesn't look like that. I bet he's just going a weird route on purpose to up the fare." Darina huffed.

"We already agreed what we'd pay him."

"Oh shut up, Lou-ser" said Darina.

We both turned to Sorcha. She ignored us, staring out at the arch.

"I just want to get to this stupid park. The dust is getting in my face," she said. "Can you tell him to, like, shut up and get going?"

The driver stopped smiling.

I paid him extra when we arrived, just in case he had understood us. He didn't look at me or acknowledge my awkward merci. So I guessed he had.

We were all surprised by the sheer weirdness of the Buddha Park. It was full of giant copies of holy statues. So here was a giant statue of Buddha lying serenely on his side, head resting on his hand. Over there was a whole row of human-size Buddhas in yoga poses, arms gracefully raised above their heads. In between were creatures with four heads, seven arms, or flowers for faces. There was a huge monstrous demon head with bared teeth and a protruding grey concrete tongue, the size of a house. You could actually walk in and climb steps to the top of it. It had empty eye sockets, big enough for a person to stand in. The face of the monster was fixed forever in a rictus grin, as tourists in shorts and t-shirts took turns to step in and out of its eyes, and smile and wave, and have their photo taken.

You could climb the giant Buddha statue too. Sorcha and Darina helped each other up, using the folds of his robes as a ladder. I stayed on the grass to take the photo. Sorcha sat on the curve of Buddha's neck, tanned legs dangling over his throat. She leaned back, slightly pushing out her chest, flicked her hair over her shoulder and pulled her perfect photo face. *Just like in every photo of her ever,* I thought. I was instantly uneasy at that cold voice in my head that I seemed to be hearing more and more. I concentrated on the shot. Darina was wedged against the Buddha's shoulder in a half sitting, half kneeling position, leaning in towards Sorcha while trying to balance, looking like she was photo-bombing her own picture.

Click click.

"Don't you want to be in the picture with your friends?"

Of course I stumbled as I spun around, startled by how close the voice was to my ear. A gorgeous American guy, maybe twenty-three, with blue eyes, a sleeveless Abercrombie t-shirt, and a perfect teeth smile.

"Er, no, that's okay, thanks. I sort of think it's a bit wrong to climb on him, 'cos it's Buddha. I mean, like, a bit disrespectful? I'm not Buddhist or anything, and I know it's only, like, a copy, but still, you know? Buddha? Also, I'm a bit clumsy, so I'd probably fall…"

He paid zero attention to my tragic babbling. He grinned up at Sorcha and Darina. Sorcha, shielding her eyes from the sun, stared right back down at him.

The American had a friend, and they each had a scooter with room for just one girl per pillion. It was fine, really, I told them. We agreed to meet up back at the hostel, and anyway, I said, didn't it give me a chance to enjoy the scenery. No problem. I watched as they all zoomed away. I felt like a labrador trying to be friends with sparrows.

But on the bus journey back I was glad to be alone. I stared out at the bluest blue sky, fields that were red brown like cocoa, and jungle lush trees. Every few miles there would be a giant wooden billboard at an angle to the road, with an old-fashioned painted picture of happy Lao people and a slogan in curved Lao writing. Without being able to read the words, they seemed to be advertising smiling.

When we reached Vientiane it was almost dark, and I had absolutely no idea where I was. The driver simply pulled over and turned off the engine. All the other passengers got off, so I followed. There was no station, no signs. I started walking down empty streets, and finally saw lights. The last few stalls of a market were being packed up, under strings of bare bulbs hanging from poles. Up ahead I could see the one true international sign I knew for 'we welcome tourists,' a battered ad for Coca-Cola. As I got closer I smelled something delicious and realised I was starving. Something told me Sorcha and Darina wouldn't be back for dinner. Still, I hesitated.

Stood there on the dark street, I heard a soft rustle from behind me, and froze. Then a metallic spark and flare of a cigarette lighter inches from my feet almost stopped my heart with fright. I ran across the road to the lights and didn't look back.

I almost fell through the door of the café and startled a group of elderly Lao women round a table into silence. We stared at each other for a few seconds. They were neat and respectable, and I was red-faced and out of breath, looming over them. Finally one stood up slowly and looked me up and down. She didn't seem happy with her findings.

"You want order?" she barked at me in English.

I nodded. She smoothed her neat blue blouse and patted her short white hair.

"Only soup. Noodle soup."

"That's okay. I mean great, yes, that's great. Thank you. Er, merci."

She nodded sourly and went into the kitchen. After a moment the ladies stood up and followed her, whispering and looking back over their shoulders at me. I wished they had stayed; my heart was still hammering with fright. But I could hear them chattering to each other in Lao and clanging pots. The café was tiny, with white plastic garden furniture. I walked to the window, and peeked through the slatted blinds. At first it was too dark to see anything, but then I saw the orange ember of a lit cigarette. It was across the street, low down near the ground, and it finally dawned on me that whoever was smoking must be sitting on the path. I could just make out the smudged outline of a small figure. It looked like a woman.

"Here is soup."

I jumped away from the window as though caught stealing. The chef and her friends stood staring at me. A steaming bowl was on the table, so I sat down, wincing as the chair creaked loudly underneath me, and flushing with shame.

They all just kept staring. I knew that look. People don't like it when a fat girl is hungry. I picked up the plastic spoon and took a mouthful of the soup. Shame and embarrassment were forgotten. I took another spoonful, and actually closed my eyes. It was just a clear broth with slivers of chicken and pale mushrooms, flat white noodles and tiny green leaves. But it tasted like a hundred things at once, like roast chicken, and hot peppers, and salt, and garlic. Something else, something almost sour... maybe lemons?

"This is the best soup I have ever had. Ever. Thank you very much. Merci beaucoup Madame, er, Mesdames."

They all turned to look at their leader. She nodded. Of course it was. She pointed to herself.

"Madame Choumally. Best cook, all Vientiane. Everyone knows. You bring your friends, you can see."

She turned and led her flock back into the kitchen. I kept eating the soup. But I looked over to see if I could see through the blinds, and if the ember was still lit across the street.

The moment I finished eating, Mrs Choumally snatched up my bowl. I hesitantly asked her for directions back to the hostel. She glared at me. She obviously considered the hostel a poor choice, and more evidence that I was not to be trusted. But she told me where I was and where to go, tracing the route on the map with a spotlessly clean and manicured finger. Then she pointed to the door.

As I stepped outside, she locked the door and turned off the outside light. I looked across the street. No ember. I crossed to the streetlight. As I turned the guidebook around to face the map in the right direction, I dropped it onto the ground. It fell open onto the pages marked with little stars and underlines in pencil, the Plain of Jars. Poor cracked book. I bent to pick it up, and suddenly a flame sparked right in front of me. I was looking into the face of a tiny old woman, sitting just feet away. She looked at me steadily for a moment. Then she smiled.

She was ancient, her face creased into deep wrinkles by her smile. Only the reflected flame glinting in her eyes made it possible to see them at all. Her hair was long and iron grey, but unlike the other Lao woman I'd seen, she wore it loose, hanging over her shoulders and down her back, almost to the path. She had bright red lipstick on, framing blackened, stumpy and missing teeth. She wore a dark sweatshirt and trousers, and sat very straight, with her legs folded gracefully beneath her. The tiny flame in her hand was from a heavy silver lighter. In her other hand she wasn't holding a cigarette, but a fat cigar. She brought the flame to the cigar, cupping her hand around it, lit it and took a long, deep drag. Still looking straight into my face, she exhaled a plume of sweet-smelling smoke, and smiled again. With an elegant little flick of her wrist she clicked the lighter shut. The flame vanished and she was in darkness again.

I took a clumsy step back, slipping off the edge of the kerb and almost falling. I stood there for a few moments, and then began backing towards the streetlight further down the road. I saw the ember of the cigar start to bob and move, first closer to the ground, and then up as the old woman rose to her feet. She moved very quietly. I turned and walked more quickly. Once I was out of the dark, I looked back over my shoulder. The old woman stepped into the light, holding her cigar in one hand and my guidebook in the other. She stopped a few feet away from me, and held it out. I hesitated, but she stood calmly, and took another drag on the cigar. Finally I walked over to her, and carefully reached out for my book, avoiding her gaze.

"You are lost?"

Her voice was low and sweet.

"No."

My voice was a rasp, my mouth parched.

She raised an eyebrow.

"You sure?"

"I... I have directions. I'm okay. Er... thanks."

She still didn't let go of the book. I looked up from the ground into her face. She looked straight back at me. Her eyes were dark and knowing, unwavering. Suddenly I couldn't move.

To me at that moment that her look said—I see you. I can see you, Louise. You don't fool me. Why would you? I know you. And you know me. Don't you?

I don't know how long we stood there. When she gently released her hold on the book, my arm dropped to my side and I took a shuddering breath that felt like waking up. I think it was the first deep breath I'd taken in a really long time.

She walked beside me all the way back. It was very dark, but after a while I could see pretty well. We didn't speak, but sometimes she would gently touch my wrist to guide me at a corner or crossing. She barely came up past my elbow, and I felt huge padding along beside her, but somehow at ease too. For once I didn't feel a panic to fill the silence. Once, she stopped and pointed down a wide street, and I could see the outline of a huge white temple with a domed and pointed golden roof that gleamed, even at night. She pressed her palms together in front of her, as if praying. But then she just nodded her head at the temple, as if casually greeting an acquaintance, a 'howaya' instead of an 'amen'. We walked on.

When we reached the hostel, she looked up at me and held out her hand. I didn't understand, and then realised, of course, she wanted money. I started fumbling in my bag for my wallet, mumbling an apology and feeling incredibly stupid.

"Sorry, sorry, I have cash, just let me get this stupid wallet..."

She shook her head, and swatted my hand away from my bag. Then once again she held out her left hand.

"I'm sorry... I don't understand..."

She looked up at me, amused. Her eyes were black and shining. She reached out and took my big hand in both of hers, held it up in front of me and drew it towards her. Then she let go, leaving my hand suspended in mid-air, and once again extended her left hand to me. I hesitantly shook it, once, twice, three times. My fat fingers covered hers entirely. But it seemed I had done the right thing. She nodded, smiled, dropped my hand and turned to walk away.

"Thank you!" I belatedly called after her. She didn't look back, and after a few minutes I couldn't see her anymore.

It must have been way after midnight when Sorcha and Darina finally got back to the hostel. I pretended to be asleep as they stumbled in, clutching each other and giggling. They made a big fake effort to be quiet, talking in whispers but throwing their stuff around, then laughing more and shushing each other.

"Look at poor old Lou, she really missed out. That was, like, so much fun?"

"Shh, D, don't be so mean. Anyway, I don't think Lou-Lou would have enjoyed it... I mean, can you imagine her trying to dance in that little bar?"

I was pretty sure they knew I was awake. But for some reason it was easy to ignore them.

This morning they were really hungover. I got them water and juice and painkillers, and asked very casually if they wanted anything else.

"I could get you stir-fried noodles? Or boiled eggs? Or maybe spicy prawn soup? That's a traditional breakfast here."

"Oh my god, will you shut up or I will totally puke!" Darina moaned.

"Oh, sorry, sorry D. Nothing to eat then... Okay, I guess I should leave you two to rest for a while. I might just go for a walk."

Sorcha sat up a bit. Maybe I overdid the casual voice.

"Where are you going?"

"I dunno, I might just explore a bit."

She looked sceptical.

"I think you should stay here, Lou. We're both, like, really unwell? It'd be really selfish of you to leave us. That's being a really bad friend."

"You left me. All last night. So I guess you're pretty bad friends too."

Sorcha was stunned. Darina stared, mouth open, her agony forgotten. I looked down at the floor.

"So... I'll see you later then."

I walked quickly out of the room before I could change my mind. It was really hard walking away from them, I guess because it was the first time I'd ever done it.

*

Now at the Talat Sao market canvas stalls on each side of the street are piled with fish and fruit I don't recognise. Cardboard signs list prices with curving black script I can't read. Red cuts of meat hang open to dust and flies, and I see live frogs being picked out of net-covered buckets and weighed. The air is soupy thick with cooking smoke and sweet, rotting vegetables. It's crowded; stalls and boxes packed into every inch of space, voices calling out, and everywhere Lao women gently haggling over prices. I navigate carefully around them, although I'm at least a foot taller, not to mention red-faced and sweating. They are all dainty and dark-eyed and golden-skinned, always in neat dresses or skirts, smiling and composed. I must look hilarious to them, pale and giant and red-haired. But anyone who catches my eye smiles and bows their head politely and I do the same. I'm really thirsty now. Maybe if I can see a peach or an orange, I'll buy it.

The street after the market is quiet and empty. I'm finishing the last of my peach as I walk, and my hands are sticky sweet with juice. You're supposed to peel fruit when you're abroad—but I dared not to with this peach. I smile, half-remembering a poem from school. As I get closer to the end of the street I'm nervous and excited at the same time, deciding what I will say to the old woman if I see her. First I want to ask her name, and tell her mine. I hope she's there. I bought a peach for her, just in case. I catch sight of myself in the window of a dusty red parked car as I pass. I look happy.

I turn the corner. The old woman isn't here. I feel like a silly child, a big dumb tourist. I walk slowly up the street, cross over and go into the café. I take a seat beside the window. Just in case. Mrs Choumally comes over and glares at me.

"You come back? Why not bring friends? More customers better than one."

She may be the sole grumpy Lao I've met. But her chicken noodle soup is the best thing I've ever tasted. Genius gets to be grumpy, I suppose. I order it again. She is unimpressed. I turn back to glance out the window. And the old woman is sitting on the street.

Today I can see that she's not sitting right on the path, but on a square of blanket. Her legs are folded underneath her, and her face is tilted up to the sun, eyes closed. She looks like a cat curled up on a windowsill, poised and elegant even when asleep, lying in exactly the right place to catch the sunlight. She looks entirely her own.

"Very bad lady!"

I jump with fright. Mrs Choumally is standing at my shoulder, pointing at the old woman and shaking her head.

"No good, no good. Ang Nam Ngum!" she says, leaning her face close to me, her mouth twisting up as though she's saying a filthy curse word.

"I... I'm sorry, I don't know what that means..."

"Pah!"

Shaking her head in contempt at my stupidity, she grabs my still half-full bowl and spoon and disappears into the kitchen.

Ang Nam something... I find it in the History section of the guidebook. Aung Nam Ngum was a prison. Communists sent undesirables there, anyone who had fraternised with the enemy. I look out through the window at the old woman, sitting in the sun. I could tell that she had been glamourous, once. Something in the way she held herself.

Two figures walk past the window. I look up and to my horror see Sorcha and Darina walking in.

"Should have guessed it Lou-ser, that you'd be off somewhere you can stuff your face without us seeing."

Darina's arm is linked with Sorcha's, and she's delighted that she's caught me. Sorcha's looking around in disdain.

"Jesus, Lou, you've probably caught something horrific from this place."

Mrs Choumally emerges and stares at them. Sorcha stares back, and then smiles sweetly. Mrs Choumally is somewhat mollified.

"You bring friends, good good. I get menus."

"Thank you!" calls Sorcha at her retreating back, and then she turns to me.

"I'm not *touching* anything she cooks."

She slumps into a chair beside me, groaning theatrically.

"I'd kill for a diet coke, though. God, Lou, you walked for miles! What's so special about this place?"

"They have nice soup."

Darina rolls her eyes, but Sorcha just stares at me, suspicious.

"You're sure it's not some cute waiter? Have you found yourself a hot tiny boyfriend? Come on, Lou. You can tell us"

"No! God. Why did you follow me anyway?"

"To keep an eye on you, Lou. That's our job!"

Darina laughs. Mrs Choumally bustles back out of the kitchen. Her smile vanishes when my friends only order drinks. She glares at me again, as though I've conned her. I stand up, knocking over my chair, and almost run out of the café.

I'm not sure why I'm so desperate to get away from here without them seeing the old woman. I don't want to share her, maybe. Or I don't want her to see the kind of people I'm friends with, says that cold voice in my head. But it's no use. Sorcha and Darina follow me and the old woman looks up. She waves. Sorcha sees it all.

"Who's that? Do you know her?"

I keep walking, speeding up.

"Hey Lou, that old woman is waving at you!"

I stop, hopeless now. I turn back, not meeting her eyes.

"She's... she's just some beggar I gave some money to yesterday. She gave me directions..."

My whole body is hot with fear, and something that for a moment had seemed light and airy in my heart shrivels up. I look over at the old woman. She's stopped waving and is now just serenely watching us.

Suddenly Mrs Choumally bursts out of the café.

"You pay! You pay now or I call police! Bad girls!"

"I'm sorry, we just forgot!"

I grab my wallet and try to count out money. I hand her more than we owe, and to be fair she hands some of it back, looking annoyed at my carelessness. She notices Sorcha looking over at the old woman.

She leans closer to Sorcha and whispers, "Bad lady. No good."

She shakes her head and pulls her disgusted face again.

"Why? What's so bad about her?" drawls Sorcha, putting on her sunglasses.

"She does not behave right. When it was the American war, she was criminal. Not proper lady, bring shame to her family. She go with different men for money, sing and dance for soldiers. Sent away to make sorry, learn behaves. After, she come back, still bad behaves. No husband, no family. Drink, smoke. Laugh all the time."

Mrs Choumally directs a look of pure venom over at the old woman, who smiles at her. The air between them almost crackles. But Mrs Choumally drops her gaze first. She stalks back into the café.

"Oh my god, Lou. You're, like, friends with the local ho-bag!" Darina shrieks with laughter and pushes me. Sorcha looks at my face.

"You gave her money? What for? Did she give you some good tips? Some nice moves the boys like? You do need all the help you can get, I suppose…"

"Jesus, do you have to be such a bitch?"

She takes a step back, stunned, as if I've slapped her. I have never, ever said anything like that to her before. That cold voice in my mind somehow got out, and now I can't take it back. Sorcha's face goes sharp. She walks over to the old woman and stands over her. The old woman looks up at her with an expression of amused interest.

I go after her, Darina following. I grab Sorcha's arm.

"Please Sorcha, please. Just leave it."

Sorcha looks at me, and smiles that sweet smile. I drop her arm.

"Sorcha. I'm asking you…"

"She's just some old slut, Lou. What's your problem anyway?"

She leans right down into the old woman's face.

"Isn't that right, granny? Just some disgusting old tramp…"

"You are stupid and cruel little girl. You are empty. And you know it. Isn't that right?"

Sorcha steps back in surprise when the old woman speaks, in that low sweet voice. She meets her eyes. Sorcha is caught, held by them. I know what that's like. I wonder what she sees.

After a long moment Sorcha backs away unsteadily like a crab. She looks pale and confused, as if she's waking up from a bad dream.

"Lou?" she says, almost in a whisper.

I slowly shake my head, and look away. She suddenly turns and walks off down the street, almost running. Darina follows and tries to link her arm. Sorcha shakes her off.

I carefully put down my bag, and sit on the red dusty ground. I look straight into the old woman's face, and she is looking right back at me. Her face is serene, her poise absolute. She takes out her silver lighter, and a cigar. I stay with her while she smokes it, enjoying the sun on my back, and breathing in the warm air and the sweet smoke. I can hear the voice in my head again, except I realise it's not cold, just honest. There's no trick, it says. It's not mystical. It's just that you can decide, one day, that you absolutely do not care what other people think of you. And then, no matter what, you are powerful.

When her cigar is finished I stand up, smile, and shake her hand. She grips my hand gently, smiles back, and waves after me as I walk away.

On the last day, we walk in silence to the river port. Sorcha and Darina have been behaving really nicely. But it doesn't make me change my mind. When we arrive at the boat, I tell them.

"I'm not going with you. I'm going to stay here for a while. Explore a bit more."

Sorcha turns to Darina.

"D. Take my bag, get on the boat and save us all seats, okay?"

Darina can't resist throwing me a dirty look for daring to cause drama. That's her job. Sorcha steps closer to me.

"What the fuck are you talking about, Lou? You're being, like, super childish?"

I shrug.

"Are you seriously telling me you'd leave me on my own with that silly cow?"

She jerks her head towards Darina, who is awkwardly climbing the gangplank carrying two rucksacks. Sorcha tries again.

"Is this because we went off with the guys? Lou-Lou, you know I didn't really want to, it's just that they said they might have a friend for you too…"

I just stare at her and say nothing. Her face hardens.

"This is because of that, that… old slut?"

"Shut up."

She looks shocked, and I almost want to take it back.

"Look Sorcha, I like it here. I'm going to go to the Plain of Jars. From the book? I think it'll be interesting."

"Oh, for fuck's sake. You can't go somewhere like that. It's really dangerous. You said there were bombs and mines and stuff, I mean, are you fucking mental?"

She's describing the dangers to me, but suddenly I see she's the one who's scared. I never realised before just how scared she is.

"It's okay, Sorcha. I'll be okay."

She stares at me, about to say something more, something real maybe. We look at each other for a long moment. Then Darina calls out,

"Oh my god Sorcha, the boat is like, leaving?"

Sorcha turns away. She carefully puts on her D&G shades and starts up the gangplank.

"Sorcha! I… I bet Phuket will be great."

She doesn't look back.

"Whatever, Lou-ser!" calls Darina, as Sorcha sits beside her.

The crew loop a chain across the gate and pull up the gangplank. The boat starts to slowly pull away, churning up the muddy brown water, and I wave at my friends. They ignore me. Maybe I look stupid, waving, but I keep doing it until the boat has turned and they can't see me anymore. I pick up my rucksack and start heading back into Vientiane. Tomorrow I'll head out, I think. Sorcha was probably right, about the danger and bombs and landmines. But other people have been there before. I'm think I'll find a path.

THE BATHTUB

KAYE SPIVEY

Late last June, the hot part at the end of the month where you can't even sleep through the night with your window open without sweating, Jenna and I drove through a town somewhere between Indiana and Colorado, and I remember that better than what happened beforehand or a lot of what happened after. The little red Subaru was kicking up clouds of dirt that marked a line from the tail end of the car back toward home. The cats were out of their carriers, one stretched across my legs, purring loud and making my lap damp. The other was perched up on Jenna, looking out the windshield, with a lazy paw on the steering wheel like he was the one driving. The car was stuffed so high that you couldn't even see out the rear view mirror, and every time we jostled over a bump something would hit the roof and both cats would bristle, but even that hardly bothered them anymore. It was hot. Hot, because the AC didn't work and the windows couldn't be rolled down because Jenna thought the drag would ruin our mileage.

The one mix CD Jenna had made for the trip had just restarted and I was hearing *Sweet Home Alabama* for the nineteenth time when we rolled through the town and Jenna changed gear and rocked her head side to side, cracking her neck. I rolled my tongue against the back of my teeth and stared out the passenger window. People actually live out in the middle of nowhere like in old Dust Bowl pictures, in those houses which are mostly brown and one storey, with sloped roofs that would go up in seconds if you tossed a match at them. I imagined people just didn't toss matches in places where the grass is so yellow it looks like something peed on it and it never grew back.

One of the brown houses with fenceless yards had a bathtub sitting between two cracked stubs that were probably once trees. It was an old porcelain thing, strung up by bungee cord and settled atop a stripped and sun-bleached hammock. Two women with wide hips and floral shirts were standing in the yard, staring at it with their hands to their mouths like,

"*I don't know how it got there, Marge. Just woke up and there it was.*"

"*Well, isn't that the darndest thing?*"

They didn't look at us as we passed, kicking rocks and spraying them with dust. I looked over at Jenna and she hadn't turned to look at them either. Her mouth was still set in a line. Behind her bug-eyed shades she may as well have been sleeping. For all I knew, the cat was the only one keeping us on the road with his one paw. He yawned wide and sneezed, then placed his other paw on the wheel to keep us on course. I shifted my legs and the cat twitched her tail and looked up at me. I laid my hand on her back.

"There was a bathtub in a hammock back there, in those people's yard," I said, and looked back at Jenna.

She waited until the end of the *Sweet Home Alabama* chorus to reply, "Yeah?"

"Yeah. I wonder what it was doing there."

"Yeah?"

"You think someone would actually take a bath in that?"

"In the yard?"

"Yeah."

"Probably not."

I lifted my hair off the back of my neck. The little town ended before our conversation did. The one gas station wasn't a company name or anything. Diesel From Dan. We were back on the highway and Jenna was making another gear shift. In minutes, we were passing by cows; big brown and black things grazing close to the road. They would also get covered by our curtain of dust.

The cat climbed up over the steering wheel and sat on the dashboard to watch them, pressing his nose to the windshield. Jenna reached out and pushed him out of her line of sight. He let himself slide, then flopped down in front of me, tail twitching while he watched them. He sneezed again. The smell of ammonium and manure reached us in a wave. I wiped my sweaty hand on the soft back of the cat in my lap, then used it to cover my nose. She was still purring.

"There are a lot of cows out here," I said.

"They kill them just down the road." Jenna pointed with one finger, hands still on the wheel. "See? You can see the slaughterhouse coming up on the right."

From the road it looked like a big barn, and the concentration of cows was dense closer to it. Some of the cows right along the fence by the road stared at us with blank eyes as we passed. I turned my head away. The people in that town probably ran that slaughterhouse—those women in their floral shirts coming to work to cut whole cows open for burgers and steak.

"We'll make a stop there," Jenna said, pointing as we passed another mile marker. I didn't see what it said. We made a stop about every two rotations of the mix CD and now *Hotel California* had started playing again.

"I wonder if the tub was a prank," I said.

"Maybe," Jenna murmured, pulling down the sun visor. I picked the cat up off my lap and hugged her. She voiced a half-hearted protest, then liquefied as cats do and slipped from my arms. She hopped over to Jenna's lap. The spot on my jeans where she'd been sitting was dark with sweat. The ammonium smell had melted away and everything smelled dusty again. The other cat sneezed. I plucked at my jeans to air them.

"It might fill up if it rains," I said.

"It probably won't."

"Why not?"

"Won't rain."

I looked out the windshield at the sky. If it didn't, I remember thinking, houses like those really might go up. The whole countryside could turn to fire. How far from the ocean would we be then? At some point you couldn't outrun it anymore. Even heroes in movies got swallowed up eventually, when there was just too much fire.

Jenna looked over at me through her bug-eye shades. "Hey," she said and waited for me to look back. "We're going to stop, okay?"

"Okay," I said, and shifted in my seat.

"Okay," she said back, then pushed a button on the stereo and restarted *Hotel California* again.

COME FLY

LIZ FLANAGAN

Caz got in at midnight. Her dad had left a bottle of whisky on the kitchen table. She poured herself a glass. It tasted worse than she'd imagined, but she forced it down, coughing away the burn. At least she'd sleep late and miss the bloody parade.

It didn't work out that way.

Sunlight crept round the edge of the blinds at seven that morning, fingers of gold, prodding her awake. First time in years it hadn't actually rained on the parade: even the weather knew that joke was getting tired. Then next door's chickens joined in, louder than any alarm clock, cackling away like they were the first birds ever to lay a sodding egg.

Caz cursed the birds. Cursed the morning. Cursed herself. She lay awake for hours, tossing and turning, mouth like sawdust and her head throbbing like a car alarm. She tortured herself, replaying the last row with Jem, imagining all the different ways it could have gone, if she'd just said… just done… just stopped being such a fucking idiot. She never thought she'd be the jealous type.

*

"You don't trust me, that's what you mean." Jem spun on her heel, yelling at Caz in the middle of the empty road outside the club.

"It's not that, Jem! But you and Ruby. I couldn't watch it any more." They'd been playing pool together, whispering and giggling, while Caz simmered on the other side of the room.

"Caz, I'm with you. Even if you won't admit it to anyone. That means I chose you. That means you can trust me. It doesn't mean I can't talk to anyone else."

"You were laughing at me." The words caught in her throat like dry crumbs.

"We were laughing. There's a difference," Jem spat, eyes narrowed.

"Not what it looked like."

"Well, if we're talking about what it looks like, how am I your girlfriend? In secret? On your terms? Caz, you don't get to be jealous and in denial." Then, quieter, "You won't even admit it to your dad."

"I'm not ready."

"Caz, no one else gives a shit. Not really! So what, they'll gossip for five minutes? Your dad gets some grief in the pub next Friday? That's it."

"That's not it. You don't get it. It's easy for you."

"It was not easy for me, but I did it. And I'm getting sick of waiting for you to be ready. You know what I think? You can't be happy. You don't think you deserve to be happy. Well, I do. Even if I have to do it on my own."

Caz watched her walk away, past the red lights at the end of the street.

*

The parade was one of the traditions that marked out the year, like Easter or Halloween. Every spring you'd go along to workshops after school, down at the big warehouse on the edge of town. Artists had it all planned out. They made vast sculptures of paper and fabric to lead the parade—eerie, beautiful, unforgettable artworks the size of a bus. And for a couple of quid you got to be part of it, you got to make your own costume. The whole town joined in, from toddlers dressed as flowers, whole families as matching mermaids, a glamorous granny in a decorated wheelchair, or the older kids pushing their luck on stilts and unicycles.

Jem would be at the warehouse getting ready. Families would be arriving. Bands rehearsing. Costumes being adjusted, headdresses tweaked. Caz thought of her firebird hat—the one she'd painted so carefully—hanging there, waiting for her, a golden eye staring blindly at the ceiling and its scarlet streamers hanging limp.

She got out of bed and stumbled to the loo, carefully avoiding her reflection. What did it say that she couldn't even meet her own eyes? She downed two glasses of water at the kitchen sink.

Caz didn't want to go. She'd vowed not to go. She was not in the mood to see any parade. But here she was, shoving phone, keys, a crumpled tenner in the back pocket of the jeans she'd slept in. Here she was, sprinting down the narrow cobbled street, joining the stream of people heading for the town centre.

In the end, she couldn't go too near, as though there was a forcefield with Jem at its centre, pushing her away. She found a high stone wall edging the marketplace and sat on it, waiting. Sunglasses didn't help the headache. She knew she was scowling when a little kid who'd been staring at her tattoos suddenly caught her glance and whimpered for his mum.

She was out of step with the world, but what else was new? The atmosphere in town was expectant, in holiday mood, ready to play. Roads were closed. Pavements overspilled with dogs, kids, pushchairs. People queued for ice cream.

Caz was on the point of giving up, crawling back under her stone, when she heard it. The distant rhythmic beat of drums. She turned and searched, tasting the air. Her stomach did one slow, roiling tumble, and she wondered if she was going to puke, right here.

Then the parade was coming. It was too late to move. Where could she go? The pavement was packed four people deep. She'd have to sprint the other way and everyone would see. She'd never hear the end. That's what Jem didn't understand. She didn't want to be public property. She'd been that for years. Didn't want all the old gossips trying to explain it away, trying to explain her: "It must be 'cos her mum died. Always knew she weren't right. Poor kid. And her dad, doing his best, but it's not the same"

Caz sucked down deep breaths of cool air. Don't flip out, don't flip out. Her fingertips grazed the brick so hard she nearly cried.

And then it broke on them like a wave: the dancers came first, with wide skirts that swooped and swirled. There was a giant swan, with a curving neck. Lots of tiny kids waddling along in alien suits. Then a team carrying a phoenix puppet on tall poles, working it so the wings spread and soared above their heads.

Caz gulped. She should be there. Right there, next to Jem.

Jem.

She had never looked so beautiful. Her face was painted, a sunburst on each cheek. Cleopatra eyes, lined in black. Dozens of bracelets shone and sang on her arms. Her dark curls escaped the headdress, snaking up, Medusa girl. She was on fire, her gold skirt catching the light. She was glittering, gorgeous, a fountain of red and orange flames.

Pain knifed Caz, between the ribs.

And there was Ruby, calling to her. They laughed together: red mouths, white teeth. Jem threw sweets to the kids in the crowd, little silver-wrapped jewels.

Time slowed. The drumbeats grew louder. Caz felt her body vibrate with it. Her head pounded, ready to burst: louder, louder, louder. She wanted to run. She wanted to be sick, but she was pinned.

Jem looked up and caught Caz's gaze. Something crackled between them, like lightning. Then Jem glanced away and danced on.

Caz gripped the brick wall, vaguely aware she was gasping, as if she'd sprinted a hundred metres. All brightness and noise moved on. A cloud covered the sun. This is what life looked like, without Jem. She sat there, unseeing. Her life loomed dully. Years and years, like one long wet Sunday afternoon …

Caz jumped off the wall and ran down the side street. Taking the back way, she circled away from the parade—ever conscious of the drums—and sprinted down the main street. She ducked past her old junior school, threw herself along the canal path, pushing on, on, on.

Near the park, crowds were thicker. She tripped over a dog's lead and sprawled out, hands forward: skinning her palms, wiping blood on her jeans. Her hair stuck to her face and neck. Her t-shirt felt glued to her back. Caz knew she looked a state, but she was past caring now. She pushed through, jostling, "Sorry, sorry, I need to find someone."

Jem was in the finale. There was a wide circular space on the field, ringed by people watching. Jem was supposed to run in and dance with five others. She'd been practising for weeks, dancing the steps in Caz's front room as she counted under her breath.

But there were only five dancers. A ragged gap where Jem should be.

"Jem? Where are you?" She searched the crowd, scanning left to right. There!

Jem stood, swaying, at the edge of circle. She was hesitant, too pale under her facepaint. One hand flew up to her forehead, trembling. Her eyes lost focus.

"Not now. Not here. Shit." Caz flew across the grass, an un-choreographed extra, because it was happening, right now and right here. She reached Jem just as she toppled like a felled tree. Jem's head crashed into her chest, winding her. Caz grabbed her shoulders and knelt slowly, laying her down on the grass before it kicked off.

"Back off! Get back. Give her some space!" Caz snapped without looking up. When she'd made sure Jem's head was cushioned on long grass, she shuffled back, too.

Jem's body trembled and shook, like leaves in the wind. The streamers on her skirt whispered gently and her bracelets clinked. Caz winced each time Jem's head hit the floor.

People leant in, blotting out the sun. Anxious women and wide-eyed kids.

Caz jumped up, circling: "Get back! Stop staring. It's fine, okay? This happens. She just needs a minute. Will you get back?" She windmilled her arms, trying to herd them away: bloody sheep. If that's how it was, she'd be the sheepdog then. Caz snapped and barked, "Back off! What don't you understand?"

They finally edged backwards, muttering and glancing at each other.

It was slowing now. Caz knew the way of it. Jem would wake in a minute, woozy and blinking. Caz's heart clenched. As the seizure left her, Caz leant over Jem. Her world shrank to this: Jem's face, drained of colour, eyelids fluttering. She reached down and touched her forehead, soft and clammy. "It's okay. It's passed. You're okay, Jem."

And finally, after far too long, Jem opened her eyes. She looked at Caz, smiled and closed them again. She rolled sideways, bringing her knees up: foetal. Without opening her eyes again, Jem reached one hand out, searching.

Caz took it in both of hers and stroked it lightly. Sometimes Jem forgot stuff, after a seizure. Had she forgotten their row? Or was she forgiven? Caz stared down at her, trying to read the truth in the side of Jem's face, the curve of her ear, the tumble of black curls down her back.

"Coming through! Paramedics!" Two green uniforms pushed through—a balding man and a younger woman—and knelt at Jem's side, reaching out for her pulse. "Alright, love? Hello, can you hear me?"

"I'm okay," Jem said, pushing the man away with her free hand. She leant on one elbow and raised her head. "Epilepsy—see?" she waved her engraved bracelet in his face.

Caz heard Ruby's voice coming closer, shrilling, "Jem? Jem? Are you okay? Let me through, I'm her friend. Oh my God, Jem! What happened, are you alright? Can you call an ambulance? I didn't believe it when Ash told me…"

Ruby pushed Caz aside and pawed at Jem's arm.

Jem ignored her and looked at Caz. There were a hundred questions in that look.

Only one answer.

Fighting the urge to run, Caz coughed. "Er, people, will you listen?" Her cheeks were on fire. "I'm not being rude, but can you all go away? Please? I think Jem just needs some peace and quiet. And maybe some water? And er, shade?" she checked back in with Jem at every word to make sure she was on the right track.

Jem nodded. A ghost of a smile.

"And you are?" The bald man asked.

"I'm her girlfriend."

Ruby gasped and gaped at Caz. "You never…"

The sunlight turned Jem's eyes to gold.

Caz wanted to bottle her smile and get drunk on it later, but she babbled on, growing in confidence, "Look, this happens, okay? She can handle it. We can handle it, honest." She raised Jem's hand to her lips and kissed it.

"Is that right?" the man checked. "Jem, is it? Is that what you want?"

"Yes," said Jem.

"Right then, sounds like you've got it covered. Here's water. Need a hand getting to the shade?"

"I've got it," Caz said. "Ready?" She slid one hand round Jem's back and helped her up.

Jem tripped on her streamers and giggled, "Health hazard. Flipping firebird." The colour was coming back to her cheeks.

Caz looked up, suddenly conscious that they'd become the entertainment in the absence of the finale. Hundreds of eyes fell on them. Kids from college. Her dad's mates, clutching tins of beer. Mrs Johns from next door, holding her grandson's hand.

Now or never.

Her heart beat faster than the drums. Her legs felt like chewed grass. She stopped.

"What's up? Am I too heavy? I'll be able to walk in a…" Jem saw Caz's face and stopped.

"Jem, I'm sorry. About last night."

"Me too."

So she did remember.

"I think I'm ready."

"'Bout bloody time." Jem's tiger eyes were full of light and hope. "Kiss me then, idiot."

So she did.

OPERATION M

ANNA SCOTT

I don't expect it was how they'd planned it. Maybe they didn't have a plan at all. Maybe they were just going to wait and wait and eventually forget that I hadn't left the house in several years, or that I was even there at all. I'd tried to explain to Dr Carroll that the triggers, the clues, they weren't working. But he said I needed to have patience and that eventually I might be able to remember the name of our first dog (Barry, apparently) or what my favourite subject at school was, or what my cousin Christine looks like, or that our neighbour used to have a budgie called Brilliant Bill who I liked to talk to when I was six (according to my sister Caitlin, Mrs Briggs was very disappointed that this wasn't one of the very first things that came back to me after I woke up). I hadn't forgotten everything. I could remember what it felt like when Mother was in hospital giving birth to my brother Alastair (like standing on the edge of a ravine). But I couldn't remember the name of Alastair's boarding school, or why he's scared of cats. And I knew almost immediately that I didn't particularly like the company of Caitlin, but I still couldn't remember her middle name, no matter how many times I'd been told it before she'd slammed yet another door in my face.

I'd been back at home a while. It didn't take me long to discover that, by not asking for anything, I collected so much more information. Just sitting and waiting for the facts to come to me, then gathering them up and storing them in my empty head, hoping they might mean something someday. Like my father always taking his phone calls at the far end of the garden, or Mother getting through twice the amount of cigarettes when they were both there at the same time. I noticed the things that weren't there too, things you'd normally associate with a home. A gathering of dust that billows up with sudden activity, living smells of food and sweat, carpets that look like they've seen grubby feet dancing across them. That place was far too beige and immaculate to be a home to anyone.

I'd given up asking them if there was somewhere else, somewhere that might feel more familiar. Mother usually said, "this is what you need right now. The fresh air here will do you a world of good." Then she took yet another drag.

The escaping part was a lot easier than I'd imagined. It didn't take long until there was a weekend when both my parents couldn't quite stand the solitude of the countryside and headed off on their own separate adventures. Caitlin was assigned to keeping an eye on me, but let's just say I wasn't the top of her priorities list that weekend. I jumped on the first bus that said 'city centre', but it didn't look like the centre of anything, not from where I was sitting on the top deck. Definitely not busy enough for what I had in mind. Nothing looked familiar. Nothing. But—and this had been my plan—if the triggers wouldn't come to me, I'd go and seek them out myself.

A couple of weeks before, I'd asked Mother where all my friends were. Surely they would have been concerned and wanted to visit? She said not to worry. She said the most important thing was to concentrate on getting better. That was her answer to everything. So I asked Father but he just smiled and patted me on the head. So then I asked Caitlin and she said "do you want the long answer or the short answer?" and then laughed like the evil person I suspect she really is. I didn't phone Alastair because like I said, I couldn't remember where he was and I wasn't quite sure if I was the sort of sister who phoned her brother to ask his advice or not.

So then I thought, what sort of person was I exactly? The sort who didn't actually have any friends? The thing was—and I'd never told anyone this, not even Dr Carroll, not even now—I was having a few problems with the feelings. Or lack of. I had become used to my family in the weeks since the accident. But there was a definite gap where something like love should have been. Dr Carroll told me not to focus too much on the person I had been and try and concentrate on the person I am now, perhaps even the person I might want to be in the future. Mother once said she imagined amnesia to be like a sort of release, to no longer feel guilt and anxiety about anything, that those elusive triggers could have downsides too—clapping your eyes on a person you'd rather forget, for example. I certainly didn't have that problem anymore.

I'd resolved to test myself. Find someone or something that any normal person wouldn't think twice about helping and see if those feelings made an appearance. And even if they didn't, to help anyway, to shape the sort of person I wanted myself to be. A nice person, a caring person. Capable of feelings. Of love.

When I stepped off the bus it was the noise that hit me first. Noisy noise. People noise. It was fantastic. A large square. Chairs and tables spilling onto paving stones. Cars, talk, echoes bouncing off old buildings, clippy-cloppy heels. I looked down at the silent beige ballet pumps, tea dress and baggy cardigan I'd liberated from Caitlin's room earlier that morning, with no clue what I usually went out in (up until that point, my attire of choice had been M&S pyjamas).

Peering through fast-moving suits, I spied an old man perched on a low wall. He remained still as everyone else flitted past around me. I arranged a smile on my face and walked towards him.

"Hello. Do you need help with anything?"

"I can sit here if I want. It's a free country."

"Is it? I haven't really thought about it. I'm looking for people to help."

"What do you want to do that for?"

He looked like he'd had a tough life. I spared him all the details.

"I'm trying to be a better person than I think I used to be."

He gave a deep sigh, almost creaking in the process.

"Well, I'm think I'm past help, dear, but thank you for your concern." He didn't react as I sat down next to him and gave a deep sigh all of my own. After a minute's silence, he lifted up his stick and waved it across the other side of the square in the direction of a crowd of people gathered in one corner.

"What about him?" I could hear a guitar being pounded on but I couldn't see a 'him'.

"Looks like he could do with a bit of cheering up. Here every day, wailing his head off, face like a slapped arse."

I smiled a thank you at my new friend before weaving my way through the stationary crowd. By the time I reached the front, he was in full flow, bashing out the chords with his eyes squeezed shut. Just as he was getting into a rhythm, he opened his mouth and a sorrowful sound emerged. It started off soft; he sung about the past as if his voice has been put through a rose-tinted filter, like it was coming out of an old record player. But as it continued this changed to raw pain, singing about how the now wasn't what once was, about how much he had lost. He swung around, turned his back to the crowd, digging deep to get everything he could out of his guitar, his eyes still shut tight.

And then it was over. The people clapped and cheered. He blinked a couple of times, scratched the back of his head then looked to the ground with the trace of a smile. Some of the people tossed coins into his open guitar case before dispersing, one of them even offering a whole note. He carefully removed his guitar and rested it against the wall and I took note of his tight jeans and worn-looking checked shirt with the sleeves rolled up, revealing a strong arm covered in a long, winding tattoo. A silhouette of a tree; roots that started at his wrist, with branches making tracks up his forearm until they disappeared under cotton.

I took a step forward. "I'm sorry, but I've only got enough for my bus fare home. I'd give you some otherwise."

He stopped still before slowly turning. Whereas before there was pain, now he looked... well, still... nothing but still. His mouth opened to answer me but no sound came out, so I carried on.

"You see, the thing is, I'm conducting a little experiment and I'm looking for people to help. And I couldn't find an old person, so I thought you might do, because your song was so sad and your face made it seem even sadder."

"Should... should you even be here? You look..."

"I know. I'm sorry about that. I've haven't been out much recently. But's it's okay, honestly. It's fine. What's your name?"

"Um, James?"

"You don't sound too sure."

He nodded. "James. Definitely James."

"Good. Hello James, I'm Miriam." It was tough, saying it out loud. I still can't say that name without my shoulders tightening. When they first told me, I laughed. Miriam? I asked Mother to go and get my birth certificate because I thought they were teasing. I certainly didn't feel like a Miriam. I still don't.

He hesitated before reaching for my outstretched hand and shaking it. I could feel the toughness of his fingertips against my skin. He shook his head and gave me a smile, similar to the slightly embarrassed one he'd given the cheering crowd.

"Hello Miriam."

"So... what was your song about? Did you lose something?"

"Um, yeah. Someone. I want to get her back, but I don't think I can. I don't think it's possible."

And there it was. I didn't even have to go too far to find it. A way I could help. My mission. My operation.

"Well... you seem nice and friendly, James. I don't see that there's any reason why you can't get her back if you put your mind to it. And you could help me, by being part of my experiment."

He bent down to collect up all the coins from his case and shoved them in the pocket of his jeans. "So what's this experiment about then?"

I watched as his hand disappeared and came back out again. Something inside me shifted, like a key slipping into a lock or a hand flicking on switches in quick succession to flood a darkened room with light. But then it was gone as soon as it happened. A fuse went and the room was dark again. But still, I bottled up the sensation; kept it for when I might need it.

Words stuck in my throat for the first time that day. I coughed. "It's a long story."

He shrugged. "I haven't got anywhere else to be."

"Well, if you're sure? Okay, I was in an accident and I nearly died, but instead of dying, I was just asleep for a while. And now I don't remember a lot of things about before. But I'm not so much worried about what I don't know, even though it's frustrating and annoying. I'm more worried about the sort of person I used to be, so I'm trying to help people. To make sure the new me turns out nice, just in case the old me wasn't. That's about it, really. Sorry, it wasn't as long a story as I thought."

"Who says you weren't nice before?"

"No one. It's more... it's more what they don't tell me. Why are you staring at my hair?"

His eyes quickly darted back to the guitar case and he fumbled around, taking his time placing the instrument back in, smoothing down surfaces and fiddling with knobs.

"Um, I'm sorry. It looks… different."

"Different from what?"

"From everybody else's."

It had certainly become a bone of contention at home. I'd done nothing to it in months and it had become long and wispy, with the ends a completely different colour to the rest. He avoided my eyes as he pulled himself up to his full height again and went back to scratching the back of his head. We stood in awkward silence before he took a deep breath and spoke up.

"Would you like to go for a coffee with me, Miriam?"

I nodded. "Yes. Yes, I would, James."

A grin of relief broke out across his face. "Okay, I've just got to… just wait here and I'll get rid of this." He picked up the case. "I've got a friend who works over there and they'll look after it. Promise me you won't move. Promise?"

"I promise."

He ran across the square towards a smart looking café and was back in less than a minute with empty hands.

"Why can't we go over there, to the café where your friend works?"

"Oh, um, it's overpriced. And does horrible coffee. I know somewhere much better."

I didn't tell him that I didn't like coffee. Didn't think I liked coffee. My drink of choice since the accident had been Ribena. Sometimes with a dash of vodka.

"So, tell me about your girlfriend. The one you want back. What's her name?"

"Em. Emma. Em for short."

"And why do you want her back? If she left you, I mean. Because that's not a very nice thing to do. Unless there's a very good reason she left you, which would make you the not very nice thing in this equation. Sorry, I'm used to saying what in my head. It's the best way to make sense of things."

The truth was, I wasn't getting any not-very-nice vibes from James at all. Quite the opposite.

"It's complicated. I know, I know, that sounds lame. But… but it's the best way of summing up everything that's in my head right now. I miss sharing everything with her. I miss telling her about my day. I miss her laughing at my songs."

"Why would she laugh at your songs? They sounded sad."

"They never used to be."

I hadn't been paying much attention to where we'd been walking as we talked, but I sensed we were quite a way away from the square by that point, having made our way down a few cobbled back streets. We reached a bridge that crossed a small river, but we didn't join the people looking over the edge, throwing pebbles and sticks into the water. It wasn't long before we were standing at the edge of an open green that had a small café nestled on the corner.

"I'm just going to get us a takeaway."

"Why can't we go inside?"

"I know a nice spot where we can sit. I'll tell you a bit more about Em and then maybe… you can work out how you can help."

Before I could ask any more questions, he darted inside. I watched through the window as he spoke to the girl behind the counter, and saw her nodding before going to fetch his order. He crossed and uncrossed his arms before being handed the two cups.

A few minutes later, we were entering a wooded area on the edge of the green. There was a pathway surrounded by overhanging trees and the dappled sunshine lit our way until we reached a clearing and a wide stump that someone had fashioned into a bench big enough for several people. He sat down and I join him, clutching my drink.

"Well, this is nice."

"Have you… been here before?"

"Well, it's quite possible, but wouldn't remember, would I?"

"No, I guess not."

He looks down and rubs his thumb along the lip of his paper cup.

I broke the silence. "So, tell me more about Em. Maybe I could talk to her, explain how much you miss her? I've discovered I'm quite good at talking to people. I could tell her that you're very kind and you took pity on a girl who doesn't remember much about anything and that you bought me a coffee."

I glanced down as my cup. I'd forgotten to tell him I don't drink coffee. Just before I opened my mouth to confess, I looked back up to see his eyes starting to flood with all that sadness again. I thought what an idiot this Em girl must be, to walk away from James. Because James was rather lovely.

"Miriam, you should drink your coffee, it's going to get cold."

"Sorry, I should have mentioned before, I…" His sadness wasn't dissipating like when he'd finished singing, so I figured one sip wasn't going to do me any harm. No need to kick a man when he's down. I peeled off the lid, but before I had a chance to bring it up to my lips, something caught my eye on the surface of the frothy milk.

"Oh look, how sweet, you put an M on the milk for me."

An M on the milk for me.

My breathing quickened. The switches were on again and this time the floodlights weren't going out. All I had to do was blink a few times for everything to become clear.

An M on the milk for me.

I knew.

I knew that Caitlin's middle name was Eliza and that she had always been a little bit evil but her heart was in the right place.

I knew Alastair's school was called Pengbourne, and I also knew that I didn't call him Alastair. I'd never called him Alastair. He'd always been Al.

And I knew that he hated cats because our cousin Christine (who looks a bit like a goat) once had a tabby cat that had attached itself to the back of his angora sweater when he was twelve and Father has to put the garden hose on it to get it off.

I knew all I cared about at school was Art.

I knew that Mrs Briggs let me conduct a funeral for Brilliant Bill when he went off to budgie heaven.

I knew that the ends of my hair were copper because that's the colour I'd religiously dyed it for the last three years.

I knew that I loved my family. As long as we weren't in the same postcode.

An M on the milk for me.

An Em on the milk for me.

And I knew what James looked like without his checked shirt on, I knew what it felt like when his fingertips moved down the small of my back, or along the inside of my thigh. I knew what his clothes smelt like because I'd borrowed them on a regular basis. I knew that I was the only person he trusted to cut his hair. I knew that he called me Em because I'd never been a Miriam, not really.

I knew all of this because we lived in a small bedsit off the main road into town and our prize possession was a vintage framed Steve McQueen poster that we found in a skip the day after we moved in. I knew that I hadn't lived with my parents for nearly two years.

As I sobbed, I never once took my eyes off the coffee.

"They told me not to visit, that it would just confuse you. I phoned every day, in the evening, once your mum had gone to bed. Your dad said to give it time. I didn't know what else to do."

We were walking back home after a gig along the street and passed a homeless guy sitting with his knees up around his ears. I only had a twenty pound note in my back pocket and we were going to get a kebab. After we put in our order, I started shivering, so James gave me his hoodie and we leant against the side of the van with our hips and lips pressed together, my hands making their way up the back of his t-shirt, thinking about when we would get back to our home and our bed again. We laughed when the guy banged on the side of the door to tell us our food was ready.

I remembered the homeless man whilst picking out some chicken with my fingers then licking them clean. Without missing a beat, my hand was in James's front pocket, lifting out the change. I went to run across the road, but came back and took the kebab out of his hands too.

The man looked pleased with his surprise dinner. It felt good.

James was standing on the other side of the road, shaking his head and laughing. I poked out my tongue at him before I put my foot out to cross.

I didn't need to look at the tree trunk we were sitting on because I already knew what was carved there.

M and J. Always.

I reached out and touched his familiar hands.

He linked his fingers around mine. "I knew you'd find me, Em. I knew you'd come back in the end."

DESTINY

JESSICA GLAISHER

I don't think this is orange juice.

Outside. Must get into the air, that'll help. Past piles of shoes removed to protect the carpet from impropriety, through the kitchen with its mounds of bread to soak up the alcohol, counter littered with bottle tops from small french beers, the hopeful soft drinks, untouched virgins, seals unbroken. Through the glass door, breathing in the tiny scent of summer hinting at romance and happy memories yet to be made. Eyes closed, I breathe in the hope of the scent and try to forget the taste of unknown alcohol in my plastic balloon-printed cup, discarded in my rush to escape the closing-in walls of the house. The garden was filled with twinkling fairy lights, festooned on fences, supported by poles and trellis, the flowers carefully avoided. A square of light from an upstairs window, where anxious parents wait for the inevitable trouble that teenage revelry causes. My task in the house forgotten for now, plastic bag thrown in the pile of shoes.

Study leave. English lessons about oxymorons spring to mind—probably they'll be in the exam. Or is it more leave to study, as in permission? I'm doing it again, that overthinking thing that Tom hates. Wants me to think less. I shake myself, try to get the thoughts out.

"Where's the drink I made you?"

He's come up behind me, a beery exhalation following his words, reaching my nostrils. Tom. I try to breathe through my mouth only to be reminded of whatever was in that cup. Definitely not orange juice. A hand now, around my wrist, clasped tight. He twirls me around, admiring the dress he bought me, that he told me to go and put on as soon as the adults had departed for the safety of upstairs. It's too small, too short to be comfortable. He expects me to gush, to be happy in the tiny pink thing that I would never have bought in a million years. Expects me to feel sexy.

"I knew it would suit you. Told you it would make you sexier."

I watch an ant move across the floor, carrying a breadcrumb, see it across the floor, make sure it's safe home. I shift my gaze to his hand, my wrist starting to hurt, the skin turning red beneath his grip. He sees me looking, I shrink back; shoulders hunched, dress riding up higher. Try to move my other hand down to pull it below my knickers, surely everyone can see them?

"No."

A dog, whacked on the nose with a newspaper. He smiles, elation at having caught me. The smile changes, or the eyes do, subtle, no one but me can see; tiny shift that tightens my muscles and makes my hands ball into fists; lump catches in my throat, breathing quickens. I try to stay quiet, try to stop my eyes from wincing shut.

My cheek stings. I bet it's red, but who can tell? I'm so embarrassed they both burn, pain hidden, damage covered by my betraying body. Two boys nearby look at me but turn their heads when they see me looking, ashamed for me, not sympathetic. He's gone now, lumbered off to try and touch up some girl from the year below. No doubt she'll be flattered by the attention of an older boy, think it's my fault that he has to do this to me. She saw, she laughed.

I watch a few more ants before I raise my head to go and find a group to lose myself in. I look across the garden and catch a pair of blue eyes looking back at me. She stares into mine, and I get the feeling she's been looking at me for some time. A small nod, an acknowledgement—I see you—before she turns away, her blue-tipped blonde hair rippling down her back, perfectly waved. A glimpse of ultramarine eyeliner.

She's talking to two boys who are trying to chat her up, no doubt on a dare. As I move towards her on my way to my friends, I can see a practiced look of disdain on her face. The boys seem undeterred, trying to impress her with various teen hero stories. *I saved a boy from drowning. Nah, mate! I saved him, you watched.* So involved in their one-up contest that they don't notice her rolling her eyes and giving me a comedy wink before returning her features to boredom.

My friends, standing in a circle, trying to look sober. A tiny bottle on the floor in the centre, currently being hopefully spun by James. No luck, it lands on Jeff, jeering, insistence, *you have to kiss him now! Nah, no, you're alright, that's gay.* Pushing them together, laughing, collapsing in a pile of giggles as they fall on each other and air-kiss like movie-stars. No one has noticed my stupid dress. Yet.

Jeff spins, moving on quickly. The bottle moves, circles interrupted by a dandelion clock, seeds dispersed by a kick of the bottle by Kate, who wants the game to move on so she can have a chance at kissing James, who was aiming for Liz. Tangled web of crushes on the wrong people.

It lands on me.

I stare down at it, shocked, realising now that by standing in the circle I was part of the game. I try to turn away but Kate grabs my arm and pushes me, along with some other hands, towards Jeff who is making kissy faces at me, and staring at my dress, he sees it now, riding up as I'm pushed, pants on show again, try to keep my legs together and still walk.

Turn my head away, wincing, eyes clamped shut, cheek turned towards him, it'll be over soon. I can't see him so miss his move around to my lips until I can feel the unfamiliar moisture. Try to move away but Kate's still there. It's like she wants the drama.

"The FUCK are you doing?"

Tom. He's seen. Abandoned his young conquest. If it wasn't directed at me, his anger would almost be funny, over the top. But it is for me. He's not yelling at Jeff, he's not even looking at Jeff, who's laughing and chugging a beer with Kate. The slap is harder this time, harder than I thought it could be, I lose my footing and fall, the heel of my stupid stupid shoe burying in the lawn and twisting my ankle around. He can't hide it this time. Everyone saw.

The laughing has stopped.

I get a lift back with Kate, staying quiet, holding my cheek. The unwritten code, don't tell the parents what happened, say I slipped on a bottle top. I'm back in my jeans, the dress still on top, hidden under a too-small Tammy Girl top that shows my stomach, breasts jutting it out where it had lain flat, it can't have been that long ago. Crazy-cat picture looking quizzically up at me where it used to look forward, happily facing the world.

Thank goodness for study leave. I don't have to watch people whisper about me. Maybe it'll have passed by the first exam, some other drama to cover my shame. Sixteen and already ashamed of my own existence.

Get organised, make a timetable. Got to pass them all. Get the highlighters out. Pick up Romeo and Juliet to re-read the party scene. And daydream about that moment when their lives change forever.

*

English. Third floor, first lesson on a Thursday. Trying to sit by the radiator in winter, the window in summer. November.

Our English teacher: Dr. Tanner, a tall woman in a crisp suit, trousers pressed in a crease, much neater than the sloppy headmaster. She likes to subvert, switch genders around, and nurture the quiet ones out with Shakespeare.

"Melanie!"

I jump. What was I doing?

"You can be Romeo today." She is smiling, so it's not punishment. Hands out the other parts. "Act one. Scene five. We'll take it from Lord Capulet's line *'Welcome, gentlemen...'*"

Kate, an over-the-top Lord Capulet, gets up with her script in hand, play-acts being drunk, crashing into tables, throwing an arm around unsuspecting classmates who were taking the opportunity to take a nap behind the scenes. I'm nervously reading through the speech I have to make in half a page's time, mouthing the words to myself, not wanting to get it wrong.

Kate sits back down, nudges me. I've missed my cue.

"What lady's that which doth enrich the hand of yonder knight?" I manage, rushing.

Dr Tanner, reading the servingman, tells me she knows not and I continue. There's a knock at the door, we all look up. I pause.

"Keep reading. Come in."

I'm further down the page, near the end of the speech, breathing a sigh of relief when the door finally opens. The frame sticks.

"Did my heart love til now? Forswear it, sight,
For I ne'er saw true beauty 'til…"

It takes me a moment to realise I'm staring, and for Dr. Tanner to say "This night?" quizzically, smirking. The new girl. The rumour went that she'd been kicked out of the private girls' school down the road for doing something to another girl in the toilets. The rumours varied on what it was she'd done. Some said she'd been completely naked, others that they hadn't even been in a stall. The guesses at specifics got more ridiculous. Our school's sex ed program was strictly heterosexual.

She's a small girl, quietly confident, our school's only known lesbian and therefore a source of safari-like curiosity. Heads turn, meerkat-like as she passes, head held high, ignoring the shouts. She's only been with us a week and already the boys have a bet going on who'll be the first to show her what 'real sex' is.

Her name is Tina, but she self-styles as Destiny. Teamed her new name with blue hair dye—carefully hidden until she's fifty metres from school, releasing it with a flourish—and matching electric eyeliner, kept behind an ear or shoved through a neat bun at the nape of her neck.

Destiny sits down in the front row, the seats left unoccupied for fear of looking too keen. Gets out her copy of the play, showing its difference by having all of its covers and pages, neatly wrapped in plastic, staring down our ancient government-gifted texts, notes from all the previous owners: Romeo's a dickhead; Juliet's fit, she can have some.

"Tina, we haven't got a Juliet yet. Will you do the honours?" Dr. Tanner winks at me. Why?

*

A knock at the door downstairs wakes me. I have to think for a moment where I am. Another knock. Remember it's only me in the house. Wednesday afternoon Shakespeare.

Tom. A bunch of cheap flowers in his hand, a sympathetic look on his face. Leans forward for a kiss.

I keep thinking, lately, how it happened that I came to be with him in the first place. I think I've got it now, what set it off, the catalyst, I think that's the word—must revise chemistry, is it on the timetable?—although I suppose this might be more like psychology, that popular kind that Mrs. Pan sneers at and always says isn't proper science. More like the kind of thing you find in pink-covered women's mags, ones that suggest that everything about you is wrong. As if most teen girls don't feel that already. As if I don't feel that already.

I think, as far as I can remember, it was the sleepover at Melissa's last October. Girls in carefully-chosen pyjamas, bottles of vodka hidden in coke. Copies of Cosmo, face masks, truth or dare. That was it: who do you fancy? A circle of giggles, the insistence. Think of a name, any name, what does it matter?

"Tom?"

Maths, and maybe Science? There were quite a few Toms, now that I thought about it, definitely one in Maths, is he an acceptable answer? Oh god, what does he look like? Hoping the rule of one question would stop them enquiring further. Should have known better from the squeals that followed.

Giving an answer, any answer, was necessary, I knew that from previous experiences, same question with no answer led to poking and probing, but you must! Weird that you have to, that it's expected you pick from a seriously limited pool of options, drooling boys in outsized shirts, trousers too short at the ankles, greasy-faced and unaware of personal space or deodorant. I don't feel safe to express this here, even with these close girls who should be, would be, confidantes if I didn't know how they gossiped when one girl was absent. Becky this time, already dissected and examined closely, called names and laughed at, in the spirit of friendship, or what passed for it.

On and on they go. Which Tom? How long? Oh, that one! He's cool! What do you like best about him? Do you like his bum? Shocked faces, nods of agreement with my choice while I desperately try to remember which Tom I've randomly attached my affection to. Maybe he's the one from History? Eventually I decide it doesn't matter. It's not like there's a test.

Monday morning Maths, face masks having made no difference, make-up washed off, truth or dare left in the living room with the sleeping bags.

A note passed along the rows.

"You fancy me, yeah? Meet me behind the science labs later."

Staring confused at the note doesn't help. Who told him? One of them, no doubt excusing it on romantic grounds. Why do they let us read Romeo and Juliet? It just encourages idiocy and unnecessary proclamations of endless love. Unless, like me, you actually bothered to read to the end and saw it for what it was: a three-day infatuation between two over-protected, over-dramatic teenagers (my planned essay hypothesis for the exam).

It was Kate. Of course. She comes to me at break all happy bouncing, wide smile expecting thanks. Greeted by silence, hoping she sees my annoyance. She doesn't, probably thinks I'm shy, wrestles the note from my hand, insists I go, offering lip gloss and mascara in the girls loos after last lesson. She bounces off, still smiling crazily at her cupid moment, assuming I'll be there.

But I wouldn't have been had nature not decided to ironically strike during Biology at the end of the day, necessitating a rush to the nearest loo to quietly rip open an Always to keep from staining yet another pair of pants. Kate catches me on my way out of the stall, drags a mascara brush over my eyes, a lipgloss wand across my lips and me, by one arm, around the back of the labs where he, whichever one he is, is laughing with a group of boys. She speaks for me as I look embarrassed at the floor, although they assume it's because I can't express my deep love for the boy (he was the one from History, not Science, but to be honest, they all blur into one). As soon as it's over and he's walked away, Kate promising my presence at the cinema that weekend, I yank my arm away and run off towards home, glad the whole stupid thing is over.

She had to bribe me to get me to go to the cinema, so involved was she in her perfect teen romance she couldn't see how much I hated it. The 'date' was uneventful, the film dull and the leaving kiss non-existent. I told Kate as much, she was undeterred but I managed to insist, and she dropped it.

Unfortunately, he hadn't. By Monday morning, the whole year seemed to be buzzing with it, clearly lacking any actual gossip. People stopped me in corridors to ask if I loved him, classmates made fortune tellers predicting our endless love. I rolled my eyes, told them all it was rubbish and tried to get on with whatever was in front of me.

He found me after school, about a week after I had expected the gossip to end. Clearly someone had been feeding it, and no amount of sighing and eyerolling was going to change that. I was walking away from Biology, leaving late after dropping all my books from my bag, the zip long past fixing. I'd been avoiding him, another effort to stop the rumour mill.

"Hey! What kind of girlfriend are you? I've not seen you properly in days!"

Girlfriend? Since when does one boring, uneventful date make me his girlfriend? I start to say this, my back to the wall of the labs, when he comes closer and pins my arms against my sides. I'm shocked. See three boys, his friends, hanging about behind him, but they're smirking, not going to help unless he needs it.

Panic.

"You listen. You belong to me now, understand? If you need help getting it, the lads can explain," he smiles round at his gang, they make threatening movements that I would have laughed at, would have found ridiculous with the girls. But the laughter had been knocked out of me.

*

Now, it's May, and here he is, lying on my bed snoring, sweating naked body too close. I feel sick. Sure that bruises will appear on my thighs, worrying about wearing skirts. I go to the bathroom, see my pale face in the mirror and don't recognise it. The flowers are limp in the sink, trying to revive. Beyond help.

*

Exams. Sports hall no longer sporty, its shiny floor and mysterious lines covered in green tarpaulins, no tape holding them down, overlaps tripping up bored teachers and nervous students alike. Checking bags, checking contents of pencil cases. I am constantly afraid of having non-regulation pens, the wrong calculator, of leaving notes or suspicious paper in the clear plastic, red-zipped pocket. Sticky air, sticky plastic seats, ripping the back of your legs on the one day you wear shorts and forget to bring a jumper to sit on. Indents in aching fingers, gripping the pen too hard to get meaning into the words.

Somehow, miraculously, I finish my first Maths exam early, with half an hour to kill. Check the answers. Check them again. Nope, still twenty minutes. Start to look around, look for bored friends, head down when the teacher makes her way through the rows. Whilst I'm looking down, a piece of paper comes into my field of vision—in the hand of the person in front of me, shaking, insisting I take it. Probably for someone else. Melanie, it says. Who from? Those blue eyes again, staring dangerously down the row, checking I've got it. Destiny.

She looks as long as she dares , then returns to staring at the wall ahead.

I open the note.

"Did you know there are 3,452 bricks in that wall?" says the note, "Want to get an ice cream after the exam? :) X"

She's looking again, I risk a smile, a nod, quick, she gives me a carefully-concealed thumbs up. A warmth spreads through me and I pass the last fifteen minutes staring happily into space. Getting up, one by one, in a line, note in my pencil case, smile still on my face. I catch Tom's eye as I leave. He doesn't look happy.

I wait outside for Destiny, relieved to have at least one Maths exam done. Kate and I discuss the questions, dissect our answers. Tom storms out before Destiny, anger in his eyes. Perhaps he missed a question.

"Why are you smiling?" He demands.

I frown. For the first time since that initial over-the-top, gang-backed meeting, his attitude seems funny. I laugh. I never laugh anymore, but still, I laugh. I laugh loudly and in his face. What a stupid question.

I catch sight of Destiny coming out of the sports hall, blue eyeliner tucked behind her ear, and wave.

My hand, still raised in the wave, doesn't managed to stop my fall. I hit the concrete with a shock that starts at my head and ripples down to my feet as they kick up and back down onto the hot, hard floor of the playground. I stare detachedly at a small pool of red liquid in front of me.

Destiny picks me up. Kate has disappeared, no help. She gives me a tissue and I walk wobbly-legged with her towards the girls' loos in the music block. There's blood on the tissue, has she given me a bloody tissue? My lip hurts.

They say your first kiss stays with you, a ghost on your lips, a veil through which all others are felt. My first kiss, with Tom, I can't even think when it was. All I remember is wetness on my mouth, and its lack anywhere else. No chills, no fireworks, no standard by which to measure all others. Just a moist unskilled tongue forcing open my pursed lips, and searching around my teeth, like a strange dental exam.

That day, in the grey girls' loos, lip still bleeding (it was my blood on the tissue, so Destiny told me) eyes open and feeling so awake, her kiss brought me to life. No inexpert groping or probing tongue, just delicate hands holding my concrete-scraped cheeks, thumb stroking away sudden happy tears. And soft, balm-covered pillows finding out my poor broken, bloodied lips, healing. Relief. What I feel most of all is relief, a long weighing pressure released from aching shoulders. It was clear, I understood.

She stops. Looks over my shoulder and, turning, I see Miss Page, must've been on duty for the exam. Busted.

The next few hours pass in shocked dream. A cold pack applied to my lip, sit down in the staff room. Dad called. Story told and repeated, to Miss Page, the head of year, written down. Destiny there, quietly propping me up. Sympathetic hands on mine, Miss Page watching from a safe distance, shaking her head, at what I'm not sure. Still worried about that kiss. They can't send Destiny away. I need her.

Back home, on the couch with (I insist) my revision notes for the last exam. Around eight, I snap out of my daze: panic. What have I done? I swore I'd never tell, not their business, just between us, all my fault, my fault for not behaving, not learning, had to show, had to teach. Breath short, hands shake.

A knock at the front door. Jump briefly from my fear and stare wide-eyed at the living room door, expecting it to open. Mum, coming from the kitchen, shouting back to Dad, no, she doesn't know who. I do.

Up the stairs, thanking whoever thought to put them in the living room and not by the front door. Into the spare room, open the window. Listen.

I can hear the arrogant smile in his voice, chance a look and catch a glimpse of yet another ugly garage-bought bunch of half-dead flowers, their heads spray painted an unnatural blue-black gradient, hints of once-white petals in missed, unseen places.

"Good evening Mrs Smith. Is Melanie in?"

"Its *Ms*."

He is confused. I like to imagine the smile slipped.

"I… what?"

"It's *Ms*, not Mrs."

Mum is giving nothing. I imagine arms folded, eyebrows raised, blocking the tiny amount of house exposed by the barely opened door.

"Is she here or not?"

A mistake. Dad has joined her at the door, I guess he's been listening to the whole thing. I can hear mum restraining herself when she next speaks.

"If you think you will ever be coming near our daughter again… get the fuck off our doorstep. You fucking dare to come back, try to speak to her, I promise you will regret it."

Mum never swears. My cheeks are wet, drips on my t-shirt, running into my ears, legs collapsed beneath me, in a heap on the floor, energy drained, panic gone.

The door slams, shaking the terrace with anger.

I wake up later on my bed, a blanket pulled up, warming shocked legs. Destiny, by my head, a pillow propping her up, one hand stroking my hair, the other holding open my battered copy of R and J. Mum must've let her in.

She sees I'm awake and reads:

"For never was a story of more woe, than this of Juliet and her Romeo."

"He's not my Romeo."

"She speaks," a warm smile, hinting at sarcasm, so beautiful, so close, I want to cry again. Like she's going to disappear at any moment. Hold her hand tight and squeeze.

One more exam. English, Shakespeare, then another party in another garden, more freedom in the air. The essay question nearly makes me break the no laughing rule so strictly enforced by our alcoholic General Studies teacher:

"Romeo and Juliet is not the greatest love story ever told, it is an over-dramatic teenage crush." Discuss.

Tom is nowhere around, rumours whisper round the walls that he's in a room elsewhere, a cell. Banish-ed.

Clock ticks, annoying until the pen starts to flow, pages filled, more paper, fingers aching to keep up with thoughts. Read it, re-read it, check the spelling. Breathe. It's over. Decisions all made, futures all put to paper, compulsory education done with, now choice, or its illusion. Life.

Warm air and late-light sky, the summer scent dancing all around, settling on my hair and skin, fresh scent, smell of smiles. Different garden, same idea, underage drinking and elation, groping in bushes and final games of spin the bottle before a long stretching summer. Last chance to tell your crush, weigh them down with your heavy feelings, hope to steal a kiss.

No tiny pink dress this time or hiding in the house, still some stares but curious now, not pitying. And Destiny, her hand in mine, blue liner twins with beaming grins. I'm suspicious my story has turned out so happy, wondering if it's deserved. Then she kisses me and squeezes my hand. My girl, my Destiny.

A THOUSAND WORDS

EMILY PAULL

After high school, I always thought the friends I graduated with would be my friends forever. The things we knew about each other seemed to bind us like wood glue, even if it was at odd angles. Those two tall boys were my bookends. We went to different universities, began dating, moved out of home, but nothing changed until that weekend. That was when I realised the three of us were hurtling down a hill towards a wall, powerless to stop. That was when I realised we had already stopped being friends. We just didn't know it yet.

*

"This is Kira," Jack said, placing his hands on the shoulders of an Asian girl in biker boots. She wore a DSLR camera around her neck. "And that's Sigmund." His cheeks swelled with pride as if the camera was a child they'd had together. Kira smiled at me, her red lipstick creasing.

"As in Sigmund Freud?" I asked, bumping my overnight bag higher on my shoulder.

"Who's that?" said Jack.

"Yes! I'm a psychology major. I love his dream theories, even though it's all been disproved."

"Who's that?" Jack repeated, louder.

"A famous psychiatrist," I said, glancing at him. Kira nodded.

Behind us, the screen door slammed and Cameron emerged from the house. His jagged front-sweeping fringe, dyed black, was hanging in his eyes. He pushed it back with a hand covered in rings. Cam was tall and becoming quite muscular. He cut an imposing figure, but he was gentle and quiet. He'd just gotten into a prestigious art programme and would be moving interstate next term. He paused, seeing us all congregated on the driveway like neighbours who'd met there by chance.

"Been waiting long, guys?" His grin was toothy and deliberate. Earlier that morning, he had managed to sleep through the queuing for the bathroom and the bickering over the mirror that ended with me abandoning hope of putting on make-up so that Jack could shave. It was just a weekend with the guys, after all—I wouldn't need to look perfect. But looking at Kira's impossible lashes, I felt grimy, invisible.

We set to work, piling our backpacks and sleeping bags into the boot, smooshing them down so that the hatch would close. Cameron and Kira climbed into the back and I slid into the passenger's seat, smoothing the map out across my lap.

"Don't be so impatient, Amy," Jack muttered, folding his long limbs into the driver's seat and putting on an extremely feminine set of sunglasses. "I have to get petrol."

"If we're stopping, I'll grab a Red Bull," said Kira, leaning forward.

"I'll buy you one," said Jack.

Of course he liked this girl. Of course she was pretending she didn't know. Of course he would spend the whole weekend performing tricks for her, like a circus dog.

"Anyone else want one? I'll get them for everyone, I mean," Jack coughed. Kira smiled towards her camera, screwing on a lens. Jack swallowed. His Adam's apple bobbed up and down.

*

Back in January, the boys had asked me if I wanted to go to a concert in Bunbury. By the time it arrived we would all be eighteen, and Cam's older sister Shelley had offered to drive us down. Cam and I loved music and went to any gigs we could. Jack wanting to go was surprising. I'd never heard him listening to anything but podcasts about science.

A few weeks later, Cam and Shelley's parents went away, and they threw a party at the house. On a trip to the bathroom, I noticed Jack leaning against the wall in the corridor. Beside him, Shelley's bedroom door was closed, and low, slow music was audible from within. Jack had a glass of beer in his hand but he was just staring at it. He glanced up at me, and I pretended not to have seen, continuing on to the loo.

*

"I can get us as far as Mandurah, then we'll have to rely on the maps," I said, offering Jack the pages I'd printed off Google. He pushed them away and shook his head.

"Just give me fair warning when there's a turn coming up. I won't remember these."

The idea of getting lost made me feel tense. I looked at the notes I'd scribbled. "It'll take about two hours to get there," I said.

"Got my iPod," mumbled Cam.

Next to him, Kira was sitting cross legged with a copy of *Lolita* open in front of her. I wondered how she could sit like that on the tiny seat.

"Hope you don't get car sick," Jack said to her, leaning around to tap her on the knee. "I have a no-vomit policy in my car."

She raised her eyebrows and kept reading. "I'm fine."

I turned the radio up a little, scanning through the stations. I could see him watching me out of the corner of his eye as the car rolled out of the driveway and bumped onto the road.

At the petrol station, he took his time, leaning against the car as if he were modeling swimwear before he jogged in to pay. I shuffled down in the passenger seat and sighed. I could hear the scratch-scratch of Cam's headphones in the back. After five minutes, when he still wasn't back, Kira unclicked her seatbelt and went in after him. He was arguing with the man at the register, hands gesticulating above the rows of shelves, and his head bobbing back and forth as he tried to be reasonable. Kira put her hand on his arm to stop him waving it. She handed her card over to the man.

*

I'd arranged for us to check in at the Ocean Motel at midday, two hours earlier than they usually allowed. My father always said I was a stern negotiator. My mother said I was pushy. I didn't really care either way; at least we wouldn't miss the first sets. We were lucky to get a room at all, let alone two. Four was out of the question. It was a popular concert and we'd booked late. We almost missed out entirely. Back in February, Jack had called me worried because Shelley still hadn't organised anything. He wouldn't call her, he said. He couldn't. I didn't tell him I knew why.

"Amy, this concert is looking like a huge deal! What if she doesn't book a place in time? We know how unreliable she is." His voice came down the line mingled with the background noise of *South Park*.

"Yeah," I said. I was trying to read the brief on my journalism class at the same time, so my voice was flat. He sighed.

"We need to find *somewhere* to stay. It's not like we can sleep in Shelley's car."

"I know." I did a quick sum in my head. "And it will be too far to drive back after. We'll need to sleep somewhere."

"Could we camp?"

I screwed up my face. "You can, but I'm getting a bed. And a shower, preferably. Think about it, Jack, it will be May. It will be muddy, and freezing."

"Yeah…"

I looked at the time on my phone. "I'll organise somewhere, okay?"

"Okay!" he said, his voice triumphant. "That's great, awesome. Thanks Amy! Make sure you book space for Shelley, too."

"I will."

"You're the best. Thank you!"

He hung up without saying goodbye. I stared at the phone for a moment, eyebrows narrowed, unable to shake the feeling that I'd been tricked. By nine that night, the accommodation was booked but we only had two beds; I would deal with who slept where later.

*

"We're looking for Fremantle Road," I said.

"Does that turn into Baldivis Road?" Kira asked.

I looked up from the map and craned my neck to read a passing sign. My stomach contracted. "Are we on Baldivis Road? Oh shit, we are. We're way off course. When did that happen?"

Jack's bottom jaw tensed. "I'll pull over."

He found a housing development, abandoned for the weekend, and pulled into the car park at the sales office. I flipped through the pages of maps, trying to find where we were. Jack was watching me with his lips pressed together.

"I'm not good with directions," I explained.

Kira patted me on the shoulder. "They probably didn't update the maps since the freeway was extended. We'll be okay."

I nodded, blinking back tears of embarrassment. "I'll just ring someone."

Jack got out of the car, slamming the door behind him. "I am so sorry Kira, she told me she knew where she was going!" he muttered, gesturing she should follow him. He stalked over to the other side of the car park, his posture suggesting a smoker without a cigarette. Kira blushed and excused herself. She stood in front of him for a while, bending her knees in an attempt to get him to look her in the eye. He gestured at me. She put her hands on his shoulders, and he folded his arms.

The home phone rang out, so I called Dad on his mobile.

"Hi Sweetheart. Are you there already? That was quick."

"No… We're a bit lost. Can you tell me what exit it is to get to Bunbury from the freeway?"

He laughed. "I don't think you take an exit. The road just ends, and there's a roundabout."

I wiped my face, shame gurgling in my gut. Cameron put his hands on my shoulders. He didn't say anything.

"Thanks, Dad," I said, and hung up. Taking a deep breath, I turned to Cam. "We need to get back on the freeway." He nodded and swung out of the car to get Jack and Kira.

While he was gone, I rooted around in my bag until I found my sunglasses. With these shoved on my face, I hoped no one would be able to tell that I was crying a little, but just in case, I stared out the window the rest of the way.

*

Just a week out from the trip, I'd had yet another confusing phone call from Jack. I'd been in the shower at the time, and the sound of my phone ringing was just loud enough for me to be unsure whether I was imagining it. I wrenched off the taps and wrapped a towel around myself, sticking my head out of the cubicle.

The phone was on the bathroom counter. I picked it up and held it just off my wet face.

"Hello?"

"Hey Amy. It's Jack."

"Oh," I said. Suddenly, it felt weird to be naked. "Uh, hey Jack, what's up?"

"I was just ringing about Bunbury. Shelley can't make it. She's going to Bali."

"What? But she bought a ticket."

"That's fine, I bought it off her."

"For who?"

He coughed. "My friend Kira. You don't know her, she's a uni friend."

I drew the towel around me tighter. Tales of Jack's sex life always made my skin crawl. He was prone to over-sharing, and I suspected, over-exaggerating.

"Do I need to get an extra room? Or will she be okay bunking with me?"

"Actually... she's going to bunk with me. I was ringing to see if you'd be okay bunking with Cam."

"Jack! There's only one bed in those rooms!"

"So?"

"So?! It would be weird me sleeping in the same bed as Cam."

"No weirder than *me* doing it. Just take separate sleeping bags and get changed in the bathroom."

I inclined my head, conceding his point.

"I really like this girl, Amy. I met her in my elective photography class. She's from Singapore, and her parents are really rich but she's so down to earth. She loves music and old films and she has really nice clothes."

I laughed, gathering my wet hair up in my free hand and twisting it up onto my head. A puddle was forming around my feet as I drip dried.

"That's really good Jack."

"I know. I was starting to think I'd *never* get a girlfriend."

"So what are you going to do? Ask her out?"

"Nah. I just want to see what happens. In Bunbury, you know? It could be so romantic."

"Bunbury? Romantic?"

"It could happen."

I nodded, biting my lip. With Jack's crushes, I'd learned not to become too invested unless he was willing to act on them. He hadn't asked a girl out since year nine, when he started going out with Jenny Robinson, who'd been nice, but also kind of fake, and had dumped him in the middle of Garden City shopping centre in the middle of a screaming hissy-fit because he *just wasn't cool enough for her, okay*. I couldn't really blame the guy for being girl-shy after that.

"Seriously, she's perfect," he said. "I just want everything to go smoothly."

*

The concert was packed, but we had a strategy. Wherever we went, the boys formed a wall behind us, which meant we went un-squashed and we never got stuck behind them where we wouldn't be able to see. Both of them were bean-pole tall, with Jack six foot two and skinny like a weed.

I was beginning to warm to Kira. As we got out of the car in Bunbury, she slipped me a foil pack of Panadol and some tissues without a word. We girls held hands and shimmied to Vampire Weekend, talking about books between songs. Our rain ponchos crinkled in the wind. Kira occasionally raised Sigmund to her eye and took photos of us, Cam pulling silly faces and me striking poses like I was Kate Moss at Coachella, just with worse hair and more body fat. I forgot that I was makeup-less. It felt like nothing had existed before that day.

Jack watched the proceedings with his arms folded and his head tilted to one side like the whole day was one of his games.

During Miami Horror, a guy tapped him on the shoulder. "Hey man, can we stand in front of you? My girlfriend can't see!" The guy was small but muscular, with a tattoo of a dragon on his bicep and a triangular goatee. Jack just stared at him. After a while they moved to get in front of him anyway, placing themselves between Jack and Cam, and Kira and me. Jack took one look at Kira, and then shoved the guy. "Fuck off!"

The guy shoved Jack back. He stumbled into Cam and righted himself, eyebrows slanted.

"Fuck you, mate," the guy said, showing Jack his middle finger. His girlfriend grabbed him by the shirt, holding him back.

"Find somewhere else to stand, we were here first!" Jack shouted.

The man said something to his girlfriend and she stood aside. He tensed his jaw and rushed at Jack with his fists in bunches.

"Don't!" I cried, running in towards them. Cam grabbed me by the arm, and

Kira by her camera strap, and pulled us both out of the way just in time. The girlfriend squealed as fist connected with jaw. Jack went down like a falling tree.

"Jack!" yelled Kira. She shook free of Cam's grasp and ran at the guy, finger pointing like a school teacher's. "Get out of here before we call security."

"Hey, he started it!"

"Get lost!" she screamed.

Cam was kneeling by Jack, shaking him. He was lucid, but his eyes were full of tears. I stood there, unable to move. The concert played on and no one seemed to care about us.

"Let's get him to first aid," said Cam, and gestured at me. Together we pulled Jack to his feet. He shook his head at us.

"Forget this," he muttered.

As he loped off, it started to pour.

He found us in the car park, waiting for him.

"Are you okay?" said Kira.

"Yep. Let's go. It's cold." His nose was pink and his teeth were chattering. He wouldn't look any of us in the eye. A bruise blossomed on his chin and his lower lip was swollen. He smelled of cheap vodka.

"Are you still upset about that guy? It wasn't your fault," I said, putting my hand on his arm.

"No, I'm not upset. And of course it wasn't my fucking fault."

I shut my mouth.

"No need to speak to her like that," said Cam, putting his hand on my shoulder.

"If she wasn't being a bitch, I wouldn't have to."

"Hey!" I called out. Suddenly I didn't care if Jack was sad or hurt. I wanted to hurt him. I peeled Cam's hand off my shoulder and advanced on Jack, and he immediately turned away, blocking me. "What is your problem?"

He didn't answer. He unlocked the car and I climbed in the back with Cam. Kira got in the front seat without speaking to any of us. Cam put his earphones in, though how he could concentrate on music after the day we'd just had, I don't know.

*

The next morning after we'd packed the car, the four of us sat on a patch of grass and daisies, sipping lukewarm instant coffee. We were all hung over with fatigue, and sick to death of each other. Jack picked a flower and handed it to Kira. She smiled and tucked it behind her ear.

"What do you think?" she said to me, holding her fingers up in a peace sign. "Could you take my picture?"

"Sure," I said. She handed Sigmund to me.

"You look beautiful," said Jack, and Kira smiled. She took the flower out of her hair and handed it to me.

"Your turn," she said. "I want to take your picture too."

I tucked the flower into a bobby pin, and stood still as Kira took my picture. My smile in that picture was genuine, although I never saw it.

"Time to go," said Jack, getting up. His face was dark and lined with worry. He stood, waiting as Cam and Kira went past him to throw away their empty cups, then fell in step with me. The word 'bitch' was still ringing in my ears.

"She clearly doesn't like me," he whispered. "She gave the flower away."

"That doesn't mean she doesn't like you," I snapped.

Exasperated, he stalked away. "What would you know," he muttered, fishing out his keys.

SPELLING IT OUT

ZOE APOSTOLIDES

I was playing Scrabble in the park when my mum called to say the chicken shop had been attacked. It looked like arson, she said. I had a triple word score, laying the "s" beside "kin"—which I'd put down earlier—and adding "gher" to the front. Two points, four points, one point, and so on. I was all ready to trounce myself.

Instead I folded the coloured cardboard and tipped the white cubes into their drawstring bag, then jogged through the trees and down the hill. Red car, blue car, Citroën, Mercedes. The air was smoky. In front of me a baby in a rickety pram was ascending, its mother puffing behind. The baby's eyes scrunched as a fire engine passed us, its mouth a perfect o, a full stop sliding to a semicolon of dribble.

Outside the chicken shop, people were standing behind police tape stretched tight around a lamppost, so you couldn't actually see the writing that said *police - do not cross,* but you knew that's what it said. Maybe they hadn't thought they'd need so much tape, that Fowl Play would be so big. I paused at the old phone box that doesn't have a phone in it any more, only flowers. They're stacked one row upon another. Flowers are notoriously tricky to spell, and every night I worried we'd be tested on them. So I waited before crossing the road, though I could see Mum waving at me, and checked. Fuchsia. Narcissus. Marigold. Oxlip. Cowslip. Gentian. Peony. Cockscomb. Chrysanthemum.

*

"The deep-fat fryer kicked off."

"So it wasn't deliberate?"

"No. That thing's been packing in for months. Janice left the lid on while she nipped to the loo. Hot oil everywhere."

We were sitting across from each other at the table, grating cheese for a béchamel sauce. I had suggested coq au vin because it was easier and we never cooked with wine, but Mum said it would only remind Janice of what she'd lost. Lasagne was what you did for people who had experienced tragedy.

Our kitchen backed onto the chicken shop's, and when I inhaled I tasted onion rings. After we'd covered the dish with aluminium and put it in the oven, Mum sat on the sofa watching *Come Dine With Me* and snorting at the desserts. I sat on the floor learning spellings.

"Want me to test you?" she said, during the break.

I hesitated. After the last competition, the one that decided who was through to the semi-final, the judges had given each of the contestants a 40-page booklet of words. They were identical, and only the words listed would be asked. We'd already worked through that booklet since then, Mum and I, and the pages had become frayed and dirty. The word 'expunge' was neatly wiped out by a glob of cream flying from a whisk. It didn't matter because I knew them all by then. The semi-final was on Monday, but I was playing the long game.

"I'm playing the long game," I told her.

She nodded seriously, slurping her tea. Then she said, "What do you mean?"

I showed her my notebook. It's bright pink with fairies along the spine, to make it look innocuous. No one's going to bother stealing or even flicking through something so salmony, I reasoned. It has my words in, the ones I'm learning on my own. They come from all over. Dictionaries—Johnson's, Oxford's, Merriman-Webster's—novels, science textbooks, sheets of music, encyclopaedias. I'd even copied out "supercalifragilisticexpialidocious" three times last week, just in case.

Mum's hair is white six days out of seven. It's short, so she doesn't wear a cap when she's cooking, and throughout the day it gets covered in flour. It's brown now though; she hadn't opened the bakery as a mark of respect.

She took the notebook as I held it out. *Come Dine With Me* came back on but she ignored it. The man and woman onscreen were looking through their host's cupboards and giggling. The woman pulled out a pair of heels and squeezed her feet into them. The man said the host's mackerel pâté tasted like effluent (nice word, I thought, for something so nasty) and the woman giggled some more. The narrator of the show made innuendoes.

Mum turned the pages of my fairy notebook.

"Jesus, I can't even pronounce most of these," she said. "I'll just test you on cakes."

Bakewell. Parkin. Tiramisu. Panettone. Pavlova. Tartin. Blondie. Buccellato. Bundt.

"Croquembouche," Mum said, yawning and patting my head as she went past.

I got that one wrong, so I wrote it in the book.

The bakery, our bakery, is called Tiers of Joy. It's at the top end of Holloway Road, just before the tube station, before the hill that leads onto the heath. We live in the flat above it.

My school's down the road, towards the playing fields at Highbury. The street gets dirtier the further down you go, and we're lucky to be sort of in the middle. The higher you climb the posher it gets; ten minutes slog up past the cemetery and you're in a different world. Thick white gates protect the mansions teetering on uneven ground, and there's no litter. It reminds me of Stepford from The Stepford Wives, which I read last summer.

On my way to school I pass the church that no one goes in, only sixth formers smoking after school, and the newsagent that sells cans of Nurishment, out-of-date pre-packaged Madeira cakes for 35p and weird racist puppets.

On Sunday we opened the shop again. Normally we would both be downstairs at 4.30am, but today Mum insisted I sleep in on account of the competition tomorrow. On a normal day we had a routine. I filled the kettle, she greased the pans and tins and trays. I weighed the flour, she lugged the industrial-sized buckets of butter from the fridges.

It was still dark when I woke up, and for a few moments it felt like I might get back to sleep again. Then I remembered tomorrow and knew it was useless. On YouTube there are videos of spelling competitions, mostly in America. There are hundreds of them. I watched three clips in a row.

A boy from Oregon stumbled on "ophidiophobia" (fear of snakes). I ran through my list of phobia spellings as the sky changed from royal to periwinkle to powder.

On Sunday nights, the Irish pub across the road locks its doors after midnight and does karaoke. Then the whole pub finishes with "She Moved Through The Fair" (it's tradition). Afterwards, the same man walks home on his own every week at half past two, kicking every bin over on Holloway Road and shouting "why?"

Normally this doesn't bother me much, but today I'm filled with panic. What if I don't sleep at all? I won't remember a thing. I'll be a laughing stock. You can't ask the audience in a spelling competition. You can't phone a friend.

Sesquipedalophobia: the fear of long words. Methyphobia: the fear of alcohol. Nomophobia: the fear of having no phone credit.

*

The Towngate Theatre in Basildon is bright red inside, velvet fur spread over hundreds of seats set across three storeys. It looked sort of like Archway library from the roadside. Inside the auditorium, every seat's empty, the curtains hanging limply, the stage with a microphone on it and nothing else. We both stood looking at it for a while, Mum biting her nails and throwing me furtive looks. I felt pretty calm at this point.

A woman dressed head to toe in black pulled open the fire escape doors and hurried over, clutching a clipboard.

"You're the first to arrive!" she trilled. "Welcome to Essex!"

We'd left the flat at 4am and arrived at Fenchurch Street an hour later. The competition started at 2pm. Mum was right—it had taken two hours to get here, and we'd been in a café since then. I'd had two coke floats, she'd had a triple espresso.

We shook hands with the woman and she walked up the aisle of the theatre, throwing her hands out and turning round to face us as she paced. I think we were expected to follow.

"How are we feeling today?" she asked, flattening a stray lock of hair across the crown of her head.

She stopped and scanned the paper on her clipboard.

"Not many of you today," she said. "What's your name, honey?"

I told her, and she ticked it off.

"Congratulations on getting to the final."

"This is the semi-final," I said. "The final's in two weeks."

The woman beamed and looked over our heads as the door swung open behind us.

"I was terrible at spelling," she whispered, hurrying over to greet the newcomers.

Slowly the others arrived; fifteen of us in total. Half an hour before kick-off I went to the ladies' bathroom and locked a cubicle, pulling the pink notepad from my bag. I chanted my lists, warming my mouth up, speaking each letter slowly and deliberately. I skimmed the booklet of words, brushed up on the easy ones and breathed in and out. The loos were polished, gleaming, the toilet paper quilted. My tongue felt heavy, the way it always did beforehand, and I noticed my pulse beating in my eardrums.

No one knows for sure why they're called "spelling bees". We call them competitions over here, anyway. It was normal in 18th-century America to call any sort of get-together a "bee", if you were helping someone out. So they had "apple bees" and "logging bees" and so on. I always call it "the bee" in my head, though. There's the hum of excitement as my name is called and I leave my seat, a peculiar buzzing that makes me feel dizzy as I get to the mic, like I'm walking through very thin oil. Mum tilts her head forward slightly as I scan for the woman asking the questions, who looks much further away now than she did a few moments ago. I'm the ninth to be called. The girl before me, Laura Something, answered two wrong. She's out, and seems delighted about it. She has a long ponytail tied with blue ribbon and she sighed heavily before answering each question. The sound of those exhalations, amplified through the theatre, set my teeth on edge. Her dad's sitting next to her now, tapping away on his phone, shooting his daughter dark looks.

"Good afternoon," the woman at the table says, looking straight at me. "Please tell us your name, age, and where you're from, please."

I do.

"Great. I'll be asking you to spell 25 words. Please speak clearly into the microphone. You're allowed a maximum of 30 seconds per word, and any misspelling will lead to disqualification."

I nod. Mum catches my eye with a thumbs-up; she's chewing a flapjack nervously, the crumbs falling into her lap.

"Your first word is locomotive."

Easy. I spell it out.

"Renaissance," said the woman.

Page 33 of the booklet. One "n", two "s". I spelled it out.

"Conundrum," she said. "C-O-N-U-N-D-R-U-M," I said. Page four.

The lights were hot on my face, being long accustomed to brightening the faces of Basildon's best. I wasn't used to them, and sweat began to trickle behind my ears. The faces in the auditorium were in deep shade. I could almost feel the will of the other contestants, praying I'd slip up. But I wasn't going to.

There were only four questions left now. The neon scoreboard beside me glowed 22. 23, 24, and then I'd done it.

"You're through to the final," said the woman, smiling for the first time. "Very well done."

I almost tripped down the stairs, my forehead burning, and walked to the back of the theatre. Two green tables were unfolded, set with water jugs with chunks of lemon floating in them. I saw Mum excusing herself from our row of seats and come hurrying towards me.

"Can we have Francis Smith next, please. Francis Smith."

I gulped the water, wiping the sheen off my face. A boy was striding up to the side of the stage, arms dangling by his side. His flannel shirt looked too big for him, black jeans hung around his hips. He made his way to the mic and faced us. I stared.

He stared back, or at least he stared out, into the crowd of parents and spellers. His hair fell slightly over one side of his face. I'd never seen him before, but then there were so many of us in the early rounds that wasn't unusual. He was chewing gum, which he pulled from his mouth and stuck behind one ear. I was equal parts horror and respect. His hands gripped the mic like he was about to close his eyes and burst into song. I could see they were trembling slightly, long fingers interlocked. Francis Smith, I thought, as Mum reached me, and we went outside just as the woman behind the judges' desk asked for his name and age. I looked behind me as the door swung shut.

*

The thing is, I'm fairly certain I'm gay. That's why my interest was disturbing. In PSHE at school, sexuality had been explained. Some of us would be heterosexual, some homosexual, some both, and some neither particularly one way or the other. The man from the Teens First! trust had a kind face, and I felt bad for him when the boys made cracks and started pretending to snog each other.

Being a lesbian had never been a big deal to me; I just knew that I was—women interested me more than men, and that was it. I remember my primary school teacher—and from some research on online forums (where I read what other lesbians said but never contributed), I came to realise most of these women had a similar story—and how keen I was to please her. I drew painstaking, elaborately designed cards for her, and mourned when she left. I've watched a lot of films, and it seems like most girls care about what boys think of them at thirteen. The girls in my class do. I didn't consider myself weird that I didn't, I just wish that I was interested in someone, someone who felt the same way.

We went to parties sometimes, my friends and I. We weren't the most popular group at school, but we weren't the least. It was a position I've always been comfortable in. The only awkward thing was boys. I liked them, mostly. There were noisy ones and quiet ones, ones who sidled up to you at parties and tried to get you to dance, ones who stood at the side being thoughtful, or something. But I wasn't fussed. I liked them, but not like that.

"Did you like boys when you were thirteen?" I'd asked Mum once.

She smirked a little smirk and turned the pages of her magazine ostentatiously. "No," she said. I knew she was lying (mendacity) but kept my mouth shut. When she didn't say anything more I tried again.

"Most likely I'm a lesbian," I said. That made her put down her magazine.

"You think?" was all she said.

"I never fancy boys."

She slurped her tea and scrubbed some icing off her knuckles. "Boys're icky," she said.

When I gave her a hard look she laughed. "So do you fancy women?"

"Jesus, Mum, I don't know," I said, blushing, though I had sort of dug my own grave here. "I admire them, I guess. I want to be like the ones I admire the most."

"You know that doesn't necessarily mean you're a lesbian, love," she said. "I admire plenty of women. Nigella. Michelle Obama. Grace Jones. Doesn't make me a lesbian."

And she was right, I suppose, but still, I knew. And as the train pulled out of the station, I wished we had stayed to hear Francis Smith's round. I hadn't even heard him speak. Everyone in the competition was either twelve or thirteen, and I suspected he was nearer the older end, just like me. So I knew that a) he could spell, b) he was my age, and c) that I found him attractive. It wasn't a whole lot to go by, really.

The train was delayed, and we arrived back in Archway just after seven. Mum had made a celebratory trifle, dotted with Morello cherries that spelled out "well done!" Later, as I drank orange juice from the carton at the fridge door, I spied another trifle, smaller, pushed to the back. This one said "never mind!" I nodded at it gravely. This was no time to be thinking about boys. I was only ever one misspelled word away from a conciliatory pile of custard.

*

September was our busiest month at Tiers of Joy. Kids from my school flooded back to Holloway Road and picked up supplies for late-summer picnics. Everyone was miserable about going back to work. Christmas was months away. We got up at 4.30 every morning, opened at seven, and then at half past I'd change into my school uniform and wait for two of my friends outside the betting shop on the corner. The final was in a week.

Every evening I scoured Wikipedia for words, returned books to the library and took new ones out. My pink notebook overflowed. An old textbook on shipping was my favourite so far. Words like admiralty, mainstay and sextant. Fishery. Lifebuoy. Rigging. Each of the finalists was sent an email detailing the date, time and place of the next bee. There were six of us, and there, in the list of addresses, was Francis Smith. fsmith95, to be precise.

The bell tinkled as the door swung open, bringing the noise and smoke of the road with it. I switched off the computer screen and stood behind the counter.

Mum was just visible through the swinging plastic beads that led into the kitchen.

"Do you have any artisan bread?"

A woman with bright yellow hair stood beaming in the doorway. She carried a Waitrose bag on one arm and a green canvas tote from Daunt Books on the other.

I did my best smile. Artisan: "(of food or drink) made in a traditional or non-mechanised way using high-quality ingredients."

We did white and wholemeal, soda bread on St Patrick's Day. Mum emerged from the kitchen, wiping her hands on her apron. "Artisan bread?" she said.

The woman nodded and surveyed the buns melting under the counter, each glacé cherry at a slight angle. She seemed unable to stop herself wrinkling her nose at the cornflake clusters, the triple-fudge brownies, the fat sausage rolls we made specially for long-evening drinkers from the pub.

I made quick eyes at Mum while the woman waited. Let me handle this.

"Of course," I said. "Let me go fetch you a loaf. We keep them back here."

"Lovely to see a proper family-run bakery," the woman was saying to Mum.

"So rare these days, you know." I willed her to stop speaking, could almost feel Mum's reptilian smile oozing through to the kitchen. I hovered behind the shelves for a moment, to make sure she wasn't about to enter into a public-relations nightmare and turf a paying customer outside without a crust. When I heard her murmured assent, I assumed the coast was clear and grabbed a loaf of brown off the shelf. In the cupboard I found a jar of poppy seeds, years old by the looks of them, and took down the box of Quaker's porridge oats. I smeared a glaze of butter and milk from the bowl Mum had been stirring, then I tipped the mixture of seeds and oats onto the top of it, and squashed the whole thing slightly between two hands. I wrapped it in greaseproof paper and tucked the edges attractively back on themselves. Artisan?

The woman beamed. "Thank you. I love supporting local business."

Mum was grinning back at the woman now, digging the nails of her right hand into her thigh.

"How much do I owe you?"

"Six pounds eighty-five," I replied promptly.

She placed the loaf carefully in the Waitrose bag and waved us goodbye from the street. Mum splayed her fingers back and raised her eyebrows at me.

I opened the till and plopped thin silver coins into their correct trays. "Artisan" was one of the words on the semi-final booklet. I felt like a shyster, but at least I had good business sense.

Returning to the computer, I stared at the name in the email list. Why was I thinking about Francis Smith? I knew nothing about him. He was good-looking, sure, but I was a lesbian. I'd had that, at least, figured out. These feelings were unwelcome and distracting. There was apple pie to bake (not nearly as easy as the saying goes, especially if you have as much trouble as I do with pastry) and words to learn. I hadn't even started on the names of countries, all 196 of them, though it was unlikely these would be asked at all. Two new-looking textbooks sat beside the computer, one on aircrafts and the other on agriculture. There must be hundreds of words in those I didn't know: any one of them could slink up on me and prove my downfall, and here I was sitting at a screen thinking about a boy I didn't even know, whose weird attraction was nothing more than a freak occurrence. I decided to act, looking at the name for a few moments more, before copying it into a new email. The subject was "Hello".

Hi, you were after me at the last comp. Hope you don't mind me emailing you. Are you nervous?

I signed my name and sent it.

That evening we set to work building a wedding cake. The couple were friends of ours, Rob and Mandy, and they wanted a five-storied lemon sponge.

The cake itself was the easy bit; the icing was hell. A pile of fresh lemons, 35 deep, was balanced precariously on the counter. Mum whistled while she worked; I flicked the pages of the cookbook back and forth. Spatchcock. Gelatinous.

Desiccated. Solidify. Treacle. I tried to put the email I'd sent to the back of my mind, but just like when someone tells you not to think of a white rabbit, all I could think of was the meaningless words zooming down the ether. The white rabbit in Monty Python looks all innocent but bites off the knights' heads. Francis Smith would snort when he read it. He and his friends would sit huddled round the computer, coming up with an insincere reply. I'd turn up to the final with a greaseproof bag over my head, like a fake-artisan loaf trying to disguise itself as the real thing.

"You're very quiet," said Mum, beating a bowl of icing sugar the size of both our heads.

"Just thinking," I muttered, then looked at her. "You know that boy? The one after me at the semi-final."

"Which boy?" she said, frowning.

"Francis Smith. They called his name just after I was finished. He had that red-checked top on. Jeans. Big fringe."

Mum stopped stirring and turned to face me. "What about him?"

"I'm not sure. I think I liked the look of him."

She did another of her smirks.

"And that's confusing for you, because you thought you liked girls."

"Well, yes," I said. I felt better for saying it out loud, despite the embarrassment. Since none of my friends knew I was gay, I was a bit short on confidantes.

I used to chat to my Aunt Nic before she moved to the States two years ago: she had a very dark sense of humour and when she came to stay she and Mum got blind drunk in the living room and danced to Fleetwood Mac. She was always asking me for "the goss" and listened when I proceeded to detail every semi-interesting thing happening at school.

She took up with a Baptist church in Idaho where everyone clapped and banged tambourines and sometimes spoke in tongues. She stopped phoning, but she did write Mum a long letter explaining how I needed to be encouraged into more "gender-appropriate" activities and made to put on a skirt once in a while. Mum didn't respond, though she did send a photo of me last year, taken at Waterlow Park. I'm coming down the slopes fast, hands gripping the bars, concentration narrowing my eyes and my hair flying behind me. Mum wrote on the back "turned thirteen last week—a dyke on a bike". I put three kisses. We haven't heard from Nic since.

"I spoke to this Francis Smith's dad, I think." Mum was doing that annoying thing where she knew she was saying something important to me but was acting all nonchalant, licking icing off her wrist.

"Well? What was he like?"

"Nice bloke, actually. Said they were from Kettering. You know where that is?"

"Nope."

"Me neither."

We chopped. We diced. We zested. We grated lemon skins and beat egg yolks into a sloppy syrupy goo. I licked the bowl. Francis Smith from Kettering. It was hardly the stuff of Nancy Mitford novels.

I decided to avoid looking at my emails again until I went to bed, which was 10.30, after we stayed up watching Jurassic Park 2. Triceratops. Troglodyte. Mosquito. I once read that women spend something crazy like 40% of their lives waiting for stuff—for all manner of weird things, and I wasn't about to start that. A six-hour break was restrained, I thought.

There were three emails in the inbox. One was from Wordsmiths.com, offering me three new quizzes that, once I clicked on them, made me feel better about next week; one from a cake blog I followed on Mum's behalf. The last was from Francis Smith.

Hi! Yeah, I remember you. Think my dad was chatting to your mum. Super nervous. Can't believe in seven days it'll all be over... Going to burn my dictionary. You're from London, right?

I stared at it. Then I started to type.

*

We had one of those wet summer storms the night before the final. I sat by the windows in Mum's room and read through my diaries of words. I'd abandoned all alphabetical order, all the groups so carefully constructed, all the different coloured pens and pages marking different topics. It was a mess, to be honest, but I'd reached that level of frenzy where I knew that by tomorrow it'd all be over and I'd be looking at these books in a totally different way.

We had emailed a lot since last week. I now knew that he went to a single-sex school (his words), that he liked running in his school team, sneaking into the cinema on Saturdays, playing cards and reading comic books. His favourite film was Annie Hall (I had no idea what this was, so read the Wikipedia page and then professed to love it too). We planned to make our parents take us for milkshakes after the final—something he suggested. Can you think of somewhere nice? he asked. I was wary. The final was in Covent Garden, in one of the main rooms they used for school visits at the Transport Museum. I'd never been. I had no idea where we might find a milkshake around there.

The water streaked down the pane. The neon sign of Standard Tandoori lit up the quiet dark under the building works opposite. The street was unusually quiet. There were always cars on Holloway Road, but for once they simply moved along, orderly, not honking their horns or blasting music. I took this as a good sign. I'd started to feel nervous earlier than usual; Mum was tetchy, too. The winner received a £2,000 cheque and a heap of book tokens. I wanted the trophy most of all, though Mum said if I did win we'd shut the bakery for two weeks and go on holiday. I wanted new rollerskates.

Words from the past week sprung out at me, glowing in the glare from the streetlamp. Symphony. Synecdoche. Pernicious. Luminescent. We had beans on toast for dinner (mine with cheese grated on top, Mum's without) and lemonade (mine with crushed ice, Mum's with wine).

"How you feeling?" she asked. The TV screen morphed into a crisscross of interconnected streets and the long, meandering snake of the river took centre stage as Eastenders began to blare out.

"Pretty freaked," I said.

"Will your friend be there?"

"Francis?"

Mum nodded. I nodded. "He got through the last round, so yeah, I guess he'll be there. We've been emailing. We were thinking of going for milkshakes afterwards."

She gave me a long look. "What if one of the two of you wins?"

I didn't know how I felt about this, so I shrugged. "I'd still like to go out for a bit with him and his dad."

"Really?"

"Maybe not, actually. If he wins we'll slink off quietly back here, I'll never speak to him again, and we'll eat the trifle of failure."

"I've made flapjacks. There's at least a hundred in the fridge. If you lose, we'll come home and eat them all. We'll make you a Shirley Temple and you can watch telly all night, eating cake."

"Deal," I said.

But I almost thought I felt the notebooks quiver slightly in my hand. All the months of trying, the memorising, the endless searches in every book I could lay my hands on. The fact that I knew I was good at this, and wanted to prove it. If Francis beat me I'd be mortified. But it was more than that. I'd worked too hard. I realised that failure to win that trophy would mean much more than just losing a spelling bee. It would tap at my head for weeks, years afterwards, come crashing at me whenever I felt sad about something else. It would sting but not drop down dead once it had stung. More like a wasp, really. Spelling wasp.

I spent the next morning wandering through the Transport Museum, checking out the old buses and train carriages. I didn't watch the others compete, so had no idea where the scores lay, and who was out, and anyway Francis would be up after me. By that point I would be finished and could watch him, actually hear his voice, without feeling sick with nerves. At ten to twelve, my name was called.

It was the same woman as before, though she was more dressed up this time. Her shirt was bright green, with a sort of tie built into the neckline. She smiled at me and I noticed her gold tooth glinting from the right side of her mouth. I deliberately didn't look at anybody else.

"For this round, as I'm sure you're aware, there are only eight questions," she said. "You have a minute to answer each. Please speak slowly and carefully into the microphone."

There was a terrible stillness in the air. My hands felt like they were dripping actual beads of sweat. The mic was standing very short before me, adjusted to the height of the person who'd stood here last. I twisted the dial and pulled it upright. I imagined I was simply standing up to bake, to whisk eighty eggs for swan-shaped meringues. I'd done this hundreds of times.

"Cymotrichous," said the woman, looking at the papers before her. Probably she'd have no idea how to spell this without them, I thought unkindly, before I licked my lip and spelled it out. I felt better after that.

"Prospicience?" she said.

I had no idea. This wasn't a word I'd ever heard.

"Can I have it in a sentence please?'

She gave it to me in a sentence. I guessed.

I got it right.

"Elucubrate."

"Stichomythia."

"Ricochet."

I didn't look at the neon scoreboard. I kept my eyes fixed ahead of me, fixed on the woman, wondering almost aloud whether she decided on the words as she went along or if she had a set for each of us. I decided it didn't matter.

My last word was pseudonym.

I got it wrong.

"Thank you," the woman said, and everyone clapped. I could see Mum standing up. My head swam. I walked off the stage, forgetting to wait, to watch Francis. I got out to the red double deckers from the 1960s just as I heard his name called, and Mum came hurrying through the swing doors. She punched my shoulder and almost threw three pieces of heavily buttered malt loaf into my face.

"You're the only one with seven correct!" she crowed.

"I haven't won," I said. "If the last two get eight, they'll win. If they get seven, we have to go to sudden death."

"Celebration trifle! Shirley Temples! Mediterranean cruise! Rollerskates!"

I didn't win, in the end. The girl after Francis fluffed a word; Francis didn't. He collected his trophy, posed for a picture with the lady in the green shirt.

I didn't really feel anything at that point. I guess, looking back, that I was shocked. Pseudonym. How many times had I copied it out, remembered the silent "p", arranged the "e" and the "u" exactly so. My memory had totally failed me, the notebooks had been a waste of time. And to top it all, having decided, happily, that I must be a lesbian, this spelling bee had only thrown me into confusion on that front too.

I waited while we were called for a finalists' group photo. The table nearest the stage held the trophy upon it, with a man slowly chiseling a name into the winner's slot. I edged forward, keeping my eyes on the name, hating him. Across the room I could see Mum talking to a man that could only be his dad; Francis was standing slightly off to one side, watching me.

I leaned over the man with the engraving tools as he wiped his forehead and paused for a moment, fiddling with some nick in the glinting metal of the prize. FRANC, the trophy said thus far, and then he went back to it. The long stem of the "i" complete, he made to move onto the curving belly of the "s", mapping out its size and place compared to the names above it. But as I stared he crossed the "i" three times, once at the top, once in the middle and again at the bottom. Frances.

I turned, my chest feeling very tight, and stared back at where they'd been standing. The adults were still there; the man rolling a cigarette and laughing at something Mum had said. Toward me was walking the boy I had found so immediately interesting, had thought about so much, had been confused by: had literally never heard speak, or even seen up close. The girl. Frances. The crowd of parents were jostling around the finalists now, pulling out combs and licking fingers to rub stray smudges off cheeks. I couldn't see her anywhere.

"Still sore about losing?" said a voice in my ear.

BREAKING GROUND

LUCY MIDDLEMASS

It's timeless in here, never quite night or day. No matter that it's summer, we've all to be back before dark. Cut my visit short that has, although they let me in early what with our Leanne the way she is. The balloon Mam brought sags behind the cot, foil so creased half the letters are in the folds. Still, it's pink, so you can guess what it says.

I take a last look at the baby, resting my hip against the back of the chair. She's clear-eyed, black eyes like a rat, looks right at me. Through me even, feels like. The wires and tubes came out two week ago and you'd never know now. Over the top of the cot, I see the others in a line. It's so hot in here there's no blankets, just wires taped to their crumpled skin. Knitted hats for the ones whose families knew what was coming, fleece for those what didn't.

Near the double doors, a girl my age is taking a photo of her own hand pressed against a cot. She hopes one day she can say she can't believe he was ever that small. My sister's baby is twice the size of hers. If she straightened her legs out her feet would touch the end, near enough.

Leanne comes back from the toilet. She's pale and drained, head bent over the baby immediately, weighed down with love. Pregnancy protected her like a forcefield but the heat in here has burned the colour out of her.

Her words are slow, it's like they're coming to me through satellite. "They're only monitoring her oxygen now. That's what the thing on her foot is. They said she could come home. She's heavy enough."

"But?"

Pause. "They won't let her come back to a place like ours."

"That's shit."

Pause. "Yeah."

She takes a cloth from her open bag on the floor and folds it onto her shoulder. The other mothers have to sit in their chairs and wait for a nurse to pass their babies down to them. Leanne picks her baby up and tips her forward to hold her upright against her chest, the way she used to with the younger kids. "What you doing, eh? What you doing?" she says to her, patting her back. Her words come easy when she's talking to the baby.

"You're good at that." I reach out to cup the baby's foot. It's colder than I expected.

She raises her shoulder and turns towards me so I can wipe up the creamy spit. "You'll be good at it too. One day. What you doing at college again? Health care or something?"

"Health and Social Care." I can't picture myself here or who I'd be here with. Leanne won't be doing this alone but she hasn't seen Kieron since two days after. Best not to get into all that.

"If you don't want none of your own, you could teach primary, or be a nurse."

"You've to go to university for that now." Leanne knows that's the finish of it. "So how long until we're moved?"

Pause. "The council is saying this month. Where are we now?" She looks at the ceiling, then at me, as if I'm about to tell her. "The fifteenth? Next month at the latest." She has her glasses back on and they could trick you into believing she's the same person she was before.

I reach behind myself to part the blind slats with one finger. The sun is sinking through the levels of the multi-storey car park opposite. There isn't time for me to ask anything else. I have to get back before dark. Back to the black mould around our kitchen window, patchy and watery like diseased skin. Back to the boxes of nappies in the bathroom, and back to smacking the front door against the pram still in its cardboard sleeves.

"Asthma's on the up all through our estate. Says so on the noticeboard when you come in the main doors downstairs," I tell Leanne. We don't look away from the baby resting her head against her shoulder. I stroke the dark curl under her ear. "Long way off, but it'll be worse once winter comes too."

Water comes through a hole in our bathroom ceiling and freezes in a pool on the windowsill. Plaster flakes into our hair like snow. When you put the electric on steam seethes through a hundred layers of paint in the back bedroom and the landlord can't say why.

Leanne puts the baby back in her cot while she sorts her words out. Mam kept her oldest daughter out of the special school and it worked out alright in the main, but she'll never live on her own. "It'll be okay. We're a priority. Top of the list now. Soon as a place comes available, it's ours."

"Right. Fuck. Good."

I should leave but I can't make myself move. There are footsteps in the corridor outside, loud enough even from here. The girl looks up over her phone but the nurse walks right by the glass in the double doors. She turns her attention back to her screen, leaning over the back of her chair, chin on her arm. She's wearing a dressing gown and fluffy slipper socks pulled right up to her knees. She probably won't hold him today.

Leanne says to me, "It's late. You need to get home. Be safer." Mam must've told her about the attacks last time she visited. She'll have been gentle about it. Leanne scares easy.

I look down at my baggy jeans. My collar is up, my trainers are new. "I'm not the type."

"There isn't a type." She brushes greasy hair out of her face. She's been in this hospital too long. A dully lit half-life, oblivious now to machinery beeps two month ago would've had her out the door shouting. "I like your hair longer like that. Suits you."

My hand goes up automatically. "Oh. I was thinking about getting it cut."

"Don't. You go on home now. It's dangerous for girls out there."

I know. Everywhere in our block, the mams put up posters about the rapes.

I wait for a double decker bus outside the hospital, jacket over my arm, low sun in my eyes. When I hold my pass against the card reader the light blinks red but I've been taking this route so much of late the driver waves me on.

Next stop, these two girls come up the stairs. They're younger than me and they don't stop talking. They're dressed like they're going all the way out to the suburbs. Their hair, blonde and clean like in an advert, hangs over the back of their seat.

The stop after that, this man comes up. The bus moves and I taste smoke as he lurches towards me. He must've stamped it out when he saw the bus coming. He's short, wearing tracksuit bottoms and although there's loads of space, he sits across the aisle from me, right behind the girls.

First time he does it, I'm not sure I saw it right. The industrial estate on their side becomes fascinating. Love security guard huts and metal fencing, me.

I wasn't wrong. He keeps touching these girls' hair. Strokes it with one knuckle so quick they don't feel it. They're still going on about the weekend. We're over the bridge when he starts jerking his other hand in his lap but when I look at his reflection he's just on his phone. I'll say something to the driver when I get off.

It's alright to look out my side now. Amber and Lily are waiting at the pedestrian crossing past the pub, collars up like mine, on their way home too. They don't see me wave from up here.

This is the first night we've to be back before dark. The papers say the girls are always followed up the stairwells. Old Mrs Ackroyd from downstairs, she says it's always at night. The police say the girls are attacked at random. Always girls in the stairwells, always after dark. Sounds anything but random to me.

I'm walking along the road to our estate before I realise I didn't say anything to the driver.

The sun hits the lower floor windows on our block. Ten up and four along, Mr Dukes is washing his pits in our kitchen sink. We're lucky to have hot water, as Mam often says, but I don't like the bug-eyed way he's looking down at me, with a face like a tongue's going to whip out of it.

The towers make hard lines against rolling June clouds. The wedges of sky between them are sliced up, handed out, no more than our fair share. A grey cat sways along a window frame on the floor above ours, one foot in front of the other. Fat as a pigeon, that cat is. It'll want to fly like one and all if it's not careful.

On the square of grass out front, Mam is bringing in our washing from Mr Dukes' line, her coat over her pyjamas as if she's walking in the grounds of an institution. There are five washing lines down here and Mr Dukes calls all of them his. We're meant to use our balcony but it's crammed with gardening stuff. It's the same for everyone now. Who doesn't owe Mr Dukes something? Mam doesn't look round so she doesn't know I'm almost back.

I'll take my time going up. Mr Dukes has these huge wet eyes behind his glasses and when he blinks he uses all the muscles in the top half of his face. I don't want him blinking at me. Maybe Mam never got dressed today. She steps back to look up, see if he's still there. She's not facing me, but when he wriggles his fingers at her I know what she's thinking. She goes inside with her basket anyway, the main door springing shut behind her.

The little kids from our tower haven't gone in yet. Their weed-thin shadows fall on the concrete, stretched in the last of the sun. They ignore me as I walk alongside the play area, the air filled with screams and dares and *you can come to my house*. A heavy chain fixes a motorcycle to the railings. Must've been there a while, there's no crowd around it.

The boys have a football. Likely it'll be cut to strips before long, kicking it about out here. When it rolls in front of me, I stop it with my foot. There's an anxious silence, even the girls stop shouting. They don't expect it, but I curl it back like I've been doing it all my life. Their noise picks up again, natural as a gust of wind. Doesn't seem long since I played here with Amber and Lily. The concrete hexagons are still here, and the little kids still love them. We jumped between them in school shoes on Saturday afternoons, hell to pay if they came home scuffed. Reckon they'll outlast us all, those hexagons will. A giant slanted disc behind them is a crashed flying saucer, a skateboard ramp and a castle, all day long until the ice-cream van starts up.

Everyone's mams are keeping us in. That's the only way it'll work, only way to keep safe, they said. Their posters have gone up on every landing on every floor. Bubble writing and stickers nicked out their girls' stashes. Just another scheme, feels like, even if our mams came up with this one themselves. Some say it was our mam who suggested it first.

Magnet for schemes, this place is. New one every other month, feels like, sometimes. Sunrise Court, our block, always first. We're four towers in a square, although one is boarded up and coming down. The kids'll be off with the scaffolding if they don't watch out. Before I go into our tower, I look back over my shoulder. See myself eight years old, jumping off that crashed saucer, coat in the air, Amber not far behind. See her smashed-up elbow on the concrete, thin bone showing through like a bird's wing.

It's not quite dark yet. I sit on the wall and kick my heels against it. They wouldn't build towers like this now; it was someone's experiment years ago. If you want beauty you've to make your own round here. Mr Dukes up there knows that better than anyone. He's an eye for the little girls too. Sits on this low wall from time to time, having himself a fussy picnic, watching them. Wipes the corners of his mouth with a serviette, enough to burn your throat to see a big man like him doing that.

The light falls strangely around me, grey overhead but bright down here like it's coming up from the earth. When all the blue has faded to grey, I get myself up and head inside.

Some man I don't recognise is just leaving. He nods to me, holds the door too, motorcycle helmet in his hand. I let the door close itself. Shuts the kids' noise right out, that does. The bottom of the stairwell reeks of cleaning fluid, reminds me of the hospital I've come from. There's not a place in this world I can close the door on and call my own.

This new scheme, Mam came up with it at the first community meeting. All the dads were silent, so the mams said. It's nothing to do with them. They come home to lean into their fridges for a can, cool the front of their work shirts. Remote control is theirs, and the pub come Friday night. Anything else is women's business. Our dad used silver paint on our beige fridge, looked new for a week until one of the kids hit it with a scooter.

Amber's dad agreed it doesn't seem fair to keep half of us in, but Amber, who won't do anything she's told, texted me to say she's going in too. Trying to make me feel better. Amber's good like that. Doesn't get dark until late this time of year so it's not so bad, she said.

There are no doormats and no letter boxes. The post you've to collect from lockers here on the ground floor. Brown envelopes to break your heart, some days. Tonight there's nothing but a hundred shiny menus the Chinese boy didn't bother to deliver. There's a noticeboard offering me a scanner for twenty quid and next to that, of course, one of the mams' posters.

As I walk down corridors lined with doors all alike, I can barely hear what's going on inside. A baby crying maybe in number 14 and the thud of music as I turn the corner, the kind you hear coming up through your feet. Walls and doors and floor and ceiling vanish into a dot in front of me.

Despite the thick doors, old Mrs Ackroyd in number 24 knows I'm coming. Has a sense for it, she does, leaning in her doorway and waiting for me. The wallpaper behind her is sticky with yellow grease and out here stinks of chip fat even when her door's shut. I used to slow down to fill myself with it, but it seems a hungry smell now.

She's wearing a checked apron and slippers, working her gums and twisting her knobbly hands. Back bent so bad she's level with my chest. "Shame," she says before I've even said hello. "It was safe in my day. A girl could walk about and no one would trouble her. All changed now. Shame to see you cooped-up, summer and all." Something's always a shame with old Mrs Ackroyd. She used to give me and Amber these weird tasting sweets that didn't come from any shop we knew.

"Yeah," I tell her, shrugging until my collar touches my earlobes. Feels like I'm faking it, as if you can fake a shrug. "What you gonna do?"

"Shame, though, isn't it?" she says again, her tongue smacking against her lips like she's hopeful I'll stay and chat.

"I've got to go." It's true. Shame.

Top of the stairs, Kiera has her door open too. There's a new piercing in the side of her face, up by her nose. She's had her brown envelope today.

"Got me a secret lover," she says, curling her tongue out of her mouth to wobble the stud in her cheek. Heels so high I'm looking right at her bra. Turns out it's a letter from the benefits people saying they've evidence she's got a man living there. She'll be back in court, no matter what. "They've printed his name too."

"They're not supposed to do that. That's their fuck-up," I tell her. "What name they put?"

"It's some whatever name, you can tell it's bullshit. Wait, wait, I've got it here, I'll show you—" foot at the bottom of the door as she leans into her flat, blood on her ankle under her sandal strap "—you'll like it. Here it is, here—" voice higher, laughter in it already "—'Richard Brown'. Richard Brown? What sort of bullshit name is that? Never heard of him." There's a bark behind her. She turns to shout then there's whimpering and the sorry clatter of nails on laminate disappearing down her hall.

I laugh for her. I'm probably like the tenth person she's told. "It's bullshit."

"How's your Leanne doing? Baby home yet?"

"Nah, she's alright though. They're saying they can't come back to this." I don't need to gesture to show her what I mean. This is the same for all of us.

"Ah, that's shit. Your Leanne deserves something good in her life. Anyway. Shouldn't keep you, should I? Home before dark, you lot." She's all giggles about that. She's seen the posters the mams put up. How could she miss them? As I walk away, I think how I don't want to be like her. Anything but like her.

134

The last scheme ended near enough a year ago. There were posters for that too, all up these stairs and on the fire glass in the doors. We were supposed to get the local news crew in but they never came. Amber and Lily got their pictures in the paper though, seed packets held up to their faces. Wilko's donated fifty trowels and spades, seventy forks and a van full of brand name compost. Then lottery cash came in, five hundred quid. Turns out it was easier to get us hands on that than money for food or bus fare.

Breaking Ground, they called that scheme. Someone fancied themselves very clever. Foreigners didn't join in, just stood in their doorways with wary eyes watching us hump growbags up the stairs. Shut their doors when we reached their floor. The mams' curfew is for them too but they keep all theirs in anyway.

There's one last Breaking Ground poster here on the ninth floor, above the fire extinguisher. Faded and tatty now, and someone's drawn cocks on the smiling apples and oranges, which always gets a smile from me too. Good luck getting an apple tree onto the twelfth floor. They announced that scheme a success in the finish, money targeted right where it's needed. Bullseye.

One woman had three trowels and twenty packets of lupin seeds but there was no food in her cupboards. Didn't speak English too well, her kids barefoot in their underwear round her legs all day. I went past when I was getting ours out the flat for Mam for an hour. This woman mimed eating the seeds, frowning at me. I tried to take them off her but she bolted back inside so quick you'd think I was mugging her. Very funny too, the kids thought that was.

There's the tap of trainers up the stairwell ahead of me. As they turn onto our landing, I see it's our Kasey. She doesn't look down like she should to check I'm someone she knows. She likes to pretend she's somewhere else. None of those clothes are hers, they're hanging off her. She wants to be someone else too, which is fine with me as long as she keeps it on her side of our bedroom.

Mam's been shopping today, there's carrier bags inside the door. She must've been dressed for that, at least. Between the bags and the pram, I can hardly get myself in. That's the next scheme, they're going for our money. This time it's the whole borough. Loaded up plastic cards, and you can't spend it just anywhere you want. You have to spend it at whatever supermarket they say. Cash-fat face from Tescos on the news confirmed it's a great idea. No good for most of us, ours comes from markets and pound shops. Mam spends all day at it sometimes, takes it that serious. Plans it out, list in her hand. Gets shorter and shorter that list does. Kasey and the others don't stop wanting. All these kids, Mam's lucky I'll never come home with news like our Leanne's.

This borough is full of families with destructive habits, that's why it's coming here first. We spend too much on problem debt, as if there's another kind. Reckless and feckless, all of us, and the national papers like a rhyme. They must've met my dad. They give one of those cards to Mam, we'll have to go back to Mr Dukes. He'll sort her out, the way he did before.

The washing basket is in the hall. I'm to empty it because I'm the only one who can tell all us socks apart. Mam's in the kitchen with her fingers at her temples, eyes shut tight. All ours are in now. Two in their primary school sweatshirts and the toddler hitting into their legs with a push along fire engine. Their noise goes right to my bones.

Uncooked chicken fillets sit on the side. Soon as I'm in the kitchen door there's a little one hanging off my neck. Mam tells me she can't cook with all these kids round her. Can't think, can't think, can't think. Can't do anything. She goes out to the balcony waist-deep in untouched gardening stuff, wrists on the railings as the sun goes down. She likes it out there. Kasey is afraid Mam might just go one day, flap her wings and take off.

After the kids' bath, I sit on the settee with the washing basket, pairing socks and piling them up. Calms me right down, breeze coming in from the balcony so nice you can forget the mould and the damp and the water Mr Dukes left on the lino. Doesn't matter if the kids are raising hell in their room, long as they don't come in here and get on to me about anything. Mam hasn't moved, likely she won't until I've gone to bed. She seems to grow closer as the light fades.

Time I go to our room, Kasey's already tucked herself in stiff. She's stuffed my clothes back in the drawers on my side. Surprised she doesn't get hell off the others for wearing them all the while. Kids like her shouldn't have to know about the rapes, it's alright she's got something else on her mind. I'm glad to step over her books too. I keep telling her they'll get soaked if she leaves them on the windowsill. Her teddies sit where I left them, three inches from the wall.

I kick my trainers off and lie on my bare mattress. The patterns in the plaster by my head have been spreading since we were moved here. "What was the worst day of your life, Kase?"

"Worst day of my life? When Dad said he'd start holding the door open for me." She didn't pause, she's that much quicker than our Leanne. Although if I'd asked her about the best day, she'd be thinking about it until the sun came up.

In the corner of the ceiling nearest the window, brown feathers into white like the cup of a mushroom. "Worse even than the day he left?" Maybe she's lucky she remembers him. The little ones only know him from the mess he made.

I look over and see she's thinking about it, her face half lost in her pillow, duvet pulled up over her mouth. "Yeah." She rolls away to face the wall.

Mam wakes me up. Been watching me sleep. She's leaning on the drawers in a strip of sunlight, holding a mug with the Breaking Ground logo on the side. There's ten or so more of those mugs in the cupboard under the sink.

"Morning." She skims the newspaper onto my legs. She's messed it up, the pages don't fit right and it sprawls.

I've kicked my coverless duvet onto the floorboards, but Kasey's bed is neat and empty, corners in tight. I lean up on one elbow; hand on the back of my head. My hair is flat and damp and there's the sharp smell of myself.

"Anything?" I squint at her in the hard light that comes in through pegged-up bedsheet curtains.

"Nothing, love," she says, face all lit up like it's Christmas morning, happiest I've seen her in a long while. "It's a success. Keeping you boys in worked."

WHERE YOU'RE GOING AND HOW YOU GET THERE

ERIN DARBY GESELL

Verica

I tiptoe across the hall to Branko's apartment. I'm going to try one last time to convince him to leave with me. We can run away to Paris or Berlin or maybe even America, anywhere but Serbia. He knows I'll do it. He knows I'll leave.

He loves me. I don't know if I love him back, but I don't want to go alone. He's my best friend. But he's too good. That goodness is what will kill him. It's what has him stuck here in this crap cycle of life. Get up, work in the meat factory, go home, eat nasty prebranac, sleep, repeat. What our parents did, our grandparents did. None of us even graduated high school.

I listen at Branko's door. It's silent. I slide my key into the lock and sneak into the living area that doubles as a kitchen. Quiet. Normally Branko sleeps on the couch and his mother, Ana, in the bedroom. There are no bathrooms in our apartments. The whole building shares a communal one on the second floor. Ana had said Branko had to go to Aleksinac for work. I haven't seen him for ten days. I know that excuse is bullshit. The factory would never send some menial seventeen-year-old to travel for work. He's up to something.

Branko has told me everything since we could talk. I don't remember a time not having him with me. Every risk I've taken, he's been there to tell me that I could break my neck jumping from the bridge into the river or get sent to juvenile court for stealing food. He's not a wuss. He just believes there are safer and more "right" ways of doing things. Branko expects to do work and get paid. I'm cynical. I'm used to being screwed over every time I turn around, so I figure I should just take what's in front of me while I can.

His empty couch fills me with dread. Even though I know his loyalty to taking care of his mama, I never imagined leaving without him.

I roll back my shoulders and check Ana's room just to make sure. He's not there. I kiss my first two fingers and hold them out to Ana. She's been just as much a mother to me as my own mama has. We all kind of take care of each other here at Cheese Palace (what Branko and I call our apartments because it smells like burnt cheese). But that's the same kind of crap thinking that gets you stuck here.

I walk away from Ana and out of the apartment for the last time. I shut the door behind me, walk down the stairs, and exit the Cheese Palace. I check my backpack for my passport, keep walking away from the building. I won't look back. I won't cry. I won't think about how devastated my grandparents will be when they see that I'm gone tomorrow morning. I won't think about what'll happen at the end of the month when they don't have my paycheck. That's not my fault. Not my problem. If my idiot brother hadn't gotten hooked on ecstasy and then heroin, and my parents before him, my grandparents would have money to take care of themselves. The rest of my family had been selfish. Now it's my turn to take care of myself.

I pull my jacket around me, not because I'm cold. Just to have something a little closer to me. I walk across to the river and refuse to look to the bank where Branko thought he could stand up to Neno Jovanovic. Thought. I ended up dropping a rock on Neno's foot so we could run away.

I walk along the train tracks outside of town. I've watched the trains for the last few weeks. I know one will be rolling through Krusevac at ten to midnight. It should catch up to me in less than fifteen minutes. Branko had been watching the trains with me, supposedly helping me with my plan to escape. Since he left, though, I wonder if he wasn't watching for himself.

Branko

Damn! A blister the size of a peach pit splits open on my palm. I drop the shovel and stare down at the ripped flesh. It's oozing. I look up, out of the hole at the night sky. The moon glows orange against the black.

Wait, what? Out of a hole? Branko, what the hell are you doing in a hole?

Yep, the shovel, the dirt, the digging. Digging a hole. Why am I digging a hole?

Dirt covers my boots, and dust streaks my jeans and flannel shirt, which is ripped across the front like a werewolf clawed my chest. Blood. My side is bleeding. How am I going to get out of this hole? The sides are just shorter than my head. What if it caves in on me?

My chest tightens. Breathing hard. Eyes bouncing to the ground, underground all around me, up, up and out, only able to see sky, where is the ground?

I'm in the ground.

I grab a root and try to hoist myself up. Pulling, scrambling out, grasping for grass, lugging body out of hole. Out, out of the ground!

I lie on my stomach, feet dangling over the mouth of the hole, left cheek resting on the grass. Breathing, sweating, blister oozing.

I can't see far in the dark. The tangerine moon is the only light, but I know in the darkness there is a field surrounded by a forest. I could be in Kosovo or back in Serbia or as far away as England for all I know. A cloud drifts over the moon, leaving me in complete darkness.

I wake with the sun and remember what I'm doing, the confusion of the night before lifts with the return of day. At first it scared me, how often I forget where I am. Now, sometimes I think it's a blessing to forget.

I'd understood what they were going to do. Knock me out, take part of my liver, stitch me up, and wake me when it was over. I knew it would be painful. But I was supposed to get $40,000 for it. Do you know how much money that is? How much food that can buy? Heat, water, food. If I just did it, then we'd be set. With Dad dead, I'm the one who needs to step up.

I thought I would go to Kosovo and the liver people would snip off the part they wanted, pay me, and send me home. Now, here I am with less than half a liver, digging holes for crazy people. Murderers, probably.

The guy who woke me in this field after my surgery had said to dig six feet by six feet, spaced three feet apart, until the entire field was full. The field is barely the size of a soccer pitch. What happens when I'm done?

I stand and immediately fall back on my ass, leaning into the nearest hole, barfing. I put my fingers on the scar. How long has it been? I sit up and count the holes. Four holes times one hole a day plus the three weeks (give or take) I was at the chop shop, "the hospital." I really have no idea how long I was there. It was a blur of waking, people wearing masks, pain, voices I didn't recognise in the dark. That means twenty-five days. At least. Twenty-five days I've been gone and mama has been without money.

I'd gone into the surgery six days after my seventeenth birthday. Six days after Mama cried because we couldn't afford anything other than canned corn, bread, butter, and a beautiful chocolate torte without the nuts—too expensive—for my birthday.

I grab my shovel and thrust the tip into the ground, pulling myself up on the handle, supporting myself to stand. I could be in any field in any country. The air is crisp, fall is coming, and it smells like dirt, soil. Holes. My gnarly, black hair flops on top of my head, dirt lives under my fingernails and probably every crevice of my body. Bones jut out everywhere, stretching my skin. No one back home in Serbia would recognise me without my usual buzz cut, scrubbed raw skin, and muscles. Verica. Verica would still recognise me. All she ever has to do is look and she knows everything that's inside me.

Verica

After almost two weeks of steadily making my way walking, hopping transportation trains, and hiding in the bathrooms of commuter trains, I hopped a wrong one in Bosnia. I meant to go north toward Hungry, but I'm definitely in Croatia. I have no religious conviction nor do I give a crap about the country that has held me in poverty my entire life, but I know if I run into the wrong person, they'll want to kill me for my accent.

I realise my mistake when I meet such a person at a park near the train station where I try to panhandle.

I mind my own business, watch people, look for someone to simply ask for money or someone whose wallet would be easy to take. Someone grabs my ponytail, yanking my head back, and whispering in my ear, "Who do you think you are, walking into someone else's territory?"

It's a girl's voice. Her accent tells me Croatian. Ever since Serbs and Croatians were forced to live together after World War II, Croats have tried to separate themselves from us, the majority, any way that they can. The same time Hitler was trying to "cleanse" Europe of the Jews, they mounted an "ethnic cleansing" campaign to kill Serbs. Serbians fought back with terror attacks. Since 1991 we've each had our own countries, but we still hate each other. I know that my education has been heavy on all of the horrible things Croats have done to my people. But I also know history is usually half lies when you only see one side of it. I'll never understand how much hatred people can build up with religion and pride.

I feel the tip of a knife against my back and the girl's breath on my neck. "I didn't mean anything by it. I'll go." I try my best at imitating her speech, but she doesn't fall for it.

"Ah, a dirty pig," she says. She whips me around to face her, knife at my stomach now. "Serbe na verbe!" All Serbs hang from willow trees.

I hold my head high and look down at her. She's about six inches shorter than me. I have a knife in the waistband of my jeans, but she looks like she actually knows how to use hers.

"What are you doing here?" she asks. Her hair is dirty and mouse-coloured. She could be fifteen or thirty-five. I can't tell with all the make-up she has on.

"Leaving," I say with a shrug.

"Sure you are. This is my spot. Since when does Erik hire pigs anyway?" She looks me up and down. "You don't even have anything to show. How's he expect you to pull in money?"

Holy shit. She thinks I'm a prostitute.

I put up my hands and try to back away from her. "I'm not here to work. I'm not trying to get in on your territory, I was just going to take someone's wallet and be on my way, but I'll go." My heart is pounding in my chest.

She keeps the knife pointed at my stomach and follows after me. "Go figure,

Serb thinks she's too good to work? You thought you'd just take someone's money?"

I keep backing away from her with my hands up. I need a plan.

The park is surrounded by a rock wall. I started only about fifty feet from the wall. If I keep walking, I'll back right into it and she'll have me.

My back hits the rock before I have a plan. It was closer than I'd thought. As the girl yells at me about this and that and all the things Serbs have done to her people, I lower my hands and run them along the wall behind me looking for a loose rock. She calls me a whore and a dumb bitch as I shake a rock loose.

"Your mother is a—"

I cut her off by spitting in her face. I slam the rock on her hand and her knife falls to the ground while she screams. I grab the knife and punch her in the face for calling me stupid. I run back toward the train station and hide in the bathroom. While I catch my breath, I hope her nose is broken so that she can't get any clients for a while.

Branko

I dig hole number thirteen.

Someone is watching. There's always someone watching. I tried to run twice and was whipped like a racehorse in a close race: swift, hard, and with a mean sense of urgency. Breakfast comes when the sun looms over the trees.

I didn't tell Verica I was leaving. I knew if I told her anything, she'd know I was lying. She's funny like that. I may have known her longer than I've known anyone, but I can't tell if she loves me or hates me. She probably knows what I had for dinner and how many times I brush my teeth every day.

"Branislav Zupan, I see you waiting for me under that tree. Don't act like I can't walk myself home. I know you aren't just passing by," she used to say when I first started at the factory, and she still got to go to school.

I hate when people call me by my given name.

A worm wiggles in the shovel full of dirt I just scooped up. Actually, I notice, I cut him in half. How does that work? That you can cut a worm in half and both halves go on living?

Verica and I grew up in the same apartment building; my mama and her grandma took turns watching us based on their shifts at the factory. We went to school together until I had to drop out. Right before I left for the chop shop, Verica had to drop out too, to go to work because her brother, Vuk, went to jail.

"I can't go work there, Branko." She yelled the night before her first day while we sat on the stoop of our apartment building. The red brick building sagged with everyone's depression. The outside smelled like piss and burnt cheese, but when I was with Verica all I could smell was her—sweet, sweet honey. Honey like her hair in the sun, reaching all the way down her back. Honey like the smoothness of her legs when she wore shorts or skirts that waved around her knees. Honey like the sweetness of her voice when she called through my window to come over. I didn't know how to respond. I knew she didn't want to work in the factory. I didn't want to work there either, but what choice did we have? I took her hand in mine.

She pulled her hand away and stood up, looking down the street. Away from our home, away from me. "I just want to stay in school, you know? Maybe if I can stay there, I can learn something. Something that will take me away from here." She leaned against the railing to the apartment stairs with her back to me.

"Where else can you go? Your family needs you," I said. I need you, I thought.

"You're too loyal, Branko. Sometimes I wish you'd just be selfish and do something for yourself. Just once. Don't be so damn responsible." She turned and stomped up the stoop into the apartment building.

I walked her to and from the factory every day if I wasn't working. I wonder what she thought when I didn't show up.

The sun is up over the trees and Lugnuts lumbers over with bread. I mean breakfast. It's always bread. Bread and water in a canteen, both of which he chucks at me like I'm waiting for a pitch. I don't know Lugnuts' real name. He just looks like he's a few lugnuts short of, well, anything that might work properly.

"Hey! What's going to happen when I dig up this whole lot?" I ask, waving my hands toward the remaining empty expanse of the field. The first few days I asked question after question, always answered by the same blank stare. After a week I gave up.

Lugnuts looks at me like I asked him to find the square root of pi, shrugs, and weaves his way back through the minefield of holes to the trees.

Verica

I jump train after train. I've gotten better at asking people for money now that I am away from Serbia, Bosnia, and Croatia. My English is decent. I've been telling people that I'm a traveling student and my mama is sick and I need to get back home to her.

Branko would say that's a terrible lie to tell people, and what if my mama really was sick, but it's working so I'm sticking to it. Knowing what hungry feels like actually helps too. I've been gone for almost four weeks now, traveling at night and sleeping on trains, then wandering whatever town or city I end up in during the day. It's not very fast travel. I sleep in a park if there isn't a train headed north or west, but since my encounter in Croatia, I've slept under the trees in the countryside. I've made it to Prague and sit outside St. Vitus Cathedral. I thought this would be a good place to ask for money—plenty of tourists—but there's already loads of beggars here.

I'm only begging until I find the city I want to stay in. Then I'll find a job. This is these people's real life. This morning a woman asked me where I am from and how I got in this mess of living on the street. When I told her I left on purpose, she said, "Baby. Family, food, a roof, you don't know that you left behind."

I thought about staying here, in Prague, but I'm not sure where I'd work or live. It's a beautiful city full of red clay roofs and bridges. I'm so sick of running with no direction. I'm starting to feel almost as trapped as I did in Serbia. I walk away from the Cathedral and see a sign for a library with a wi-fi symbol. In my high school, we had one computer per grade.

I wander into the library. I sit at a computer next to a girl who looks to be only a couple of years older than me. She has a stack of books next to her and a pen in her mouth as she wrinkles her nose at the computer screen.

School.

College.

My heart starts to beat faster. I search cheap colleges in Europe. Bam. Countries with free college tuition. Germany is my closest option. I don't speak German, but I think I could get by in English. I don't have any papers and no degree, but maybe I could work and take the tests to get accepted. I could really do it. I read more and more. Leaving home is one thing, making it's another. I fully intend to make it.

I walk out of the library hungry but full of focus. It's starting to get dark and the library is closing. I finally have an intention. I retrace my steps back to the Cathedral to find someone who'll help me get food. I cut through an alley that I think will make the walk shorter, when someone grabs me from a doorway. He covers my mouth with a cloth. The light at the end of the alley is the last thing I see.

Branko

Lugnuts and Ski Mask, the guy who whipped me on my first day, interrupt the digging of hole number fourteen. They motion for me to follow them. We walk through the trees with only the sound of our feet and nothing to give me any indication as to where we are. A forest. With clearings. On Earth, I assume.

We arrive in another clearing. A flat-bed truck loaded with half a dozen white barrels about three feet in diameter and four feet tall is parked in the middle of it. I wonder what would happen if I ran.

Lugnuts motions for me to jump up onto the bed with the barrels. I climb up. "What's in the barrels?" I ask. Verica would be so happy for me. I used to never question anything. Just did what I was told. Verica says knowledge is power.

I didn't want to leave school. Verica was right. Education was the only way we were getting out of the Cheese Palace and Serbia, but how could we get out if our very survival depended on us earning money in the factory? That's what I'd thought until I heard I could sell an organ on the black market. Look how great rebellion did me. I'd thought the worst thing that would happen for selling an organ was a fine and jail time. I didn't even consider getting sick or dying. Just getting in trouble. Now I wonder if I'd rather be sick and dying than in the trouble I'm in.

I lift one of the barrels at Lugnuts' motion. "What's in the barrels?" I ask again.

"You don't need to know," Ski Mask answers me. His voice is rough and he has an accent I can't place. At least I know he speaks Serbian.

"Heroin?" I ask.

Ski Mask doesn't look at me. Lugnuts shrugs.

That has to be what it is. This is not what my life is supposed to be.

Verica

The people who took me speak English but not Serbian. They talk to me in English and to each other in a language I don't recognise. Not that that's saying much, I only learned two languages before I had to leave school. We've been driving at night for the last three nights. During the day one of the guys, Red Hair, stays with me in a cheap hotel while the other two, Big Nose and Lumberjack Beard, go out and do some kind of business. At night they all count money. They don't talk to me except to say shut up to my questions. None of them have touched me yet, other than the one who grabbed me from the alley, so my questions get bolder and more persistent. "Who are you?" "Where are you taking me?" "Where'd you get the money?" I even try things like what's for lunch and get no answer other than "Shut. Up." I'm beginning to wonder whether they might let me go out of pure annoyance.

Branko

It's drugs. I knew it was drugs. What else would you bury in the woods in waterproof containers by freaking pounds. Better drugs than bodies, I guess, which was my original thought. I haven't dug any more holes since number thirteen. I did help bring the barrels to the holes, though. I've lost more strength than I thought. Before the surgery I could've taken both of these guys, no questions asked. Now I'm just as weak as the dweeby kid I was in junior high, when I was afraid to jump in the river, and all the girls were taller than me until I was fifteen.

The crap is really about to hit the fan, now, and I'm not sure what I can do about it. Lugnuts finally talked to me. We're in the truck; driving into town (I still don't know what town or even what country. When I asked he said it didn't matter). He's going to drop me on a corner. I'm to walk two streets down to the northeast corner of that street and wait for someone who'll say, "it looks like rain in the east." I think that sounds stupid. I mean, who really says that, but whatever, it looks like rain. Then, get this, I'm supposed to hug the person like we're old friends and slip them the goods—a piece of paper with a locker number and combination. I can only assume the locker is at a train station nearby and stuffed with drugs. Lugnuts will have me in his line of shot at all times. He says for me to be out and back with no piss down my leg and brains still in my head. He gives me a clean shirt and stops at a rest stop along the way so I can wash my face and hair.

As we drive, I lay my head against the window. I consider my options. I can do as Lugnuts says and live and be a total wuss for the rest of my life working for a drug lord. I can refuse to do it and maybe Lugnuts will shoot me and put me out of my misery. But I don't want to die. I know I can get back to see my mama. To see Verica. I could risk running. But what if there are people around? What if Lugnuts tries to shoot me and he hits someone else?

Verica

We're in Italy. I may have never left Krusevac my whole life, but I'm sure that's where we have to be. The windy roads, the mountains, the way we have to slow down so often because there's town after town, the food we ate this morning, the salty air that has to be the smell of the ocean. I've read about all kinds of places. I know that Italy has mountains and volcanoes. I know there are millions and millions of people that live there.

I don't know how knowing where I am is going to help me escape, but the knowledge gives me a rush of adrenaline.

Red Hair brought me new clothes this morning. Nicer clothes than I've ever seen in real life. A black leather jacket, loose fitting white tank top, and tight jeans. The pair of shoes he brought me were black ankle high boots with fringe and huge heels. I could've cried when I saw them. All of my life I've dreamed of walking across stages in heels and waving to millions of people. I couldn't decide if I loved the shoes or if I should try to knock Red Hair out with the heel.

When I'm dressed, I stand in front of the hotel mirror. My hair is down around my shoulders. I look nothing like myself. This is what I thought I would look like when I left Serbia, but this girl in the clothes still isn't me.

When I come out of the bathroom, Red Hair is waiting. He has a gun in his lap. In his accented English he tells me, "You are going to help us. We'll buy you more clothes. We'll buy you jewellery. We'll keep you safe. You'll do our trades for us. If you do well, maybe we'll start to pay you. You do badly? I'll have to shoot you."

I swallow, roll my shoulders back, and stand straighter. "What do you expect me to do?"

Branko

I'm at the corner. I shift from one foot to the other, a nervous habit I started in grade school. I sucked at soccer. I had this thing with my ankles. They were super weak and I sprained them all the time. My dad taught me to practice balancing on one foot and then the other for as long as I could.

There are so many people out. So many people here. It's got to be a Saturday or something. There are kids and parents and the sun is shining, and it's all I can do to put one foot in front of the other. I'm sweating and shaking. I wonder if the paper will shake right out of my hand and onto the street.

The corner where I wait is on a street that doesn't allow traffic. This walkway turns into a bridge on the other side of the square. I can see a river below. A boy and girl are throwing rocks or pennies or something into the water. I send them my wishes. I wish for my mama to be taken care of. I wish for Verica to be okay and to find her way out of Serbia. I wish for me to not screw this up and hurt anyone. I get to the corner. I want to sit down on the cement. I want to lie down and not get up.

Something grabs my elbow and I turn, ready to swing, my heart pounding in my ears. Then I'm face to face with Verica! Before I can say anything, she pulls me close for a hug and hisses in my ear, "It looks like rain in the east."

I pull away and grip her arms, holding her out in front of me. "What the hell?" I ask.

"Who else would look so out of place here? I knew you had to be the person," she says. "And who else other than my Branko would stand practicing his balance on a street corner?"

"Yeah, but what? How? We have to get out of here." I look around. I can't see the van but I know Lugnuts is watching me. Someone has to be watching Verica too. The scene hasn't changed. Kids are still playing, people are still living normal lives around us, while our corner spirals out of control.

"Well, my plan was to use the other person as a body shield as I ran away." Verica shrugs like it's my fault her plan is ruined.

"So you aren't dealing drugs on purpose, right?"

"For the love of God, Branko! No. Notice how I didn't assume that of you? Jeez." Verica's eyebrows crawl together like two sweet little caterpillars, and I want to kiss her more than anything else in the world. I have to get her out of here. Going against Lugnuts and whoever is after Verica isn't safe or smart, but it's the right thing to do. I didn't give up half a liver to become a drug mule.

Verica

We're at least thirty feet from the nearest building. I can see why they chose this meeting spot. Nowhere to run or hide. Plus, neither of us knows our surroundings so we wouldn't even know where to go. There are no cars on this street. Just the walkways and the bridge.

And the river.

It's not very wide. But I'm certain going toward the river would draw any gunshots away from the people in the square.

"Can you still swim fully-clothed?" I ask Branko.

He nods and smiles. He doesn't need to answer because he knows my plan. We take off in a sprint toward the water. As we run, I lose the jacket and the shoes. I hear a gunshot and people screaming.

When the gunshot goes off, I can feel Branko start to turn back. I grab his hand and tug him forward. He has to keep moving. He has to keep going with me. We jump off the bridge and know that whoever is shooting at us will have to run all the way through the square and to the river's edge to get a shot off. I know Red Hair, Lumberjack, and Big Nose were at least two blocks away in the car and only one or two of them could have followed because they wouldn't have abandoned the car. We swim with the current. It's not moving fast, but it's enough to help us get away faster.

We make our way toward the other side as we move downstream. Branko nods towards the bank and we haul ourselves onto the other side. We are both panting like dogs from the swim and the rush of escape.

"We can't sit here. We have to keep moving," I say, offering him a hand up. It's quiet except for the running of the river.

Branko's hand is rough and calloused on my skin. His grip is strong, but his hand feels smaller than before. He looks like he could be thirty pounds lighter than when I last saw him. We walk along the river, sticking close to buildings, and keeping our heads down. When we get outside of town we slow our pace slightly and move in a ditch along the road rather than on it. We fill each other in on the last month and a half. I tell him my plan about college.

Branko

"We could do it together, you know," Verica says. "We could both get jobs and rent a place together and study and go back to school."

"I can't leave my mama. I have to go home," I tell her, shaking my head.

"Why, Branko? Why can't you do something for you for a change? I love our families too, but there comes a point where you have to go out on your own." The sun is setting behind her. When I look at her, she glows and my heart breaks. Why can't she just go home with me?

"Once we get settled, we could bring our families wherever we go if that's really everything," she says. "We just can't go back."

I can keep walking with Verica, jump a train to Germany, start a new life that is unknown and possibly, probably, better. I can jump a train and work my way back home. Neither choice is perfect.

We walk in silence as I imagine what we'll study and where we'll work. Somewhere that doesn't involve dead animals like the factory at home. I could send money back to my mama. I'm never going to make a difference or be different if I go home. I'll be the same Branko with no money, working twelve-hour shifts and smelling like death.

Verica

I knew he wouldn't go with me the moment we found an Italian train station.

I look at the map and the timetables, contemplating my next move. Away from Serbia, I can be someone. Anyone I want to. I can start over. I still have my passport and some change I had stuffed in my shirt before the goon squad took me. I can sneak onto a train this afternoon to Assisi, Italy. If I hide in the bathroom and try to only stay on a train for an hour or so and hop off, I should be able to make it out of Italy in a day or so. And what's the worst that could happen if I get caught without a ticket? They kick me off? I smile to myself. I've just been shot at and used as a drug dealer, I've seen worse.

I give Branko part of my change to call the single phone in the apartment building. I tell him not to tell anyone he saw me. "Maybe you'll come join me some day," I say.

He can't look at me in the eye. "Come home with me," he says. "After what we've been through, it can't be worse at home."

I shake my head. "I don't know where I'm going, but I know what's back there. I can't live like that forever. Ahead is always better than back." I stand on my toes and kiss his cheek. I turn away from him, toward the platform, and know that I won't look back.

NOTHING

EVANGELINE JENNINGS

Nothing. Nothingness. That's the dream.

The board says the train is one minute away.

It would be so easy.

How much could it hurt?

An absolute fuckload, that's how much. But only for a moment.

Long enough to register? I don't think so. But can I take the risk?

People who jump off bridges frequently change their minds as soon as it's too late. I read that in a newspaper so it must be true. I couldn't bear to feel that eternal instant of infinite regret. Also I'm not big on agony.

What about the driver? The other passengers? Is it fair to traumatise them, and make them late for work? For school? To make my death an integral part of the driver's life?

Fuck the other passengers. What have they done for me lately? And all the other kids can suck my dick. If I had a dick, which contrary to rumour I do not.

Here comes Kennedy now. Fucking bitch. Prancing along. Skirt too short for school—if they ever applied the rules—but look at those legs. I'd die for legs like hers.

The man next to me turns to watch her once she is past and catwalking towards her friends at the far end of the platform. His newspaper—the Telegraph—is tucked beneath his arm. He's carrying a briefcase and umbrella. What century is this? Fucking Victorian perv.

I don't know anyone else named Kennedy. It's an American thing. A President and his brother. We did them in history, and last year the newspapers ran a story about the two of them and Marilyn Monroe. The first and biggest sex tape of them all. Allegedly.

Victorian Perv licks his lower lip.

It isn't only her legs. Everything about Kennedy is to die for.

Could I make it look like she pushed me?

Would I want to?

Maybe. Maybe not. I don't know.

The board says the train is here.

I can see lights in the tunnel.

I'm going to not jump again today.

This carriage is fucking rammed. None of these twats know they could have been late for work, and the driver has no idea how lucky he's been. If he struggles to sleep tonight, he won't be blaming me.

All the other girls are at the front of the train because they want to be first to the lift after we arrive. I was waiting at the wrong end of the platform because it's the best place to jump and I don't fucking care about the lift. School can wait, and I have a date.

He's there on the platform as the train pulls in.

At least, I think it's him.

Can't be sure.

The doors open with a sigh, and I turn my back. Focus on the advert on the wall outside the train.

It is him, I'm sure.

I recognise the air he brings with him.

The weight of his body presses back against mine.

No erection. He's facing away from me. His leg is against my arse. My head rests against his shoulder blade. He's taller than I am. Thinner too. His fingers stroke my thigh.

He wasn't here on Wednesday. I could ask him why but talking is against all our unspoken rules.

His hand creeps up my leg.

A shudder runs through me.

The man is a pale reflection in the window. He's reading a newspaper. Telling the world he has no idea I exist. The headlines disappear into the smears and grime.

His grip tightens on my arse. My breath is steam on the glass. My face fades away. I can't recognise myself. We have four stops together. Sometimes it's enough.

He stays on the train when I leave. I ask him to excuse me, please, as I brush past. I don't look at his face. I don't try to catch the other girls.

English. Maths. Latin. Uneventful.

Science. Fucking boring.

Kennedy and her friends aren't picking on me today. Probably lulling me into a false sense of something. Those bitches always have a plan.

Have they realised I don't do Facebook anymore?

This classroom looks out on the school grounds. The sports pavilion burned down a month ago. We had the press, photographers, police, the fucking works. The headmaster all but sobbed when he asked us for information. Idiot should have offered a reward.

My first time was a rock concert. I was on my own. Ribs and elbows braced against the edge of the stage.

The lights went down. The band came on. And I forgot my name. I was nothing. I became no one.

The first indication was a hand on my hip. My right hip. His right hand. I did not know why. It was no accident, that much was clear. His grip was tight with intent.

Squirrels play in the trees while the groundskeeper rolls the square. Cricket is such a fucking boring game. They have to change in the gym now and walk down to the field. The school has launched an appeal. They still haven't cleared all the wreckage away. They'll probably name the new pavilion after the headmaster. The Cries Like a Bitch Pavilion.

The first song ended. The singer loved London. Were we ready to rock? The band was going to kick our asses for us.

Talking of which. A second hand pressed against me, squeezed my arse. I assumed it was his. I didn't know how many men treated girls like that—possibly all of them—but the chances were good it was his. It felt like a left hand.

An old familiar riff introduced the next song. Lights exploded from behind the drum riser and blinded me. He released my arse, taking me by both hips.

He pulled me back an inch, maybe two or three, and I felt his cock.

I didn't know what to do.

If I open this window and jump, I don't think I'll die. The second floor isn't high enough. Broken legs won't do. Not mine.

His right hand lifted my band t-shirt and slipped inside, squeezing and rubbing my belly. His dick stabbed my arse. I didn't know how to stop him, so I didn't try. I let him have whatever he wanted to take.

Maybe I could get onto the roof.

He took his time.

His breath was in my ear, his hand inside my bra, when I felt him jerk and twitch against my arse. It went on and on and on, like a drum solo. I cried out when he pinched my nipple and twisted hard. Nobody heard above the sound of the band.

I didn't turn around.

I didn't want to know.

I didn't want to spoil anything.

He played with my breasts before he left. Tugged my bra down. Tucked in my t-shirt. Patted my arse. A true gentleman.

On the platform, after the show, waiting for the tube, I studied every face, wondering.

No matter what Kennedy says, I'm not stupid. I always get good grades and I know the man on the train can't be the man from the show. I must give off a vibe.

The boys at school can smell it. Six months ago, three of them grabbed me in the hallway after school and dragged me into the basement.

On my knees, my back up against the water pipes, Martin Kingsley put his cock in my mouth.

Kennedy watched.

I fucking hate her.

I fucking hate myself.

Two weeks later, Martin was there again, waiting for me. He twisted my wrist behind my back and took me down the stairs. Called me names, slapped my face, and said no one would believe me if I ever tried to grass him up.

Who was there to tell? Who would care?

Is there something uniquely wrong with me, that I attract this attention, appear to welcome it? Or is this commonplace—a secret between men and all the girls who can't say no?

Martin doesn't hurt me anymore. He split up with Kennedy and started texting me. Once or twice a week, he tells me when and where. The first time was behind the sports pavilion. He had me well trained by then. I knelt for him and swallowed every drop. He thanked me before he walked away. Another gentleman.

There is an obligation for people who suicide. I think.

I don't jump in front of the train again after school. What would be the point? There might be something decent on TV.

I travel home alone. Work keeps the man later than school ever detains me.

I may never throw myself in front of a train.

The way I would like to end my life? A posh hotel. A warm bath. Alcohol. An overdose. A fresh razor blade. But I can't do that to the maid.

The roof of the school would be high enough. So would the Archway Bridge. But what if I change my mind halfway down? What if I land on someone's car?

I don't want to leave a body for anyone to find. I want to disappear. Like that boy from that band. They say he went off a bridge.

"How was your day?" My mother only ever has one question.

"It was a day." I only need one reply.

We speak but we never talk. How can I tell her? How can I tell anyone how I feel?

I've never been kissed but I've had fingers inside me.

Martin Kingsley comes in my mouth whenever he feels the need. A month ago he did it on his way to Sasha's house. He told me to meet him after school behind the pavilion. He thanked me afterwards, while I was wiping my chin. Said it would help him when he took Sasha to bed. That was when I set the fire. I watched the pavilion burn through the window of the Chinese takeaway.

I could shoot myself on the bridge where that guitarist jumped. Stand on the guardrail so my corpse would drop and disappear.

Where would I get a gun?

Is there anything good on TV tonight?

In the bath, I shave.

How easy would it be to break this plastic razor apart?

Why the fuck should I?

In the morning, on the train, when his hand cups my arse, my fingers reach for his. He hisses with surprise—I'm breaking all the rules—but he takes the note anyway.

I can't focus in class.

Latin is Greek to me.

I was up half the night, and have no fucks for Kennedy or her bitch posse.

I told the man I wanted to meet at a nice hotel. Told him I needed more that the train. Said he could have whatever he wanted from me. Tie me up. Blindfold me. Put it anywhere.

I promised I would wear my uniform. I didn't mention I would have a knife.

He will be the first.

I have made a list.

I will not be nothing anymore.

Does Kennedy even know her famous American namesakes were both killed?

ANIMAL HEART

COURI JOHNSON

In the barn with the Griffin is where he kept me. The man with no heart. It was my sister's fault, me being there. I had six of them, all older than me. All of them as dumb and trusting as fawns. My eldest sister was going to sell the lot of us to a family of brothers. Marriage is what they called it. I was too young to understand what it was, other than it had a lot to do with washing dishes, making beds.

The brothers were taking us home when an old man stopped us in the woods. He turned each one into stone. Except for me. I couldn't say if my life would've been much different had they not been turned to stone. Because mostly I washed dishes. I made beds. Probably the big difference was that I lived in a barn with a Griffin, but who knows how different that really is from living in a house with a man? I didn't.

The Griffin didn't talk much on account of the muzzle. The only time the old man took it off was to feed him. Then the Griffin let loose a terrible wail until the old man got the bucket of mash over his mouth. If the Griffin had given up screaming maybe the old man wouldn't have muzzled him. He could have had his mouth, like me. I gave up on screaming after the third night. My throat got sore. After that I didn't see the point in screaming. But if the Griffin didn't have the muzzle, maybe I would have. 'Cause he would have warned me. About the old man's intentions. About the proper meaning behind the word marriage.

*

"Child" is what the man with no heart called me, and one day he called me in by that name. He had just finished breakfast. I was outside cleaning his bedpan, and airing out his sheets. "Child," he called and child came. For a few moments he let his scaly eyes rest on my face before he reached to run a thumb over the curve of my cheek. The man with no heart had hands that felt like soil. Moist and crumbly.

"You got straw in your hair, child," he said, picking it out.

"I sleep in a barn," I said back. It was a risk, talking back like that. He could take it as cheek, and get angry. Or he could just take it as fact and let it go. That is what it was, and that was all I ever meant to speak in. Facts. Cheekiness was for girls who didn't live with men with no hearts. Girls who did got wiliness, if they were lucky. And a girl can't have much luck if she's living with a man with no heart.

"Ain't proper for a girl your age," he said after some time, and his voice was silky in a way that made me shiver. "And look at the rags you have on. Boy clothes. You've outgrown 'em. We should start putting you in dresses."

"Got none," I said. He let his hand trail down the length of my neck to rest on my shoulder. A few years I had been living with the man with no heart by then, and never had he ever touched me without it being in discipline. Somehow, this was worse. It made every inch of my skin feel like fresh hatched fly eggs.

"I'm going to head towards the town tonight to buy you a few. You mind your brothers and sisters, and you say goodbye to the barn. When I get back we'll be moving you in to the house."

I blinked and said thank you, because the barn was cold in the winter, hot in the summer, and smelt like Griffin piss year round. So moving into the house seemed like something nice. Like maybe a reward. Like maybe the man without a heart actually had a heart afterall.

But it wasn't so. You can see, clearly, where this was really headed.

*

My sisters and so-called brothers hadn't changed a bit since the day the man with no heart took me. They were locked in at the very age that they were then, even had the same expressions. Each of them with their mouths hung slightly open. By the time the man with no heart had told me he was moving me out of the barn, I was close in age to my middle sister. She was maybe seventeen. The one in between us, she was fourteen when the marriages were agreed upon. Me? I'd been eleven. Baby-faced. But when our eldest sister said anything it became our truths, no matter what. And she said marriage, and she said go, and then she was stone.

It may seem cruel to say, but I liked them fine as stone. They argued less and needed me more. Every day or so, I would go out and scrape bird dung off of them, make sure the weather wasn't wearing them down too much. And we'd talk. It was about the only conversation I had.

"Guess what?" I said that day, setting my bucket down at the feet of my eldest sister. She had her stone arm wrapped around her intended's, and the two of them were staring forever at each other. Which I figured must get boring after so much time. I stepped up on her toe so that I could wedge my own face in between the two of them and grinned. "I'm going to be moving in to the house soon as the old man gets home."

She just went on staring open mouthed. I rubbed at her cheek where there was a smudge and stepped down. Grabbed the wet rag out of the bucket and moved down the line, going on and on about how comfortable my new life would be.

"That's right," I told my other sister, then nodded to her beau. "Real nice." Turned to smile full toothed at my groom-to-be so he could see how happy I was. But their eyes just stayed flat and dull. It wasn't as satisfying, talking to stone, as I got older.

I let the rag fall out of my hand and into the bucket. Stood there waiting in the silence, looked around the stone faces once more, and set off back to the barn. Maybe, I thought, it would feel better telling the Griffin. Sure, he didn't talk back either, but I knew he could at least listen. And ain't that why people talk in the first place? Just to be heard?

*

The barn was meant for more animals than just me and Griffin, so space wasn't much of an issue. There was also plenty of hay to make a bed, but it was dark because we only had one lantern. The man liked to keep it hung up on this one center pole so he could see that the Griffin was where he was supposed to be.

When I came in the Griffin was in one of his down and out moods. He was curled up on the ground with his beak resting on his forearms, his wings folded over him to make a sort of tent. His big old eyes were open and just following along the floor like he was chasing imaginary horizons, recatching old kills. This was one of two ways the Griffin would usually be. The other was raging, his head tossing and his claws snapping at the muzzle.

"Master is real pleased with me," I said. Griffin rolled his eyes up to watch as I slumped down into my own pile of hay across the way. They looked misty and sad as all hell. For a moment I thought maybe I shouldn't brag at him, him being trapped and chained and muzzled as he was. But Griffin probably didn't give one lick about living in a house, so I figured there wasn't too much harm in it. "You won't even believe me when I tell you this, but he's gonna go ahead and let me live up in his house with him. Stroked my cheek and everything. I must be doing good work."

While I was talking I had begun getting ready to sleep, beating down the hay so as to kill some of the bugs and scare off any vermin, then spreading it out the way I liked. While I'd been doing this the Griffin had stood up. He had his eyes locked on me something fierce.

He lifted one claw and beckoned me, like the man with no heart would sometimes do.

I paused then, 'cause he never did anything like that. Every time I had talked at him he had mostly just laid there, watching me. Never had he ever shown any inclination that he was listening. And never had he summoned me.

I thought of the stone faces. I thought of the last joke I had told. To my fourteen-year-old sister nearly five years ago. It was a beautiful one, about a milkmaid and this bull. She hadn't even laughed. Just straightened her shoulders and acted like I was the wind.

It was nice being acknowledged.

And it was my last night in the barn, and I didn't even know what the Griffin sounded like when he wasn't wailing. I realised I might never get the chance to know. So I stepped across the barn for the first time and got really close to the Griffin.

"You gonna bite me if I take that thing off?"

The Griffin bowed his head, gave it the smallest of shakes. I wrapped my arms around his neck and felt his feathers tickle the insides of my arms. I found the clasp and undid it. Stepped back quick to half-hide behind the pole.

"You have to run," the Griffin said, his voice just a small, brittle twig snapping in his throat. "You have to run tonight."

*

The Griffin told me all sorts of things I didn't want to hear. Things about the man with no heart. Things about what he'd do to me that made my joke about the milkmaid and the bull seem like child's play.

He said the old man was going to marry me and not in the make the bed, do the dishes way. I told him I was already supposed to be getting married, thank you, to the stone boy in the woods. That we were very happy. The Griffin tossed his great head and shook his feathers. Went on explaining, until my blood was all cool and my clothes were soaked through with a whole pond's worth of sweat.

"I don't believe you," I told him. He'd been going on for hours and dawn would be coming any minute.

"Fine then," he moaned, falling back down into his down and out curl. "But you'll see. He'll do as I said."

"If he tries, then I'll kill 'im."

"He can't be killed. He has no heart."

"Ain't a soul that can't be killed. You stab 'em enough, they're gonna die."

"You have to get his heart to do it, and you'll never find it. I know where he keeps it, but only he can speak where it is."

I narrowed my eyes at him. "You're trying to trick me into letting you go." I scratched at myself and pointed my nose in the air.

"You couldn't if you wanted. Only the key round his neck can let me out of this." He shook his back leg where the chain keeping him in place was hooked. "And he keeps that on him, always."

"Well, still, you're trying to trick me," I said. "'Cause you're jealous."

"Believe what you must. I've tried to tell you but it's no use. Go ahead, girl. Put the muzzle back on. But you'll see. Tomorrow."

I crossed the room carefully and picked the muzzle up off the ground where I left it. I was sure that he was going to try and nip me, or hurt me in someway, but when I lifted it up he just bowed his head into it.

*

The next day I only had a little time to spend with my sisters and the boys, and I had to leave most of them uncleaned. I told them short bits of what the Griffin had told me, and nodded in appreciation at their wide mouths, their horrified stares.

"I know," I said. I turned and laid a hand on one of my sister's shoulders. "I'm really sorry you had to hear that. But imagine me having to listen to it all in the dead of night."

I nodded for a moment while scrubbing away a patch of filth on one of the brothers' faces. "You're right. I won't have to put up with it again. And I am lucky. If the old man knew I'd taken the muzzle off—"

At that moment, however, I felt a tingle go up my spine and heard "child" being called from the road. He was coming. I dropped the rag and overturned the bucket. Slung my arm through the handle and ran towards the road without saying goodbye. He didn't like to be kept waiting.

*

The man with no heart led me inside his home. Over his one arm he had a sheer white dress hanging. He held it up against my body.

"Go and change, child," he said, and so I turned to go back outside to the barn. He stopped me by my elbow and pointed me towards the door to his bedroom instead. "In there."

I hesitated, thinking of the Griffin, before setting my shoulders and heading into his room. I pulled off my clothes and the smell of my body caught me off guard. Honest, I hadn't washed my clothes, or myself in a week or so. Maybe even longer. There was a tick sticking off of the side of my knee that I hadn't noticed. I popped it off with my nails.

Seemed a real shame, putting on a nice new white dress when I was dirty as I was. I should have asked for a bucket of water. Something. But I'd never asked the man with no heart for anything. Least not after the first three days when I knew he wasn't gonna let me go. Wasn't gonna turn my family back.

Run, the Griffin had said. But where to? It's not like I hadn't thought about it, I was just sure that it was hopeless. Besides, all I'd ever had to do was keep house. That had been what I was heading for anyhow. What had changed? Really?

I pulled the dress over my head and looked down at how it fell in graceful folds just above my ankle. I swung one of my legs back and forth to watch it flutter. Turned on my toe.

The old man was standing behind me in the doorway, arms opened wide.

"Darling," he called me. He came forward, wrapped a hand around my waist, and pulled me towards him. His mouth gaping open, his tongue lolling out from between his lips.

*

When I got to the barn the dress was already stained. With dirt on the knees from where I fell. With blood at the sleeve. From the man with no heart. Already the Griffin had been on his feet, waiting for me. He bowed his head as I came close and I undid his muzzle.

"What happened?" He asked.

"What you said." I replied. I slipped under his wing and crouched down at his leg. I had to hitch the dress up to give my hips room to move.

"And?"

"I knocked him out. I pushed him and he fell against the bedpost. He's going to kill me when he wakes up, I know it."

"Well, he'll be up soon. He doesn't hurt for long without a heart."

"I've got the key," I told the Griffin, and I fumbled with it and the lock. My sweat kept making it slip. I batted my hair back and leaned in close. "Stay steady." I hooked the key into the lock and it clicked into place. The shackle fell away and the Griffin stretched out his long leg.

"On," he said and kneeled. And on I went.

The Griffin lowered his head and I hooked my bare feet under the joints of his wings, buried my hands in the feathers of his neck. He charged forward, burst out of the barn and ran down the lane. His wings unfolded. I felt us tilt as we lifted. Made it a few feet into the air, fast as you could blink.

And then there was a quick jerk, like a snag, and he fell back to the ground. We landed in a heap, his body crushing my own, his wing bent crooked under my back.

"What's wrong?" I asked.

"I can't fly," he gasped. "They won't work."

I struggled out from under him, crushing more of his wing feathers as I went. He rose slow and unsteadily to his feet. Took a step and slipped again. His eyes were bugged and rolling the way they were when he went mad.

"He's waking," the Griffin said. "I can feel it. You should run."

"Come on." I wedged my hands under him and heaved as hard as I could to pull him up. "We've just got to get to the trees. Get up." The Griffin snapped his beak, and rolled his head back on his neck so he could look me in the eyes. His pupils shrunk to small little slits, like cat eyes, until all that I could see was the strange gold of them and one tiny black line.

"I don't know how to do it alone," I said.

The Griffin's pupils swelled again and he gave one shuddering push. Rose up to his feet.

*

We made it into the woods. It was slow going, the Griffin limping the whole time. Every now and then he'd try to stretch his wings out, and I'd hear a pop or a snap and he'd let out one piteous caw. After what I judged to be a few hours of this, the Griffin collapsed to the forest floor between the roots of a tree. "Stop," he told me. "For a moment. I have to rest."

I put my arms around myself and shivered. The dress wasn't enough cover for the woods at night. It was impractical and stupid. I wished I'd never put it on. At the bottom it was torn and didn't even fall like it had. Dirty, all the way up to my knees.

The Griffin nodded his head, beckoning me to come and sit down. I nestled up in the curve of his body and he laid his head over my lap. He closed his eyes.

"What are we going to do?" I asked, eventually.

"The only hope I have of keeping him from me is to find and kill his heart," the Griffin said. "He'll pursue me to the ends of the Earth and beyond otherwise. But you, you could go on. There are plenty of wild children in the world for the catching. One of you is never missed for long."

"I won't know what to do alone," I said. The Griffin popped open an eye and looked up at me. Shook his head slightly and I felt his throat expand with one great sigh.

"He's going to catch us. And when he catches us he'll kill you. If not for fighting him than for setting me free."

"And what about you? He won't kill you?"

"He is neither allowed to kill me, nor let me die," the Griffin said. "Which is worse." The Griffin raised his head up and tilted his neck back to look above at the canopy of tree branches. "I was in that barn a long time. Much longer than you can imagine. I don't want to go back."

"He won't catch us if we keep moving," I said.

"Listening isn't one of your talents, is it, child?" the Griffin asked, but he said child in a completely different way than the man with no heart said it. Like the word was goose down.

"It ain't like I had anyone to practice it on," I said back. The Griffin raised one of his front claws and began to lick it softly. There was dried blood there, and one of his talons was near snapped off. He cleaned all of the old blood away, and then with one sharp jerk of his beak, ripped the damaged nail off.

He spat it into my lap. "Well, try and listen to this. Because when I say so, I need you to do exactly as I tell you. I need you to keep that claw. And when the man with no heart catches up with us, I need you to bury it deep in my throat, right at the hollow. I need you to cut my chest open, and eat my heart."

"And what then?" I asked, taking the claw in my hands.

"Then you'll know what to do."

*

Despite my pushing, the Griffin insisted we stay at the roots of the tree awhile longer. He lapped at his bleeding claw, he put his head back in my lap, and he slept for some time. Every second I thought I could feel the man with no heart getting closer. Every breaking tree branch, every moan of wood, was certainly him creeping up. I could not sleep, picturing his tongue, haired and yellow, coming towards me. Pressing against my neck.

But eventually the Griffin woke and got to his feet and I followed him further into the woods, his claw clutched in my hand. We found a stream, we followed it. Every now and then a breeze would kick up and he would lift his face into it and gently I could hear him sigh, his wings spreading out just slightly.

"To fly again," he'd murmur while paused, and then move on.

We made good time. Dawn was approaching. I thought there must be a town coming soon. A break in the woods. A place we could hide. A place we could rest. He needn't have to die and I needn't have to kill.

And then I heard it. The word child. Just so softly. I felt my pulse jump like a wild hare. The Griffin stiffened. His head snapped towards me. He reared up on his hind legs.

"You have to do it now," he said.

I stalled, fumbled with the claw. Wanted to throw it from me but found it gripped upward inbetween both my hands instead. "But—"

The Griffin fell forward, his neck stretched back. Landed full force on the talon and very nearly knocked me down. He pushed down onto it and I felt blood, slick and warm, spread up and coat my bare arms.

"Don't stop," he croaked, and blood pooled on his tongue, flowed over the crest of his beak. "You promised."

He fell over dead into the leaves, his own claw still sticking out of his neck.

Child hung on the air, drawing in and in. Already I could feel eyes all over my skin, my hairs rising with goosepimples. I hitched up the dress and knelt by the Griffin. I dragged the claw downward and his flesh and bone split apart as easily as cake. Down past his neck into his chest, which opened up, ribs and all, to show me his fat purple heart.

I reached in, took it in my fist, and pulled it loose.

Swallowed it down in one choking gulp, and fell ontop of his body shuddering. I breathed in, and felt little pricks of tears at the corners of my eyes. I turned and curled up next to the Griffin's body and lay there shivering.

The Griffin's heart had given me wiliness. I knew what I had to do.

*

The man with no heart found me with the body of the Griffin. For a moment it gave him quite the pause, and I saw a small wild joy over take him, him thinking the secret of his heart had died with the beast. I'd never have seen it without the Griffin's heart inside me. He jerked me to my feet by my wrist and dragged me back through the forest without saying a word.

I didn't fight, I knew I ought not to. Not because I feared him but because it was what the Griffin's heart told me to do. When we got back to his cottage he threw me into the barn and shackled me up by my hands and feet so I had to stand arms stretched above my head, for three days and three nights.

Three times a day, the man with no heart came in and dumped a bucket of ice cold water over my head, and fed me a bowl of mash. Each time he did I said what the Griffin's heart told me to say.

First day, I stood there apologising. Singing his praises. Saying how wrong I'd been to run.

Second day, I told him what a liar the Griffin was. I told him he had told me that the man with no heart meant to kill me dead.

Third day I told him how I figured it all out. How I knew he would treat me kinder than anyone I ever knew, than anyone ever could. How I wasn't good enough to give myself to him. To be the wife he deserved. But if he let me, I would try.

The whole time the man with no heart acted like he wasn't listening, but I knew in my Griffin's heart he was. And the third time he came that third night he brought a key and undid the chains.

"You say you'll behave, child?" The man with no heart said, his voice cold, and I nodded in earnest. "Then show me." The locks clinked open and I could move again. I dropped my arms and the man with no heart put his arms around me once more. Before he could bring his tongue out I had my hands up between us.

"Before I can be a proper wife to you, I have to make your heart happy," I told him. "But whenever I'm near I cannot hear it beat."

"Child," said the man with no heart, "that's impossible. My heart isn't in my chest. It beats, I assure you, but you will never hear it."

"Then where is it? I must hear it before we are really wed."

The man with no heart tilted his head back and looked me long in the face.

"Have you always had such gold eyes?"

"Always," I said. "For you. Where is it that you keep your heart? So that I can be sure that I bring it joy?"

"Under my mattress, child."

"Then give me tonight to plan how to be its delight."

The old man left me then, and went back to his own bed, and I curled up in the Griffin's stall. I fell asleep listening to the Griffin's heart pumping alongside my heart. Pumping fresh blood, and little whispered words.

*

The next day, while the man with no heart was away, I went out into the garden and gathered up an arm full of flowers. I weaved them into a large wreath and laid it on his bed sheets. I scattered flowers all along the floor by his bed. When he came in I was kneeling among them, my ear pressed to the mattress, face drawn with concentration.

"What are you doing, child?" He asked.

"I have tried to make your heart joyful but still can't hear a thing," I said, fretting my hands in my lap.

The man with no heart came to me, his eyes crinkled up and his mouth sneering at my foolishness. "Darling, dear, of course you can't hear a thing. There is no need to worry. That is not where my heart is at all."

"Why did you lie to me?" I asked, and began to cry in earnest. The man with no heart tried to quiet me, tried to calm me. His hands moved frantically over my shoulders, my hair, my face, but I kept rocking back and forth with sobs.

"It is impossible for you to reach my heart, darling. That's all."

"Because you don't feel for me?" I asked. The man with no heart tutted and tutted, shaking his head.

"No, no, no," he said, massaging my arms with his oily fingers. "It's just too far away and too dangerous. You would never be able to get to it."

"Why don't you tell me then? So that I know for sure?" I asked, pulling away from him and narrowing my eyes.

"Your teeth," the old man said, his fingers pushing against my lips. "Have your teeth always been that sharp?" The Griffin's heart heard the note of hysteria in his voice and purred loud in my blood. I took his wrist and guided his fingers along my lips.

"I'm sorry I'm so ugly," I said, resting my head against his heartless chest. "That's why you won't tell me."

"Darling, it is through the woods, to the north, beyond a canyon. My heart. In a nest on the highest branch hanging above. It lives in a blue jay that sleeps there, and no person can put their hands on it. That is why you can not hear it beat."

"I understand," I said.

166

"And so now will you stop with this foolishness?"

I nodded, slowly. "Let me go and clean myself up. Fetch you something to drink. Let me make it up to you. Let me make up everything."

I stood up and left the old man by his door. Went into his cottage, into his kitchen, where I fetched down a glass, some wine, and from the highest cupboard, a pinch of belladonna. Together, I mixed them all. I splashed water on my face to dry away the tracks of my tears and went out to him, smiling.

*

Belladonna will not kill a man with no heart, but it will buy hours. This the Griffin heart told me. Hours I had to use wisely. Once the old man drank down the wine and his lids closed I went out the door and to the north, my double hearts beating like drums as my legs carried me faster than I'd ever run before. Faster than I ever thought any person could go.

A moment struck as I hit the height of my speed, I stretched my arms out and could have sworn I felt wind beneath feathers, the rocking pull of the Earth falling away. I closed my eyes and tilted my face into the breeze. My double hearts cawed.

Even with all that speed it took hours for me to reach the lip of the cavern the old man had described. The woods thinned out and the ground grew barren and black, ending suddenly in a steep dive. The canyon stretched from one horizon to the other, and was so deep I couldn't see the end of it. On the other side I could just see the hazy shape of land; a snarling bramble of forest tearing at the sky, and one massive tree up front, reaching toward the heavens. A thick, sturdy branch extended midway across the canyon, hanging miles above.

There, the old man's heart lived.

At the lip of the canyon I sat down and listened to the beat of my hearts slow, my blood cool, and my breath gather in my chest. What must be done now? I thought.

Jump, the Griffin's heart told me. Jump.

I looked down into the canyon and saw its darkness, heavy and full, reaching up to catch at my ankles. Saw myself plummeting like a stone down.

I can't alone, I thought. I'd never done anything alone.

You've gotten here, the Griffin's heart told me. And I am here with you.

I turned from the lip of the canyon and paced back towards the wood. Turned on my toe and kicked my leg out a few times, feeling its spring. Then I lowered my head and charged. Kept charging until I felt the last bit of earth under my toe get ready to give to nothingness. And I leapt.

The wind lifted me up by my underarms and I was carried. I felt my back stretch, and tear, and tingle. I gave a great thrust and rose higher. I kept rising until my hands wrapped round the branch above.

Into the tree with the heart I climbed. Crawled to the nest, hand over hand until I came to the nest. There the blue jay sat, fat and feathered. I ran my tongue over my teeth and tasted blood. I could hear my hearts leaping. The blue jay's eyes cracked open and locked on me. It fluffed its wings out. I reared back.

The blue jay took to flight and I plunged after it, arms out, towards the mouth of the canyon below.

*

A mile beyond his cottage, the old man was laying against a tree's roots, palm pressed to his chest and gasping. I found him there, the bird clenched in my fist. As I came close I could feel the pulse of the blue jay's body rise, jump, fall, rise. It was warm. Hot, even.

"Child," he gasped, lifting his limp arm and holding his palm out. "Give that to me now. You've made it leap quite enough."

"Have I?" I asked. I squeezed the blue jay in my palm and watched him wince.

"Wings," he wheezed. "When did you ever—"

I brought the blue jay to my lips and opened up my mouth. Between my teeth I took its head. I snapped my jaw closed. I chewed. Swallowed. I opened my mouth and stuffed the body in.

On the ground the man with no heart writhed, then stilled. I dabbed a bit of blood from the corner of my mouth. Stretched my back, and felt the wind run through the fibers of my feathers.

I pointed my face into the breeze.

*

I collected seeds in the forest, and there is a garden now outside the cottage of the man with no heart. Flowers of all shapes and sizes spring up at the statues' feet, curling around their ankles. I keep the house. Feed the pigs and hens in the barn, and keep it well lit so that they can see. When the breeze is good I stretch my wings, watching the horizon roll ever away, away, away. Animals and people slink on the ground, indistinguishable shadows. When the flowers bloom I gather them up and make wreaths. I hang them around the necks of my sisters, and even my brothers, too. I put my ear to their chests and listen, but there's never anything there. How might their hearts sound, if life had been different?

It does not matter. I have plenty to listen to. When I close my eyes I can hear my hearts leaping. One after the other after the other.

CONTENT WARNINGS

KIN SELECTION   Adoption

THE ORIGINAL   Illness

DISHARMONY   Racial segregation/violence

DESTINY   Violence

BREAKING GROUND   Poverty, mention of rape

WHEN YOU'RE GOING...   Violence, drugs

NOTHING   Rape, violence, suicide

ANIMAL HEART   Kidnap

BIOGRAPHIES

Zoe Apostolides is a writer and journalist. She grew up in Tooting and graduated from Oxford University in 2012. She has written for *FT Weekend, Erotic Review, For Books' Sake, Spiked, Lifetime, Planet Ivy, White Coffee, Screen Robot, Student Beans,* and various local newspapers. She lives with her girlfriend in London. Find her on Twitter @zoeapostolides

Tanvi Berwah is a literature and pop-culture enthusiast with a keen interest in world politics and human rights. She has been writing since a young age and holds a master's degree in English Literature from University of Delhi. Currently juggling her life as an entertainment blogger and a YA writer, she actively believes in the need for diverse books.
She can be found on Twitter @xginnyx

Elizabeth Byrne is a writer and award-winning documentary film-maker. She worked in BBC Current Affairs for ten years, and produced programmes for Panorama and Spotlight, as well as producing and directing three acclaimed films for BBC Three. Originally from Dublin, she now lives in Belfast, where she is a member of the Green Shoot Irish Migration Writing Group, and the Belfast Comedy Writers group. She recently completed an MA in Creative Writing at the Seamus Heaney Centre, Queen's University Belfast, and is currently working on her first novel.

Liz Flanagan writes for children and teenagers. Her books for children are *Starlight Grey, Cara and the Wizard,* and *Dara's Clever Trap* (all *Barefoot Books*). She's currently studying for a PhD in Creative Writing: Teen Fiction, at Leeds Trinity University. Liz lives in Hebden Bridge. Till recently she was Centre Director at Lumb Bank, the Ted Hughes Arvon Centre, hosting creative writing courses at that beautiful house all year round. Before that, she lived in London and Brighton, and worked in children's book publishing.Liz blogs at lizflanagan. co.uk/blog, interviewing leading YA authors about their writing process. You can also find her on Twitter @lizziebooks.

Katie M. Flynn's fiction has appeared in *A Cappella Zoo, Barrelhouse, Bellingham Review, Fugue, Temenos,* and elsewhere, and has been nominated for a *Pushcart Prize.* She holds an MFA from the University of San Francisco and recently completed her first novel, set in the Nevada desert at the height of the War on Terror.

Erin Darby Gesell is a writer, personal trainer, triathlete, yogi, and lover of chocolate, dogs, and all things fictional from Norfolk, Nebraska. She now lives in Omaha where she obtained her BFA from the University of Nebraska at Omaha in Creative Writing and Spanish. She obtained her MFA in Creative Writing for Young People from Antioch University in Los Angeles. Her short story *Good Boy* was published by *The Magnolia Review* in July 2015 and her flash fiction piece *Living* was published by *Riding Light Review* in summer 2015. Both of these pieces were written for adults, however, she is currently working on a novel for teens.

Jessica Glaisher lives in London and works in theatre as a freelance lighting technician and designer, fitting writing in around her career and taking inspiration from her own life and those around her. She is often to be found procrastinating with cake. Jessica can be found @jglaisher on twitter and at imaginationadded.blogspot

Valerie Hunter is a high school English teacher and freelance writer, and enjoys combining the historical with the fantastical. Her young adult stories have appeared in magazines including *Cicada* and *Inaccurate Realities,* and in anthologies including *Brave New Girls, Real Girls Don't Rust,* and *Cleavage.*

Evangeline Jennings is a former young adult and a very unreliable narrator Born and raised in Liverpool, Evangeline has lived in Austin, Texas, for the last eleven years. Evangeline's novella *No Christmas* was shortlisted for a 2015 award for "excellence in independent publishing". Mostly, she writes stories about girls. She believes in equality, so she writes about that. She also writes about gender, sexuality, and violence against women. Her characters often seek bloody satisfaction. Sometimes, they find it.

Couri Johnson is a recent graduate of the North Eastern Ohio Master of Fine Arts. She is currently working on a collection of fabulist tales and publishing a novel. She spends a disproportionate amount of her time at the playground for a girl her age, and can be found on Twitter @a_couri

Angela Kanter, as a teenager, had a cool job as a radio presenter but now she sits in a newspaper office all day drinking coffee. She studied English and the art of making toast on an electric fire at Somerville College, Oxford. Published work includes *The Princess and the Pets* and *Dear Meena*. She is represented by Ben Illis at The BIA. @AngelaKanter

Ioanna Mavrou is a writer from Nicosia, Cyprus. Her short stories have appeared in *Electric Literature, Okey-Panky, The Rumpus, The Letters Page,* and elsewhere. She runs a tiny publishing house called *Book Ex Machina* and is the editor of *Matchbook Stories*: a literary magazine in matchbook form.

Lucy Middlemass has contributed stories to three YA collections, *Heathers, Mermaids* and *Moremaids*. She also wrote the standalone Kindle single, *Mothers,* and co-authored a second single, *Convertible*. Find her on Twitter @LucyMiddlemass

Emily Paull is an emerging writer from Perth Western Australia who blogs in her spare time at emilypaull.com She was a young writer in residence at the *Katharine Susannah Prichard Writer's Centre* in 2014 and helps run the *Book Length Project Group* at the WA branch of the *Fellowship of Australian Writers*. She is also a bookseller.

Eliana Ramage holds a BA and MA in creative writing from Dartmouth College and Bar-Ilan University, respectively. She was awarded a *Scholastic Art and Writing Awards* silver medal in 2009, and later signed on as a fiction co-editor for *Compose Journal*. A proud Cherokee Nation citizen, she is at work on a collection of linked stories concerning indigenous girls and women. One will be in an anthology of finalists for the *Galtelli Literary Prize,* and others have appeared or are forthcoming in the *Beloit Fiction Journal, Four Chambers,* and *The Baltimore Review.*

Anna Scott is a copywriter by day, aspiring YA writer by night, Anna can be found discussing books on her blog Anna Scott Jots (annascottjots.blogpost. com) and on twitter @scottyjotty. She used to sell wine for a living but now develops mild obsessions over TV shows whilst teaching her daughters about the importance of '80s' movies, '90s' kids' telly and feminism. Her favourite colour is turquoise and her favourite food is crisps.

Kaye Spivey is a Pacific Northwest writer who recently published her first poetry chapbook, *An Isolated Storm,* and has had poetry previously published in such literary journals as *Northwest Boulevard, Sterling Mag,* and *Written River.*

Alaina Symanovich is a graduate student at Florida State University concentrating in creative nonfiction. Her work has appeared or is forthcoming in *Fourth River, The Offbeat, Word Riot,* and other journals.

For Books' Sake is the charitable organisation that centres, supports and champions writing by women and girls. Founded in 2010, For Books' Sake celebrates classic and contemporary writing by established, emerging and marginalised women authors through a national programme of live events, creative writing workshops, publishing imprint and other projects.

For Books' Sake aims to challenge and counteract systemic, institutionalised biases impacting women writers. The organisation provides an alternative platform and resources for writers, readers, publishers, educators and more, challenging inequality and empowering women and girls of all backgrounds and abilities to tell their stories and have their voices heard.

Previous For Books' Sake publications:
Tongue in Cheek: The Best New Erotica Written by Women (2015)
Furies: A Poetry Anthology of Women Warriors (2014)
Derby Shorts: The Best New Fiction from the Roller Derby Track (2013)
Short Stack: The Best New Pulp Fiction Written by Women (2012)

www.forbookssake.net